CW01064233

HOW TO FIX A BROKEN HEART

NICOLA MAY

Storm

This is a work of fiction. Names, characters, businesses, places, events and incidents are either the products of the author's imagination or used in a fictitious manner. Any resemblance to actual persons, living or dead, or actual events is purely coincidental.

Copyright © Nicola May, 2015, 2017, 2025

The moral right of the author has been asserted.

Previously published in 2015 as *The SW19 Club* by Accent Press and in 2017 as *The Women of Wimbledon Common* by Nowell Publishing.

All rights reserved. No part of this book may be reproduced or used in any manner without the prior written permission of the copyright owner. This prohibition includes, but is not limited to, any reproduction or use for the purpose of training artificial intelligence technologies or systems.

To request permissions, contact the publisher at rights@stormpublishing.co

Ebook ISBN: 978-1-80508-958-2
Paperback ISBN: 978-1-80508-960-5

Cover design: Jo Thomson
Cover images: Shutterstock

Published by Storm Publishing.
For further information, visit:
www.stormpublishing.co

ALSO BY NICOLA MAY

How Do I Tell You?

Cockleberry Bay

The Corner Shop in Cockleberry Bay
Meet Me in Cockleberry Bay
The Gift of Cockleberry Bay
Christmas in Cockleberry Bay

Ferry Lane Market

Welcome to Ferry Lane Market
Starry Skies in Ferry Lane Market
Rainbows End in Ferry Lane Market
A Holiday Romance in Ferry Lane Market

Ruby Matthews

Working it Out
Let Love Win

Star Fish
The School Gates
Better Together
Love Me Tinder
Christmas Evie
Escape to Futtingbrook Farm

To mothers... in every beautiful form.

PROLOGUE

The pain was so great inside and out that even Gracie's scream was shocked into submission. Instead, she sat motionless on the toilet, whimpering like a frightened puppy. She knew Lewis was outside, just the other side of the door, but she couldn't find the strength to call his name. She was in this alone. It was happening to her, alone.

She was aware that blood was pouring from her. Feeling suddenly woozy, her head lolled forward as if she were a ragdoll.

Losing consciousness, she had just one last wish – never to wake up from this insurmountable nightmare.

ONE

'A full fat cappuccino with nutmeg sprinkles and a flapjack, please.'

'Gracie, did you really say a flapjack? It's eight o'clock in the morning!'

Gracie grinned and then pretended to look shocked. 'Oh, no – is it really? I didn't realise cakes cared what time they were eaten.'

Annalize – spelled 'with a z' – shuffled her weight slightly from one designer trainer to another. Her *Pretty in Pink* nail varnish matched her expensive Nike sports top, which clung snugly to her trim figure. 'It's just, you know... maybe it's time you thought of losing your baby weight.'

Gracie shut her eyes to stop the tears and took a deep breath.

'And maybe it's time you weren't so bloody insensitive,' the petite blonde behind the coffee shop counter butted in. Gracie noticed her very slight Eastern European accent and her tiny diamond nose stud. She wished that she could be brave enough to wear such a thing.

Shocked into silence by the stranger, Annalize downed her two-shot espresso and headed for the door.

Doing some sort of weird arm-stretch, she called back, 'Gracie, darling. I'm running to the Monument and back, should be at my desk for nine twenty. Cover me if Warhurst is on the warpath.'

Leaving a trail of strong expensive French perfume behind her, she jogged off.

'God, that's pungent.' Gracie turned her nose up. 'Wonder what it is?'

'*Eau de Bitch*, I expect.' The blonde barista smiled and passed Gracie her coffee. 'I'm Maya, by the way.'

'Gracie. Gracie Davies. I work just down the street at Lemon Aid. *For charity events that wow and deliver,*' she recited in a comically high-pitched voice. 'So, this is my local caffeine stop. You're new here, aren't you?'

'Yes, first day.' A queue had started to form. 'I'd better get on.'

'Yes, of course,' Gracie said, 'good luck and thanks again for sticking up for me.'

* * *

'Gracie Davies, it's 9.04,' Rob Warhurst's deep voice boomed as Gracie took her seat at her desk. His grey beard made him look older than his forty-one years; his twinkling blue eyes gave away the fact that he wasn't cross at all.

Gracie glanced at her phone while flicking open her laptop. 'No, it's not. It's 9.01.'

'So you're still one minute late. Where's Lara Croft anyway?'

'Last seen in running gear in Marcy's.' Gracie laughed. 'It's a good job she isn't in earshot.'

'What do you mean, she'd love that comparison.' He

checked his watch again. 'You all have it far too easy these days, the lot of you; even with all this flexible working malarkey you still can't make it on time on a day you're in the office.' He huffed.

Gracie's relationship with her MD, Rob Warhurst, was one based on humour and mutual understanding. It was an ongoing joke between them about her arrival time, because Rob knew that an old boss of hers used to monitor her every movement. In the end she had left that job because of her hatred of being micro-managed.

Rob tolerated Annalize mainly because she was great at business development and, with Lemon Aid being a small company, he needed her. Her bad timekeeping didn't really bother him at all, but he wasn't going to let her know that, as the excuses that Gracie conjured up for her colleague usually made his morning.

Twenty minutes later, a red-cheeked Annalize shimmied across the open-plan office, her tight pencil skirt accentuating her perfectly round little bottom, her stilettos making her already long legs look even leaner. Her stylish black bob didn't have a hair out of place. She removed her coat and elegantly sat down at her desk.

After two years of sitting opposite Annalize – and having accepted her own love of flapjacks and scorn for any kind of exercise that made her too out of breath – Gracie had given up on comparing herself to Madame Perfect.

'He's on the proper warpath,' she managed to whisper as Rob threw a file onto Annalize's desk with such force its contents flew out all over the place.

'You're late.'

'Didn't Gracie explain?' The 'perfect one' made a questioning face across the desk as Gracie scrabbled on the floor to pick up the errant papers.

'Of course I did. I said you had a really bad stomach and

were going to sit in Marcy's until your wind had subsided. Black coffee and no cake does that to you, you know.'

Annalize closed her eyes in mortification.

Rob didn't look up for fear of catching Gracie's eye. 'Right, ladies – to work. Shits or no shits, we've got a tender to get out of the door.'

TWO

The light wasn't working outside her two-bedroom flat in Wandsworth when Gracie returned home from work. She sighed and flashed her mobile phone into her handbag to hunt for her keys.

Inside, she cast off her coat in the hall, flung the keys onto the kitchen worktop and went to the fridge. Pouring herself a large glass of Sauvignon Blanc, she walked across the hall and did something she hadn't done in days – slowly pushed open the 'nursery' door.

The two little Moses baskets stood patiently side by side, their soft white sheets still awaiting the delicious smell of baby. The teddy bears on the border that Gracie and Lewis had taken so long to choose looked back at her sadly. They had decided not to find out the babies' sex, hence the plain white walls – thought it would add to the excitement. It had also made for many fun nights of choosing names that went together, be it two girls, two boys or a boy and a girl.

Shutting the door behind her quietly, as if not to wake them, she took a large swig of her chilled wine then plonked herself down on the sofa. Tears fell down her cheeks. She sniffed loudly.

As hard as it had been to hear, Annalize was right. It was about time she thought about losing her baby weight. But in a way knowing she would never again have baby weight to lose made her want to hang on to it – remain comforted by it, almost pretend those precious babies of hers were still inside of her. Growing and kicking. Making her a mummy. She would never be a mummy, because losing the twins had resulted in her ultimately losing her womb too.

'Barren' was such an awful word. But that was what she was. Barren. Desolate. Empty. Unable to have biological children of her own. Never. Ever.

The worst question (which people asked more often than Gracie could ever have thought possible) was: 'So, do you have children?'

By thirty-eight, people expected to have kids, but for Gracie Davies even when the time was right, and the man was right, it hadn't been easy. In fact, it had been bloody hard. Three rounds of IVF hard. But then, when it had happened, when that test came back positive... oh my. It was like the best birthday she had ever had, quadrupled a million times. That feeling of completeness, of belonging. Starting a family. Her dream.

Gracie wiped her eyes and drained her glass. She glanced down at her stomach. Yes, there was a muffin top. A distinct bulge over her smart black work trousers. She felt more comfortable in a baggy cardie than a tight dress. Leggings were her friend rather than jeans.

Looking at her favourite photo next to the TV, she put a hand through her hair. OK, maybe she had changed.

She remembered so clearly when the photo had been taken. There was the lovely Lewis, flashing his beautiful white teeth. Her five-foot-eleven, dark-haired, handsome sales director partner of seven years. She had poked him in the ribs to make him laugh. Her sister, Naomi, had caught this magical moment on a sunny Dorset beach six years ago. The look of happiness. The look of love.

Hearing his key in the door, Gracie flicked on the television. She used to look forward to that sound. The 'hi, honey, I'm home' sound. The sound of union. That instant sigh of relief. *We're both in and safe. We can have a lovely dinner together, chat about our day, then snuggle up together. Make love and face the next one – together.*

THREE

Lewis didn't even kiss her hello anymore. Lifting his glasses and rubbing his eyes, he went straight to the fridge. 'Any beers?'

'No, all gone, sorry. There's some wine in there, though.'

Lewis turned, frowning. 'There's football on tonight, too.' He sighed. 'I'll see if Connor's about. He might want to go down the pub and watch it. What's for dinner, anyway?'

Gracie was now engrossed in the news. 'I thought we could get a takeaway.'

'Gracie, you know we're still paying the bloody IVF off and I thought you were trying to be good this week.' She sighed as Lewis went on, 'And I'm sure it would make you feel better losing some of that weight of yours.'

'Not you as well!' Gracie couldn't listen to any more. 'What is it with everyone today? It's *my* body, it's *my* problem. If I don't want to lose weight, then I won't.' Her face reddened. 'And as for not being made of money, it's all right for you to piss off down the pub and spend more than a takeaway costs without a worry.' She was on a roll now. '"Gracie, are there beers?" "Gracie, what's for dinner?" We're a partnership, Lewis. Or we used to be, at least. So, no, don't stay in with me and have a nice evening. No, you just go, meet Connor, do what you do with him. Talk shit, watch football. I don't really know what your problem is anymore.'

'Problem? The problem –' Lewis was shouting too, '– is that we haven't had sex for weeks, Gracie. Weeks! And do you want to know why?'

Gracie bit her lip, dreading but already guessing what was coming.

'I just... I'm struggling to love you as you are.'

Too late, Lewis realised the enormity of what he'd said, and ran to her side to hug her. But the words could never be taken back. That was it, they were out there. Hurtful words swirling around the room, like a wasps' nest of secrets – one of which had just stung Gracie right in the face.

Like a bull about to go into the Plaza de Toros Las Ventas, Gracie's nostrils flared. Stifling a sob, she fled to the bedroom, slammed the door and locked it.

Fired by his guilt, Lewis nearly pulled the handle off as he tried to open it. 'Oh God, I'm so sorry. I shouldn't have said that when you are feeling this way. But shutting yourself away in there again, well it's not going to help. We never spend time together. Your head is always stuck in that bloody computer. There are only so many Hyster Sisters you can talk to, surely?' His voice now shook with emotion. 'And as for money, I've said before, we could always get a lodger. It's not healthy keeping the spare room as a bloody shrine.' He paused, sounding more contrite when he spoke again. 'Life needs to move on, Gracie. There are no babies and there won't be any babies.'

Silence. Realising he had now stepped over the line in magnificent fashion, Lewis's voice softened. 'If you're going to be like this, Gracie, I'm going to go out now. We do need to talk, I know that. Let's have a date night on Thursday, like we used to in the good old days, eh? We can work it out, I'm sure.'

Still no answer.

Lewis sighed, grabbed his coat, closed the front door quietly behind him and walked slowly down the stairs.

Feeling ashamed and like he had been watching the same old sad drama over and over again for the past six months, a massive wave of sadness washed over him.

They had been his babies too.

* * *

Sighing heavily, Gracie pulled her laptop out from under the bed and placed it on the bedside table. So what if she wanted to chat to women who'd been through similar situations? She needed their support at the moment.

It was a relief to her that Lewis had gone out, to be honest. The fact was, they hadn't had sex for weeks. Quite frankly, it hadn't bothered her. By not mentioning it, she had hoped he wouldn't even think about it. But who was she kidding? He was a man in his sexual prime and, to give Lewis his due, this was the first time he had moaned about the lack of it, so he wasn't that bad. Unless he was getting it elsewhere, of course? No. Gracie shook her head just thinking that. Whatever Lewis's faults, he would never be unfaithful. He had always had the ultimate respect for her and she for him. It was just so bloody sad that it had come to this.

Before their baby-making had commenced, she had adored sex too. They could never get enough of each other. They had been known to sneak out of work to have a quickie in a lunch hour on more than one occasion.

But as soon as there was another reason for the whole love-making thing, God, how things changed! Her ovulation date turned sex into a military operation. And if, for some reason, Lewis was working away or just not in the mood, she would fly into a foul temper, distressed at the thought of her body clock ticking away loudly for yet another month.

Poor Lewis, he said he had felt like a performing seal. Even with the promise of a daily blow job, it wasn't fun anymore. They started living the cliché that too much of a good thing drains away the excitement.

And now she knew that she couldn't have children, she was the one who wanted it less. Secretly, she was slightly scared that she might never want sex ever again.

Some of the Hyster Sisters (one of the many self-help websites Gracie had frequented since her hysterectomy) had said that the operation had been the best thing that had ever happened to them: that they were horny all of the time and, with no periods to stop them, had the sex drive of a twentysomething again. She imagined they were all older than her, had kids already, and that probably most of them were lying. Gracie didn't even have the urge to masturbate.

She undressed to her pants – too big, too grey, not sexy – and checked herself in the full-length mirror in the bedroom. She moved her forefinger across the dark red hysterectomy scar that ran above her pubic line. She hated that scar. It depicted *loss* – and what man in their right mind would find that attractive? A long ugly line across such a delicate area.

They had to cut her a little wider than normal as it was an emergency and they had found a fibroid as big as a melon – the reason that her babies had been kicked out, apparently. God knows why they had not picked that up on the scan. Her sister had said she should make a case against the hospital. Gracie had neither the mental capacity nor the inclination to do this.

When she came round, weak, white as a sheet, with tears spontaneously flowing down her cheeks, she was told that there had been complications. She had lost nearly all the blood in her body and there had been no option but to take away her womb and ovaries.

She was evidently a very lucky girl to be alive.

Gracie didn't feel lucky.

Unable to walk unaided, she spent the next four weeks looking at her bedroom ceiling and living off porridge and soup. And when not surrounded by the distraction of friendly faces, she was wrapped in a shroud of complete despair.

How useless was she not to be able to keep those little dots safe and warm? To have let some big ball of muscle fibre take over and take away her new life: her new life as a family of four.

Now a shelf of flesh loomed above the scar. She felt she looked awful. All that bullshit about love being more than skin deep: it was no wonder that Lewis didn't fancy her anymore. He obviously didn't love her enough. Gracie was glad that she had a therapy session tomorrow.

After her 'operation', Rob Warhurst – so much more than just her boss – had softly and kindly suggested that therapy might help and offered to pay for six sessions for her. He was a good and wise confidant, so Gracie took heed, acknowledging that she still needed to let out so much anger and grief.

She pulled on one of Lewis's big T-shirts and, despite it being just 7 p.m., got into bed. She flicked on her laptop. Her screensaver flashed up and she had to shut her eyes. She knew she should delete it.

It was a scan of the twins. They had danced around that day, not staying still for long enough to be measured. The 3D photos were in her sock drawer. She had only been able to look at them once since she had lost them. Lewis had said that maybe it would be cathartic to throw them away.

Lewis, she thought, *is a dick.*

FOUR

'Promise me you'll still fuck me like that when you're grey and old, Professor.'

Maya Bakova glided confidently across the room to pull up the sash window of the tatty Victorian flat she was renting, her lover's eyes following every single agile movement of her taut, naked body. A tattoo of a blue dragon wound its way down the left side of her smooth, supple back.

'You know I never promise, apologise or explain, little bird.' The professor's voice was low and throaty.

Maya shimmied back under the crisp white covers. Two purple satin scarves now hung limply from the ornate white French-style bedframe.

The professor raised himself up onto his elbow and looked down at her. 'But bloody hell, you are so goddamn sexy and I'm so ready to ruin you again.' Maya put her hand down to his erect penis. He groaned in pleasure, then jumped up in his full glory. 'Bollocks. I've got a lecture this afternoon and I need to prepare.'

'Spoilsport. You have to promise to whip me within an inch of my life next time now.'

'You're an insatiable little minx, that's what you are. Now, are your housemates out?'

'Yes, yes, of course, it's lunchtime – they are all at work. I'm the only one lucky enough to work shifts and get lunchtime callers.'

'Callers? Not sure if I like the plural of that.'

'Just a slip of the Czech tongue.' She winked. 'Now go and impart all that knowledge of yours to your lucky students, before I suck it out of you again.'

FIVE

Professor Scott Princeton hated being late. Especially as he drilled it into his students that lateness was the epitome of rudeness.

He scurried across the university campus, swearing to himself. His floppy fair locks caught in the late-March wind and blew about like mad sheaves of corn in a field. He knew it was only a matter of time before he would have to shave it off. He was receding badly and long hair coming from the middle of his head wouldn't be a good look.

At forty-five he still looked all right and the fact he could pull someone as hot as Maya surely meant he still had it. Although, he thought she was more turned on by the fact that he was a professor, more than double her age, with an exceptionally large cock, than by his personality and wit. Some of his students were her age. Was it wrong? No. It was a relief to have someone so fit and nubile to keep him from being tempted by the many students who made it their business to flirt outrageously with him on a daily basis.

Sex with Maya was what it was.

No holds barred, non-committed, pure unadulterated filth

between two consenting adults. And he was certain she was aware of that, too. For stupid was something Maya Bakova definitely wasn't. He had never mentioned that he was married and she had never asked.

Lecture over, Scott nodded to one of his colleagues in the corridor, and unlocked the door to his office, sitting down at his desk with a huge sigh, to go quickly over tomorrow's course notes. *That* desk. The one he had fucked Maya over the day he had met her cleaning his office a year ago. He had been working late. She had stretched up to dust a cobweb from the ceiling, ruching her T-shirt up with her. He noticed her smooth, tattooed back – and that had been it. He loved a girl with tattoos. It didn't take much. Just her noticing the slight bulge in his trousers, and him asking her if she had ever considered sleeping with an older man. That was enough. Before he had even had a chance to ask her on a date, his zip was down and she was giving him the best blow job he had ever had in his life. Thirty minutes later, they were both buck naked fucking like rabbits over his leather-topped desk.

Just thinking about it now gave him a slight swelling. Right, he must concentrate, he had a job to do. He checked the diary on his phone. 'Oh crap!' He had forgotten he had a therapy session at six. *Gracie Davies*. He racked his brain. Oh yes – pleasant girl, lost twins, struggling to get over it. Relationship now struggling. Straightforward stuff really.

He grabbed his papers and threw them into his worn brown leather briefcase. He swore as he tried to do it up. The catch had broken. He was fiddling around trying to fix it so as not to waste money on a new one when his phone rang.

'Scott, darling?'

'I'm in a rush, Cynthia, what is it?'

'You couldn't pick up Emma from Georgia's later, could you, around six? It's my Ashtanga yoga night with Pearl.'

'No, I've got two therapy sessions – in fact, I won't be home until ten. She's eighteen, Cyn. Leave some money in the emergency pot and she can get a taxi, surely?'

'OK, OK. I just thought for once you might be home at a reasonable hour. Especially as it's our wedding anniversary. God forbid!' She hung up.

Scott sighed again. His second therapy session had been an invention. He had planned to go back to Maya and now for the semblance of peace, he had no option other than to give that up.

* * *

Checking his watch, the Professor swore loudly as he rushed around making his office look half-reasonable. Sweeping his arm across his desk, he turned his nose up as he spotted a mouldy supermarket sandwich in its plastic wrapping, which had been sitting there for two days. He realised he hadn't put on a bet in the 5.30 at Plumpton. Lesson Learnt was the mare's name. It would be a bloody lesson learnt to try and get a bit more organised when he had after-lecture commitments.

'Bugger!'

He squirted some Jo Malone room spray that one of his students had given him for Christmas. Then, taking a pillow from the cupboard behind the door, plumped it up and threw it absent-mindedly on the chaise longue in the corner. One of the many pieces of furniture he had inherited when his father had died, just months after his mother, two years ago.

Despite being highly intelligent – his mother an English teacher, his dad a GP – both had smoked. And both had died of lung cancer in their early seventies. There was little effort required for the grave digger when Scott's father was buried, as the soil on his mother's grave was still loose. Scott had only to re-instruct the stonemason regarding the headstone and that was that. *Rest in Peace – Rose and Benedict Princeton. Much loved parents of only son Scott.*

Scott had been born more academic than organised. He also had never acquired much regard for money. With his PhD in Psychology and Behavioural Studies he wanted to make a difference: write as many papers as he could that would benefit society; help students achieve the best grades with the least amount of stress possible; and then, of course, give something back in his guise as a therapist.

He had enjoyed the therapy he administered, learning a lot about himself – not all of it good – along the way. And the fifty quid an hour came in handy too. Insisting on cash payment, it covered the odd gift for Maya, plus funded his horse-racing addiction.

Perhaps his disinterest in money had arisen because he had never lacked it. His wife earned well as a barrister. And now that his parents were gone, he had inherited a townhouse in Battersea, as well as a magnificent holiday home overlooking the sea at Looe in Cornwall.

Cynthia, his wife, and his daughter, Emma, had visited Cornwall a lot more than he had. He preferred work to relaxation. In fact, he loved it when they went away, as it meant he could fuck Maya without worrying about the time.

He loved Emma, the result of a honeymoon period of perpetual sex in the first year of his relationship with Cynthia. But the passionate attraction to his wife had faded years ago and, if he was really honest, he wouldn't have chosen to have children: having discovered that even one child brought too many demands on his time. Despite this, he didn't like being on his own, and was too lazy to find someone to replace Cynthia. The pair of them led fairly separate lives, but the bond of all those years in common – a certain comfortableness and, of course, Emma – kept them together. Now that Emma was eighteen, she didn't really need them. Soon she would be at Oxford and then definitely wouldn't need them – well, apart from financially, of course.

Scott opened the door to his office and looked down the corridor. Good, it seemed quiet. He had not told anyone that he conducted therapy sessions in his college room. He didn't know if he needed some sort of special insurance, or permission from the university, or even if it was legal. He didn't really care. If anyone asked, he was just giving extra study.

The childless one was always punctual. He liked that.

* * *

Gracie knocked gently on the door as previously instructed, smiled at the professor and laid her coat at the end of the chaise longue, her home for the next hour.

This was her fourth session and they both acknowledged now that not a word was spoken when she arrived. She lay back, nestled her head into the middle of the really quite vile flowery peach pillowcase, and shut her eyes.

'There are tissues and water as usual underneath,' Scott instructed.

Gracie, soothed by the professor's low, throaty voice, took a deep breath and felt instantly at ease.

Scott noticed she had a lower-cut top on than usual; he could see the soft curve of her breasts spilling over the top. He had never seen her cleavage before.

'So, how's your week been?'

The professor watched Gracie as she replied. Her habit was to keep her eyes closed for the whole hour, unless she had a full sob going on, when she had to sit up and blow her nose for fear of choking.

She faltered, before saying quietly, 'Lewis doesn't find me attractive anymore.'

'Was that exactly what he said to you?'

'Hmm, he said he was finding it difficult to love me as I was.'

'OK.' Scott nodded wisely. 'So your interpretation immediately went to your body image?'

'Well... yes.'

'And how does that make you feel?'

'I'm not surprised, to be honest,' Gracie confessed. 'I know I'm not very pretty naked at the moment. And I'm certainly not the woman he first met. And... well... well, it's almost like I don't want him – Lewis, I mean – to find me attractive.' She let out a huge sigh. 'And well, it can't be easy to live me with me at the moment. I'm a mess.'

The professor took a sip of water from a bottle on his desk. He was looking at Gracie in a different way today. Her round face was half-hidden by her wavy, dark brown, shoulder-length hair. He had noticed how beautiful her big green eyes were before she had shut them tight: full of expression and feeling, despite being drowned with sadness. He hadn't taken in her long, mascaraed eyelashes before today. Her cheeks were flushed and she just had a smudge of gloss on her full lips. She was a naturally attractive woman and, despite all that she had been through, looked younger than her thirty-eight years. *Probably because she doesn't have children*, he thought to himself. *No constant worry or sleepless nights.*

She was missing a little bit of soul at the moment, but it was his intention to help her get it back.

He looked down her body. He could see the line of her leg through her black leggings. He could never say it to her, but she had the figure of a mother who had just given birth. Curvy and desirable.

'And why do you think you don't want him to find you attractive now?'

'Oh, I don't know. No, actually, I do know. I don't want sex. No, it's not that. It's the association with sex and Lewis and loss.'

'That must be so difficult for you,' Scott said gently as a tear rolled down Gracie's cheek.

'Yes, it is. And being honest I don't know if I love him anymore or not. I feel a bit devoid of emotion at the moment, to be honest. It's as if I need to get strong myself before I can give any love back. And I know it's been six months since, you know... since what happened.'

'Losing the twins, you mean, Gracie?'

'Yes.' She took a massive breath; even saying the word 'twins' still made her feel a bit sick.

It seemed, since she'd lost them, that she had never seen so many twins in her whole life. Or met so many people who were one of a twin, or saw so many women who were pregnant and kept harping on about it. But that had been her not so long ago. Pregnant and proud.

'What do you think would happen if you did instigate intimacy, Gracie?'

'He'd probably run a mile.' Gracie sighed.

'Like rules, walls are put in place to protect us,' Scott replied gently. 'Sometimes, we just need to break them down.'

Gracie almost had a skip in her step as she walked back to her car outside the university campus. She felt slightly better than when she had arrived and knew exactly what she was going to do. Professor Princeton had really helped today.

Lewis was at football practice for his local pub team so she had time to prepare.

She luxuriated in a deep bubble bath. Shutting her eyes, she thought back to a particularly romantic weekend they had spent in the South of France. They'd stayed in an amazing hotel in the hills, where they ate, drank, laughed, danced and made love all weekend. The memory itself made her feel a little bit horny. Yes! Professor Princeton's words were ringing true. Maybe she wouldn't be a barren old bag who would never have sex again. She was a sensual, sexual woman who deserved to be loved. It wasn't that Lewis didn't find her attractive physically, it was just the grief had been all-consuming and she had lost herself along the way. Had lost the person he had fallen in love with. She wanted to feel better, to feel attractive again, and it was only her thoughts and attitude that could change this.

After applying copious amounts of her favourite shower gel, she shaved herself smooth. Then, opening her wardrobe, rifled around for the best matching underwear she could find – stockings, suspenders, the lot. Her highest heels were donned. And to complete this outfit of seduction, a short black mac she hadn't worn for years.

The minute he walked through that bedroom door, Lewis Blair was going to get what she hoped was a very happy surprise.

SIX

Maya Bakova checked her phone. Where was he? She tried to call him and was greeted by the very annoying – *this person's phone appears to be switched off.*

'Yes, thanks, I gathered that,' she said aloud, then swore in Czech.

The professor never failed to turn up when he said he would. He said he'd be with her after seven thirty but it was gone ten. She could have worked tonight if she had known.

It annoyed her that he had begun to have such a hold on her emotions. She had tried so hard to keep him at arm's length, keep whatever this relationship was, purely sexual. But he was different. Never ordinary in bed or in conversation. He intrigued her. Excited her. Made her laugh with his eccentricities. And despite trying to push them away, she couldn't deny that she was beginning to have feelings for him. Feelings that she hadn't felt before in her twenty-two years on this planet. Feelings she knew she could never divulge to a married man. It would be so much easier if he was one of her paying clients. She would never allow the lines to get blurred. But he wasn't and they were, and she really wasn't sure what she was going to do about it.

SEVEN

'Bollocks! Bollocks! Bollocks!'

Scott Princeton realised he'd left his phone at the university and that he hadn't texted Maya. It was just as well, though, that she couldn't call him now he was home, especially as it was his wedding anniversary. It was a bonus, too, that he could use the excuse that he couldn't reach Emma to sort picking her up, since he'd also forgotten all about that.

He'd had twenty quid on a five-to-one winner, so had gone to a bar, had a bottle of white and a burger and was now home awaiting Cynthia's return from her Ashtanga class. He had managed to find a dozen red roses on a flower stall outside the Tube station. She didn't usually eat after yoga, so they could sit and share a bottle of Saint-Émilion and have a chat.

He was even considering going to Cynthia's bedroom tonight as he was feeling horny just thinking of Maya tying him up earlier. God, he loved having sex with her. In fact, he quite liked her company, too. She was dismissive of him, unlike the fawning students he was around all day, and it actually turned him on more. She was intelligent and streetwise. Yes, definitely streetwise: something he had never really been. His brain was full of unnecessary facts, and he wished he could be more down to earth like her. He also wished he could switch off his whirring mind sometimes. Tonight had been a rare event. He loved eating alone, watching the world go by. For despite his job involving the study of the human mind, he didn't actually like people very much.

If he stopped and thought about it, he knew that it was wrong to be having an affair with Maya, especially as she was just four years older than his daughter. But, for the past few years, he had had minimal sex with his wife, so seeking relief elsewhere didn't amount to unfaithfulness in his mind. Maybe Cynthia wouldn't have quite the same view in her menopausal state. Or maybe that was all a ruse for her lack of libido, and she was doing exactly the same as him! He batted the thought away, not sure that he would like that scenario.

Their ten-year age gap had never been a problem. Cynthia didn't look her age. And added to that her position of power, he quite often noticed other men ogling her. She still had a sensual edginess. Like Helena Bonham Carter. In fact, she looked a lot like her.

He often thought that the complexities of men and women should never allow them to live together in perfect harmony as a couple. He also thought it interesting that after having had a thing for older women in his youth, he was now craving the love of someone younger. But it wasn't love, was it? It was pure non-committed sex.

A harem would be a far better scenario. For Cynthia still stimulated his brain; Maya stimulated both his cock and his mid-life crisis. He had free access to both a barrister and a barista, what more could a man want!

Emma appeared in the doorway of the conservatory. Scott had his head in his iPad, catching up on the day's news.

'Hey, Dad.'

'Emma, darling. Sorry I couldn't collect you earlier. All OK?'

'Yes, all good. Mum called a while back. She's gone out for dinner with Pearl, said she wasn't wasting her night waiting in for you.'

'Ah, OK. Totally understandable. Do you want to join me for a glass of wine?'

'No thanks. Josh is upstairs.'

'Then why on earth would you?' He winked as his daughter shook her head and ran off up to her top-floor bedroom.

He looked at his watch. Ten o'clock. Maybe he could go to Maya.

Gracie came into his mind. She had had a good session with him that evening. She had left him with a bounce in her step. He hoped that she was doing exactly as he had suggested and was seducing that man of hers right at this minute. If anyone deserved happiness that poor girl did.

EIGHT

It was 3 a.m. Lewis sat in the black cab with his head in his hands. He was in that awful stage when the drink was wearing off and the hangover was beginning to start. What had he done? In seven years he had never been unfaithful to his beautiful Gracie. And he had been so unkind to her yesterday, too.

Losing the babies had not only made them drop the ball on their relationship, but on real life as they knew it as well. They had never been very good at communicating and last night, something just snapped. How could he have been such an arsehole?

'You all right, mate?' the cabbie enquired, noticing tears in his fare's eyes as he looked in the rear-view mirror.

'Yeah, yeah. Got an allergy, you know.' Lewis stumbled out onto the pavement and handed a twenty-pound note through the half-open window. 'Keep the change.'

'Thanks, mate.' The cabbie put his thumb up. 'And women, eh? They're not worth it, most of 'em, you know that.'

Thinking that Gracie wasn't most of them, Lewis forced a lopsided smile. That woman, she was one in a million.

He clambered up the stairs and put his key as quietly as he

could in the door. He undressed in the lounge and quickly hand-held the shower over himself. He'd never had to do anything like this before and he didn't like it. He didn't like it one bit.

He crept into the bedroom and put his hand over his mouth. For there was Gracie, fast asleep, spread-eagled on top of the covers, wearing the underwear he had always adored her in. The bedside light was still on and an empty bottle of wine lay on the floor. Her make-up was perfect, apart from the tracks of her tears down the middle of her cheeks.

Never before had he realised just how much he loved her.

NINE

Gracie woke with a start. In her drunken stupor she had forgotten to set her alarm. She was surprised that Lewis hadn't woken her. She put her hand to his side of the bed. It was cold. She quickly checked her phone. Nothing. Groaning, she walked to the kitchen, still in full underwear regalia, to flick the kettle on. She glanced at the clock. Luckily it was only seven, so she wouldn't be late for work. Although the way she was feeling, she was quite tempted to ring in sick.

There was a note by the kettle.

Gigi, get yourself dolled up tonight, for we shall wine, dine &
69 XX

Then in brackets:

(Sorry, got pissed after football and slept on sofa so as not to wake
you.)

'Aw,' Gracie said aloud and got on with making her tea. He hadn't called her Gigi for months. She found she wasn't even cross now about him being late last night. By the time she had finished getting ready, she had downed a whole bottle of wine on an empty stomach, had cried her eyes out to her sister on the phone, and had crashed out by nine. She'd have been fit for nothing anyway by the time he'd got in after the pub had closed. The pleasure had been in making an effort. In making herself feel good.

She got back into bed and thought of Lewis. His note was so sweet. He was thinking of her, for once. Maybe the outburst the other night *had* cleared the air? He would have talked to Connor that night and chatted to his other mates after football practice. Maybe they had helped him through it. As a couple they had never been very good at communicating. Hopefully now they could emerge from the smog of grief and work things out.

They had met, bizarrely, at the bar during a Coldplay concert. If love at first sight was a thing, then she was sure they had experienced it. She thought back to the time that they first had sex, on their first date following the concert. They had met for a drink in Soho and couldn't keep their hands off each other. The lust was so great that she saw no point in waiting. Sod all that 'will he respect you in the morning' malarkey. Lewis took her back to the house he shared in Brixton that Friday night and they didn't make it out of bed until the Sunday lunchtime. Seven years on they were still together.

She bit her lip, feeling something she hadn't felt in a long while. She texted Lewis.

69, you say? I take it that means times?

TEN

Ping. Gracie heard a message land in her phone as she sat down at her desk. She smiled, thinking it would be Lewis's reply. Instead it was Annalize.

> Gracie – hungover. Throwing up! Can you cover for me if the walrus is in please?

Gracie replied:

> Only if you promise to get me a bacon roll on the way in. With ketchup. Thanks!

> Ta! Might even get one myself.

Gracie thought it must be some level of hangover if Madame Perfect was considering letting a crumb of carbohydrate pass her immaculately glossed lips.

Rob Warhurst scurried in with a huge smile on his grey-bearded face and his 'Lemon Aid' branded backpack on as usual.

'Morning, Gracie. Wow, you're looking lovely today.'

'Thanks. I haven't done anything different.'

'Well, your face has a little glow to it, something I haven't seen for a while.'

'It's probably too much wine last night,' Gracie laughed. 'What's in your bag today, then?'

'You just wait. It's a new gadget. Actually, I have two that I want to show you. An apple corer and peeler and a pasta basher. Both amazing!'

There was never a dull moment with her crazy boss, who was always either buying a gadget or trying out a new hobby.

'I look forward to seeing both in action.'

'I wish Mrs Warhurst shared the same excitement. After twenty years, she is what I call... gadget worn.' They both laughed. 'Right, work time! It's 9.05, any word from Mz Good?'

Gracie rolled her eyes.

'She's hungover *and* running late.'

'Oh God. She's going to be more intolerable than usual.'

As he spoke, Annalize hung her tailored jacket neatly on the coat rack and sashayed across the office. Though perhaps a little tired under the eyes, she looked perfect in every other way. Not a hair out of place, wearing a beautiful Chanel-inspired black-and-white shift dress with high black stilettos.

She put a white paper bag on Gracie's desk and sat down quietly opposite her. Gracie, with relief, noticed an imperfection.

'You've lost an earring, Annalize.'

Annalize put her thumb and forefingers to both ears. A diamanté butterfly hung from her left lobe.

'Shit, I love these too. They're hook-throughs, not backed, so they come off quite easily. How annoying!'

She took the other one off and put it in her purse.

'Maybe it shot down the toilet when you were sick.'

'Yeah, thanks for that, Gracie. It'll be at home somewhere, I'm sure. They get caught in clothing when I undress usually.'

'Annalize, good afternoon,' Rob piped up extra loudly.

'I thought Gracie would have told you I was going to be late?'

'Yes, I said that you had run out of haemorrhoid cream and couldn't even think of sitting at your desk all day without it.'

Annalize grimaced and shot Gracie a furious look. Gracie laughed. Would she ever learn?

Rob got up to go to the kitchen for coffee. 'Well, ladies, we have *piles* of work to get on with, so let's get on, shall we?'

'Gracie,' Annalize hissed. 'Why can't you just think of a normal, not embarrassing excuse for once?'

'Because I've run out of them, you're late so many times.'

Gracie didn't dare tell Annalize that it was her and Rob's standing joke; she'd be even more mortified.

'Fair point.' Annalize exhaled loudly. She seemed to be missing her usual composure today.

'Are you OK?'

'I'm hanging, Gracie. I think I may have to go home early. Stopped off at Marcy's to get your bacon roll and had to be sick again in the toilet when the smell of food hit my nose.'

'Ew. Thanks for getting it, anyway. Here.' Gracie handed her some money.

'No, no, my treat. I insist.'

Blimey, Annalize must be ill! A show of kindness and generosity in one morning!

'Where did you go anyway?'

'I... I don't remember the name of the bar.'

'So were you with girlfriends, or on a mystery date you failed to tell me about?'

Annalize suddenly went green and rushed off in the direction of the toilet.

Gracie's phone pinged and she found tears pricking her eyes.

I love you Gigi x

ELEVEN

'Are you sure you're not guilty of something, Lewis?' Gracie said casually as Lewis arrived home from work and handed her a single red rose. She grinned as she put the single bloom to her nose. 'A gift and a table booked at our favourite restaurant? It's like the old days.'

'Don't be silly. I've just had a wake-up call, Gracie, that's all. We need to talk. I'm so, so sorry about what I said the other night. I didn't...'

'Ssh now.' She kissed him softly on the nose. 'No talking required just now, big boy. Just take me to bed or lose me forever. I've had the hangover horn all day.'

Lewis watched as Gracie dropped her silky robe to reveal the brand-new underwear she had bought in her lunch hour. High heels accentuated her shapely legs. She had had her hair blow dried and amazingly Annalize had managed to do her make-up perfectly before she left early to go home.

She really did look beautiful.

'Whoa!' Lewis took a step back. 'Where have you been, sexy lady?'

'It's not where I've been, it's where we're going now.'

Lewis was wide-eyed at this newfound confidence in Gracie. As she led him by the tie to the bedroom, pushed him back on the bed and roughly began to pull off his trousers, he bit his lip in anticipation.

God, he had missed her. Missed her soft lips knowing exactly what to do to give him pleasure. Gracie Davies *was* the complete package.

Yes, last night he had been faced with a nigh-on perfect body, taut, fit, not an ounce of fat. But that's all it had been: a shell. There was no love, no feeling, no softness of curve or strength of character.

When he was as hard as he could be, Gracie jumped on top and writhed confidently, moaning at the sheer pleasure of sex again. Her voluptuous breasts bounced around in front of Lewis's face.

'Take me from behind,' she gasped.

After a sweaty session of much needed love-making, Gracie screamed louder than she had in seven years as they came together.

Lewis was finding it hard to push back tears. It was ironic, and made him feel weak, that his act of betrayal had finally made him realise just how much he felt for his partner.

Should he tell her now? Could he live with himself? No, it would destroy her. But what if she found out? It would destroy her anyway, especially as she had just got her confidence back to sleep with him again. No, he would keep quiet. They could move forward from here; they could talk everything through. Sex had been as much a major hurdle as their lack of communication. It would take a while, but he knew they could put the terrible time they had both been through behind them.

Gracie had always wanted to get married. They had put that on hold while they were paying for the IVF, but now there was nothing to stop them. Yes, they had debts but they could get engaged and save. They could start the life they had always wanted. He found it hard to imagine a life without children, but he found it harder to imagine a life without his Gracie. They could adopt. There were only barriers now if he created them.

Gracie snuggled in to him and kissed him on the lips.

'I love you, Lewis Blair.'

'I love you too, Gracie Davies.'

It got to ten o'clock and Lewis propped himself up and looked over to her.

'I don't know about you but I'm bloody starving. It's too late for Zitas now. Shall I order a takeaway?'

'Didn't I just say I'm going to watch my weight from now on?'

'Oh, Gracie, come on – last treat. You've burnt off enough calories tonight, so start your health kick tomorrow, and it won't take you long to get back to where you want to be, you know that.'

'OK, OK. I'll go and get the menus, what do you fancy?'

'You up against the wall.' Lewis smacked her bum as she got up.

'Oi!' Gracie smirked as she walked through to the lounge.

On seeing the jumper Lewis had been wearing last night scrumpled on the floor, she folded it and went to put it on the arm of the sofa. As she did so, she noticed something sparkly sticking out of it.

Looking closer, she gulped. And as her heart began to beat at one hundred miles an hour, she felt physically sick. For there, staring back at her, was a diamanté earring in the shape of a butterfly.

TWELVE

Still flushed from their love-making earlier, Gracie stood in the kitchen trying to control her emotions. There was no doubt this was Annalize's earring. Stuck right there in her boyfriend's jumper. The jumper he had been wearing last night. The night that Annalize had gone out and got drunk, too. It all made sense. Her over-generosity, her helping with her make-up! She would never be able to look at a butterfly as a creature of beauty ever again.

Sinking her face into the jumper, her worst fears were realised, as the undeniable scent of 'Eau de Bitch' filled her nostrils.

As she marched through to the bedroom, she found Lewis laughing out loud at an old episode of *Friends*.

Dropping the earring from a height onto his duvet-covered crotch, she knew his face would tell her the truth. It took all of her mental strength to remain calm. 'I just saw this stuck to your jumper, and it's not mine?'

To her despair, his face had guilt written all over it.

He sat up abruptly. 'It's not what you think. I can explain.'

Gracie started to pull on jeans and a jumper.

'Where are you going, Gigi?'

'Nowhere, until you tell me what the fuck is going on. I bloody knew you fancied her. You bastard, Lewis.' She tried her hardest not to cry. 'I work with the woman. I have to look at her every single day – what the hell were you thinking?'

Lewis got up and clumsily pulled on his joggers. He took a huge breath and ran towards Gracie and held her by the shoulders. 'It was a silly mistake, Gracie. I was drunk. We'd had a row. I was horny! She was there. Randomly, in the same pub as me after football. We got talking. She came on to me.'

Gracie pulled herself away, her voice now a growl. 'We had a row and you were horny! What the fuck! *No* is a very short word to remember, Lewis.'

'It meant nothing, I promise you. In fact, it's made me realise how much I love you, Gigi. I don't want her. I don't want anyone else. I love you, Gracie. I really do. So much. And I swear on my mother's life that I have never done anything like this before and I promise I will *never* do it again.'

'Cut the Gigi and the crap, Lewis. Did you have sex with her?'

Lewis jumped up and held Gracie by both arms again.

'Look at me, Gracie, you have to believe me. It was a one-off, it was nothing to me. It was purely physical.'

'Did you fuck her?' Gracie growled.

'She's fake, she has nothing to offer me. You are far more beautiful.'

'Just answer me, Lewis, I have to know or I can't deal with it. I have to know everything.'

Lewis paced over to the window and put his head in his hands.

'Yeah, we had sex. It was shit. I am *so, so* sorry, I really am. You have to forgive me. It meant nothing.'

'Did you arrange to see her again?'

'No, of course I didn't. It was what it was. Sex. Plain sex. Nothing more, nothing less.'

'To you it was, Lewis. To me, it spells the end of our relationship. I thought nothing could hurt me as much as losing the twins but – do you know what? – I think you've matched it.' She wiped her eyes clumsily with her right hand. He went over to her and tried to hug her.

'Get your filthy, philandering hands off me. I trusted you, Lewis. I trusted you.'

She started throwing things into a bag.

'Where are you going?' Lewis was crying now.

'I don't know.'

'We need to talk about this, Gracie. If things had been running smoothly, it never would have happened.'

'So, every time we have a row now, or I may not fancy sex and you go out, what do you think I'll be thinking?'

'You can't just run out on me, Gracie.'

'Watch me!'

THIRTEEN

'Why is Auntie Grace crying, Mummy?'

Naomi Davies handed her sister a tissue. Gracie blew her nose loudly and ruffled her nephew's hair.

'Me and Uncle Lewis had a row, that's all, darling. I'm fine, don't you worry about me, little man.'

'Why did you have a row?' The innocent inquisitiveness continued.

'Be a good boy and eat your cereal or you'll be late for school.' Naomi dragged her dark long hair up into an untidy ponytail.

'But Mum...' Five-year-old Jack bashed his spoon down and milk flew across the kitchen table.

'No buts, eat!'

Naomi Davies looked a little worn for her forty years. Her previous sex, drugs and rock and roll lifestyle, plus the stress of single parenting, were beginning to catch up with her.

She had never really wanted kids, preferring a free-spirited hippy lifestyle. But while on holiday in Croatia, a one-night stand with a Hollywood actor who happened to be filming there, no less, had put paid to that.

Gracie had gone along with her to the abortion clinic, but Naomi couldn't go through with it. And nine months later, baby Jack was born. It was just the two of them – and that's how it had stayed.

Long-term relationships had never been on her agenda either. In fact, having slept with half the male population of London and become increasingly frustrated at the lack of compatibility, Naomi had found herself more and more attracted to women.

'Phew, that's him out of my hair until three.' Naomi returned from the school run and flicked the kettle on. She looked to a puffy-eyed Gracie. 'So, firstly, little sis, what are you going to do about work?'

'I'll have to resign, won't I? I mean, how on earth can I face the bitch? I just can't.'

'What did you say to Rob this morning?'

'I told him what had happened. I couldn't lie to him, he's been so good to me. He was great as usual, there's no urgency on any events at the moment, so he said take the week off. Have a good think about what I want to do.' Gracie ran her hands through her hair. 'He doesn't want to lose me, but *she* does bring in a hell of a lot of business. It's not his problem, is it? Oh God, Noms! I can't believe this is happening.'

'I never thought the scumbag gave you enough attention after you lost the babies, to be honest, Grace.'

'Yeah, I know all that, but I love him and he's been through it, too.'

'Still, no bloody excuse to sleep with someone else. Especially a woman you work with!'

'I know, I know. I don't know what to do, Noms. I mean if I leave him where will I live? And I can't leave work, I need the money. But I seriously don't think I could ever trust him again now. Or work with her, for that matter.'

'You can't stay with someone just because you've got nowhere else to go.'

'Give me a break, sis.' Gracie blew out a huge breath. 'I need to get my head around it all.'

'I realise that, Grace. But, how dare he? You're so beautiful. You lost those precious little babies and he does this to you. What an arse.'

Gracie sighed deeply. 'I've been hell to live with.'

'I'm not buying that.' Naomi's voice softened. You can move in here. I don't need any money from you, you know that.'

'You make it sound so black and white.' Gracie blew out a huge breath. 'And out of anyone you should know that relationships aren't ever that.'

Noms gripped her sister's shoulder. 'I'm so sorry this is happening to you.'

Suddenly appreciating what Naomi had gone through herself, Gracie removed her sister's hand, put it momentarily to her lips, then went to fill the kettle with water.

The Hollywood actor had said that if Naomi kept quiet about the baby, she would want for nothing. So a three-bedroomed house in Wimbledon had been purchased and five hundred thousand popped into her bank account. She had signed an NDA to say that she would never publicly out him, and that was it. She would watch him in his movies with a wry smile, and could already see his brooding good looks developing in her handsome young son. Gracie was the only person in the world who knew.

Gracie and Noms's parents hadn't questioned anything. They had assumed that Naomi had been her usual black-sheep self but was doing very well at selling the bespoke handbags she made, and could afford the house she lived in.

John and Deidre Davies had emigrated to Spain when the

girls were in their early twenties and no love had been lost between them since. Their distance had been another factor in Gracie's sometimes depressive state. The one woman she had wanted by her side when she lost her babies was her mum, who didn't even bother to book a flight to the UK. Noms had been her rock instead.

'Go and sit down, do you want coffee or tea, I'll make it?'

'Coffee and fuck it, two sugars, please.' Gracie let out something between a laugh and a cry.

'That's my girl and if it makes you feel better, why don't you just fill the fridge for the three of us, as I know you'll want to pay your way somehow. Workwise, get your CV up to date, so if you do decide to move on, you'll be ready to go. Maybe you should go away for a week, get your head around everything, decide whether you really do want to be with Lewis or not.'

Gracie sighed deeply. 'So many bloody decisions.'

They were interrupted by a bark and Naomi smiled.

'Hello, Boris, you little munchkin. Where have you been, you scamp?'

The lively Patterdale Terrier jumped up at Gracie's knees. Gracie bent down to stroke him as her sister continued.

'He's like a teenager, hilarious. He literally lies in his crate and waits for me to come back from the school run when he knows it's walk time.' She whispered the word *walk* for fear of him getting even more excited.

'I'll take him out, if you like. Forget the coffee for now. The fresh air will do me good – give me time to think.'

'If you're sure, Grace, that would be great. I'm doing a talk about my bag making and setting up a stall at the WI at eleven. I know, don't say it, I'm still so rock and roll.'

Gracie managed a smile. 'That, dear sis, you are. Now, where's this little fella's lead?'

FOURTEEN

Gracie pulled into the packed car park. What was it with all these women who didn't have to work? She looked around at all the 4x4s, the odd Smart car and the space-age-looking electric cars. There were also a couple of dog-walking branded vans. Naomi had told her that quite a lot of famous people walked their spoilt pooches here, too. There was actually nothing common at all about Wimbledon Common!

As soon as Gracie opened the passenger door of her red Ford Puma, Boris jumped out, barking and running around her feet in excitement.

Gracie liked the comfort that having a dog on a lead brought. It gave her the same comfort she felt pushing a pram. She had loved looking after Jack when he was a baby. The love she felt for him was so intense, she thought it must almost be like having a baby of her own. She tried to convince herself of this. Yes, her nephew obviously loved her dearly, but he would never be hers, not properly. The familiar sadness of knowing that nobody would ever call her Mum washed over her.

She set off on her trail, breathing in the early April air and enjoying the feeling of sun on her face. If she closed her eyes maybe, just maybe, she could magic all her angst away; she would wake up and still be pregnant, still have Lewis, her lover, by her side. A Lewis who hadn't cheated. A Lewis who hadn't ruined everything between them. The Lewis she had been so in love with.

Boris was in his element off the lead. He knew the paths of the common like the backs of his paws.

Gracie didn't think she had ever seen so many dogs in one place. A lot of them were with the professional dog walkers, some of whom were walking seven at a time. Some were with joggers, most with yummy mummies bitching about one thing or another, in the knowledge that their little Jemimas and Scarlets had been safely deposited at their respective private schools.

All these people had the dog code down to a T. You didn't really acknowledge the person, just talked about little Pooks, Rudi or Poppytail, then off you went. Mummy duties set aside, the talk now turned from dirty nappies and school uniforms to poo bags and studded collars.

Gracie chose not to join in. Caught up by a mixture of hurt and hatred, she wasn't in the mood for conversation and, when her button decided to pop right off her jeans, complete self-loathing, too. When Boris decided to have a poo in the most open part of the path, it was just about the last straw.

'Oh, you little devil, couldn't you have done it in the woody part?' She put a hand through her hair in despair and sat down on a bench which, she noticed had been skilfully carved out of a tree trunk.

'Well, I'm glad he didn't. I'm always getting shit on my boots. Have you got any bags?' The North London accent was evident.

'Oh God, no, I didn't think.' The man in front of her was grinning at her agitation.

'Here, let me. I always carry a couple. I can't bear the

bloody mess.' He ripped a bag from a roll and swiftly picked up the offensive-smelling litter.

'I haven't seen you here before. I work here, see, get used to everyone who comes through. Same old faces, same old habits, same dirty bitches, oh, and their dogs.' He smiled broadly.

Gracie noticed a good set of teeth along with cropped brown hair, a slightly outgrown goatee beard which she didn't mind, even though Lewis had always been clean shaven. She also noticed his smouldering brown eyes and beautifully shaped big lips. She loved big lips on a man. He was in his late twenties, she reckoned.

'You didn't have to do that, you know.' His small act of kindness made Gracie feel like she wanted to cry and just not stop. 'But thank you. Thank you very much.'

'I know I didn't, but I did. By the way, my name's Ed. I would shake your hand but...'

Gracie smiled, looking at the green bag hanging from his finger.

'So what do you do here then, Ed?' She felt she ought to make a bit of an effort as he had just picked up her dog's shit and he was rather handsome.

'Ground work on the common. Keep it shipshape, you know. I charge around on my quad bike, trying not to run over any posh birds and get sued.' Gracie liked his devil-may-care attitude. 'Well, good to meet you...' Ed hung waiting for answer.

'Gracie, my name's Gracie, and this is Boris.' Boris was now dragging around a stick wider than the length of his body and growling. 'And he's actually my sister's, hence my amateur attempt at canine shit disposal.'

'Well, he's a lucky boy having you at the end of his lead.' Ruffling Boris's brown coat, the handsome one winked. 'Right. I'd better do some work.'

Gracie, not sure what to do with this obvious flirtation,

stood up, then swore loudly as her jeans began to slowly slip down her hips. She sat down again abruptly.

'You OK?' Ed called back.

'Not really, but I'll get over it. Seeing all these runners makes me think I should get fit.'

'You look fit enough to me.' He grinned. 'Bu if you need a bit of a push there's a running club that meets here regularly.' He assumed a posh voice. 'The SW19 Club,' he laughed. 'There should be details on the café noticeboard.'

With that he leapt on his bike and whizzed past her with a smile and a wave.

FIFTEEN

A week later Gracie sat opposite her boss in Marcy's. To avoid the elephant in the room she began talking about everything from the weather to the forthcoming summer party for their biggest client – until Rob cleared his throat and said casually, 'Just so you know before you make any rash decisions, *she's* gone.'

'What do you mean, she's gone?' Gracie took a sip of her cooling coffee.

'Annalize. She's gone. Resigned.' Rob Warhurst wiped cappuccino froth from his beard.

'Really?'

'Yes, really. Now come on, finish your coffee, I've been flying solo for too long and I could really do with your help,'

Rob Warhurst had never been a very good liar. Of course Annalize hadn't resigned; she had been on good money at Lemon Aid and was very much a career woman. But Rob's heart was stronger than his head. She had upset his lovely Gracie and he couldn't bear to have her anywhere near him, much less lose his favourite employee. Gracie was a fantastic, empathetic events organiser. He could replace a salesperson such as Annalize more easily than her, he hoped.

He had made Annalize redundant with immediate effect. She hadn't kicked up a fuss probably because he had offered her a tidy pay-off in order for her not to threaten a lawsuit, which he assumed she would try to do. He was sure that her passive exit had nothing to do with guilt, as he was doubtful that that was an emotion ever to have troubled her.

Gracie lightly put her palm on top of her kind boss's hand. 'Well, that's a relief. I thought I may have to resign. I do need to ask you something, though.'

'Go on.'

'I'd like to be a bit flexible with my hours, if that's OK? I've found a running group on the common, but they seem to not fit in with the nine to five. I haven't been yet but I want to try and go as many times as I can. I will make up my hours – start early, work late...'

'Gracie, of course that's fine. I know you know the devil's in the detail with events. You're experienced enough to work out what needs doing when, and you sure enough put in the hours, even weekends when needed. And I certainly don't want to lose you. You're special, you know.'

Gracie felt herself welling up. 'It's going to take me a while to get over this and I love you a little bit more now, you know that.' Gracie kissed her boss on the cheek, which she noticed reddened immediately.

Gracie was putting on her coat when Maya approached.

'Gracie, isn't it?'

'Yes, hi. How you doing? I'm so sorry, I've forgotten your name.'

'Maya, I'm Maya.'

Gracie had nose-piercing envy as the diamond in the young Czech girl's nose caught the sunlight that was streaming through the café window.

'I promise I'm not being nosy, but I did overhear about a running club and I really could do with getting fit. I bloody smoke too much. My lungs could do with an airing.'

Gracie smiled. 'It's on Wimbledon Common. They set off at eight thirty and four thirty. The meeting point is the Windmill Café.'

'Perfect. I can do the later one. That's great, thank you, Gracie. Hope to see you there.'

Rob was making 'hurry up' gestures.

'I'd better go. The boss has got ants in his pants.' Gracie smiled.

As she sat back at her desk, Gracie felt momentarily peaceful. Work was sorted, tick! And she need never look at the harlot that was Annalize Good ever again; she was going to get fit and may even have made a new friend to boot. Then a dark cloud of realisation swept through her. Who was she kidding? Peaceful? Lewis had messaged her earlier wanting to take her out for dinner on Friday night.

This was probably just the calm before a very big storm ahead.

SIXTEEN

Lewis smiled nervously as he got up to greet Gracie at the bar at Zitas. She noticed his fitted blue jumper. She had always said how much she liked him in it. He had shaved, too, and she detected the swoon-inducing aftershave that he had been wearing the very night they met.

'Hey,' he said softly, handing her a bunch of daffodils, her 'favourite flower in the whole world'.

'Thanks.' She held them to her chest.

'You look beautiful.' He moved to kiss her but she turned her head away. Feeling she had been foolish to agree to meet him so soon, she had an overwhelming urge to just run.

Suddenly faced with her future, Gracie felt far from beautiful. She felt sad, scared, unhappy and angry all at the same time. Why couldn't life just give her a break? Just a teeny tiny one. It didn't need to be a side-splitting guffaw of a break; an ongoing smile for a few months or so would do.

Here she was standing in front of the man to whom she had given seven years of her life. The man she had so wanted to be the father of her children. And suddenly he seemed like a stranger. She was thirty-eight years old, childless and at a cross-roads in her life with no idea in which direction to turn.

The smart Italian waiter saw them to their table and pulled out her chair. With a heavy heart and a watery-eyed 'thank you', she took a deep breath and sat down.

SEVENTEEN

Cynthia Princeton pushed back on her comfy office chair and pulled up the large sash window of her wood-panelled office. She looked at the case file in front of her. Rape, her speciality. And she had dealt with enough criminals to know an innocent when she was faced with one. This poor lad was so likeable, came across as so honest, too. Which was great for a jury if it went that far.

Her colleagues would say that she should never be so confident, as it would get her into trouble one day. She most certainly had intuition on this one, but admittedly not a lot of evidence. It was the young girl's word against his. Always tricky, always grey. But his family were putting up the money for a top defence lawyer and a top defence lawyer was what they were going to get.

She was just about to call her assistant when a text came through. It was her husband.

Therapy tonight, be home 9ish. I'll eat en route.

'*Quelle surprise,*' she said aloud. She honestly didn't know why she stayed married to Scott. She knew he was sleeping with someone or other at the moment, as she had smelt cheap perfume on him all too frequently. They had separate rooms, aside from the occasional drunken coitus, lived separate lives, really, but they occasionally rolled each other out for a necessary dinner party and they did genuinely like each other.

Scott Princeton made a good friend but a diabolical husband. The romance had long gone, but until Emma was at university, there was no way that she would leave him. Cynthia's childhood home had been broken when she was small and, despite her very successful career, it had done her no favours.

She pushed her glasses to the end of her nose, undid a button on her crisp white shirt and called the new intern through. He sat himself nervously down in front of her. She could tell he was trying not to look at the tiny glimpse of white lace bra that was now showing. Imagining his firm ebony skin pressing against her paleness, she leant forward slightly.

'Luke, I'm going to my Cornwall house this weekend to get my head around the Duke/Simpson case.'

'That sounds like a sensible idea, Mrs Princeton.'

Cynthia pushed her glasses up and nonchalantly asked, 'Do you think you could come with me?'

EIGHTEEN

'So, I've met with Lewis,' Gracie said quietly from her lying-down position.

Professor Princeton put a fresh box of tissues on the table next to the chaise. He knew this was going to be quite a session. The last one had been traumatic enough, after the poor girl had found out that she'd been cheated on.

'OK, and how was it?'

'It was sad.' Gracie kept her eyes closed and sniffed loudly. 'He bought me daffodils. I love daffodils.'

'Why do you like daffodils, do you think?'

'They are just such a bright and happy flower. Make me think of spring, of new beginnings.'

'Ah, right.' The professor quietly jotted something down in his patients' notebook.

'He is truly sorry. I know that, but...'

'But what, Gracie?'

'I don't know what to do.' Her voice started to crack. 'The past few months have been so unsettling, that it's almost as if being in his company reminds me of the loss. And now that he's cheated, I don't think I can bear to look at him, because all I can think of is him sleeping with somebody else.'

'Maybe relationship counselling would help?' Scott quietly shut his notebook.

Gracie sighed deeply. 'I think it's gone beyond that.'

'And did you say that to him?'

'Well... yes, sort of. I said I thought that I needed to clear my head of everything that had happened. Needed some time alone, to grieve, I guess.' She put her right hand to her forehead and made a groaning noise. 'It's hard when you lose little souls that you didn't even meet. It's not like you can miss them as people because you never knew them, touched them, smelt them. They were just inside me, little bundles of energy that I knew were there, but weren't. Sorry, I'm making no sense.'

Scott cleared his throat. He didn't completely understand what she meant, but thinking back to the love he had felt for his daughter when he had first been handed her in the hospital, he felt sadness wash over him. What a terrible thing Gracie had been through, and she was such a decent human being. It wasn't fair.

'Don't apologise, Gracie. You have a right to feel how you are feeling. You've been through a terrible experience. A lesser person would be lying in a darkened room beating their fists, saying, "why me?" You've been so strong. But maybe now it is time to let go. To think of you, and just you.'

The professor looked down on her pretty round face and could see it contorting in anguish. He gently placed a tissue in her hand as he knew she wouldn't open her eyes. Her lips wobbled, she turned to the wall, curled up in the foetal position, and let out an almighty sob.

Gracie stayed like that for five minutes. It wasn't until she sat up to blow her nose that the professor spoke.

'Do you feel better for that?'

'I don't know. What I do know, though, is that everything I

felt for him has gone. For Lewis, I mean. I have no respect for him. I'm glad I told him it was over.' She sniffed again loudly. Lines of mascara tracked her tears. 'Oh God, but how can you just stop loving someone like that? Bastard!' she shouted, then softened. 'I'm so bloody confused, Professor Princeton.'

'How did he take it when you said you were leaving?'

'He said he thought I was being stupid, as he had made a dreadful mistake and now realised just how much he loved me. He thinks we can still work it out.' Gracie let out a sarcastic laugh.

'And do you think in time maybe you could? Maybe forgive him. You *were* going through a bad time in your relationship.'

'No. He committed the ultimate sin. He crossed the line. And if you love someone you don't do that. I didn't even stay for dinner. I walked out on him. There was nothing for me to say.'

'OK. So on a practical note, what are you going to do about living arrangements?'

'He's going to stay in the flat. It's rented, and he can afford it on his own. I'm going to stay with my sister for a while, until I sort myself out.' Gracie suddenly stood up. 'I don't want to talk about it anymore. I just want to go now. Thank you for listening.'

'Oh, OK, that was quick and – well, that is my job, listening, I mean.' Scott smiled a lopsided smile. 'If you need to book any more sessions do let me know.'

'I will do, but I'm going to go it alone now, I think. I have to. A new start. No one is going to hurt me ever again.'

'Don't close everything off, though, Gracie, including these sessions. Think about it. It's good to get these feelings out, without judgement.'

'I'll see.' Gracie felt agitated.

'Your heart is bruised at the moment, but someone will come along and fill it with love again one day, you mark my words. You're a pretty and intelligent woman. And if I don't see you again, you deserve the best. Don't forget that, eh?'

'I'll try.' Gracie handed over his cash, which he tucked into the pocket of his jeans.

She declared her thoughts. 'It's so weird telling a stranger so many intimate things but it kind of works.'

'Yes, yes. Goodbye, Gracie. Take care.'

Scott closed the door behind her and reached for his *Racing Post*. If he was quick, he'd still get a bet on the 7.20 at Southwell.

NINETEEN

Lewis Blair sat at his desk staring into space. His secretary knocked lightly and put a cup of coffee down in front of him.

'All OK?' she enquired politely.

'Actually, I'm not feeling so good, Rosie. Think I might be coming down with something. I'm going to work from home this afternoon. Can you shut the door behind you, please?'

He reached into his pocket and opened the small red jewellery box that had been there since that awful night with Gracie. The sun coming through the window lit up the beautiful diamond ring which threw glints of light onto the wall.

He put his head in his hands in despair. Why, oh why had he been so incredibly stupid?

TWENTY

Gracie was only half a mile into her first run and already felt like she was going to die. Her cheeks had gone bright red and her heart was beating way too hard under her new Nike T-shirt.

'Keep up now, stragglers,' Keen Kate, the posh organiser of the running club, shouted from the front.

Maya raised her eyes to Gracie, who managed to splutter between wheezes, 'Jeez, if I'd realised it was going to be this hard, I might have thought twice.'

'Keep going, Gracie, we will feel better for doing it, I'm sure. Mind you, I might have to stop and have a fag in a minute.'

Gracie laughed. 'Quick, over here.' She ushered Maya off the path and onto the carved bench she had found herself on last week. 'You have your cigarette, I need a bloody sit down.'

Maya laughed. 'Yes, sod this for a game of shoulders, that is what you say, isn't it?'

'That's funny. No, it's soldiers.'

'Ah, mind you, this is like being on an army training camp. I think I may stick to sex, it must burn as many calories and at least it's enjoyable.' Maya retrieved her fags and a lighter from a pocket in her leggings.

Gracie's face dropped. 'Chance would be a fine thing.'

'It's not so bad being single, you know, Gracie. I am. And you can still have sex without all the messiness of a relationship. That's what I do, anyway.'

'I don't think I could do that non-connected sex thing. I'm just out of a very long-term relationship.'

'All the more reason, then. Get out there, Gracie, have some fun.'

'But you're young, Maya.'

'And what's age got to do with anything? Life's all about fun and it looks like you could do with some right now.'

'I need to adopt your attitude.'

'You do. You're a sexy woman, Gracie. And you need to grab life by the balls.'

Gracie leant back on the bench, her breath having returned. 'You speak very good English, by the way.'

'Thanks. I started learning it at school when I was five and have been over here for four years now. I've picked it up as I've gone along, really. But still not quite up on all the English slang, as I just proved.'

Maya lit a cigarette and inhaled deeply. Just as Gracie leant forward to tighten her laces, a quad bike came speeding round the corner at full pelt and screeched to a sudden halt right in front of them. She didn't know whether to be pleased or mortified. Pleased that it was handsome Ed or mortified that she must look a red sweaty mess.

The handsome one jumped off the bike. 'Afternoon, ladies.' He caught Gracie's eye and she could feel herself going even redder. Maya stubbed her cigarette out on the ground. 'Not sure if that's part of the workout, and I trust that butt is going in the bin?' He winked at Maya. 'So you followed my advice then, Gracie?'

She nodded, trying discreetly to wipe away the sweat that was now dripping down her nose. 'Well, sort of. I mean, we didn't even do half a mile and had to stop.' She was flattered that he had remembered her name.

'Well, it's a start, eh? You're looking good on it already.'

Gracie was mortified to realise that wet, sweaty marks had formed under her boobs.

'Yeah, right.'

'No borrowed dog today, then?'

'No, I thought I'd be too fast for him.' Gracie smiled.

Ed smiled back. 'Humour as well as beauty, I like that.'

'I do my best.' Oh God, she was flirting as much as he was.

'Well, good to see you both.' He smirked. 'See you again soon, I hope.' Before she had a chance to answer he hopped back on his quad and sped off.

'Whoa! Talk about him not taking his eyes off you, Gracie.'

'Shut up. With someone as young and fit as you next to me, I don't think so.'

'No, he fancies you. I can tell.'

'Really?'

'Yes, really.' Maya smiled. 'See, you've still got it going on, girl. Be confident in who you are.'

Suddenly the shrill tones of Keen Kate and the stomping feet of ten yummy mummies could be heard approaching.

'Quick!' Maya took Gracie's hand and dragged her behind the bench. Gracie thought she was going to wet herself for laughing. 'Come on now.'

They joined the rear of the pack, still both laughing, and jogged back to the café.

'Well done for keeping up on your first go, ladies.' Kate beamed as she appeared from the café with a steaming skinny latte. 'I trust I will see you again?'

'Oh yes,' Maya and Gracie lied in unison.

'Drink?' Maya pushed open the door to the café.

'Yes, a Diet Coke would be good, thanks.'

'So *are* you going to come again?' Gracie enquired as they sat drinking their Cokes on the wooden benches outside.

'Not sure they are really my kind of people, to be honest.' Maya took a drink.

'Nor mine. But if you're up for exercising together, I'd like that.'

'I'd like that too. Ooh, watch out, your young man is approaching.'

Ed appeared in football kit from inside the café. Gracie noticed how firm his thighs were. He squeezed up next to her on the bench.

'Twice in one day, now there's a treat.'

'You're such a charmer.' Gracie felt herself reddening again.

'Always! Glad I've seen you, though. Nice trainers, I know my sister would love a pair like that. Why don't you text me the details? Got a mind like a butterfly. Gotta dash.' He placed a business card into her hand. 'See you soon, I hope.'

'See.' Maya lit a cigarette and was promptly asked to put it out by a snooty-looking woman on the table next to them. There were no 'no smoking' signs and they were outside anyway, so she feigned deafness and carried on. 'Told you. I've never heard of such a roundabout way of getting your number, though. You have to text him.'

'Really?'

'Oh, stop it, Gracie, you know you do. You have what is known as... just pulled.'

'He must be at least ten years my junior.'

'Who cares, age is just a number. We're all the same age lying down.'

Gracie grinned. 'That's hilarious. Shouldn't that be height?'

'Whatever. If you don't, I will.'

'I've literally just said goodbye to my ex.'

'Like I said before, all the more reason.' Maya smirked.

Gracie screwed up her face. 'What do I say if I do text him, then?'

'Gracie, you are out of practice, aren't you?' The pretty Czech took the card from her hand.

She read aloud. 'Edward Duke. Landscaper – so you say, *Hi, Ed, it's Gracie from the common. My trainers are from wherever. How big is your cock?*'

'Maya!'

'Or you could say, *Hi Ed, blah blah re trainers and yes, I'd love to, thanks. Tomorrow, outside the café at six?*'

'I couldn't be so forward.'

'Oh, you so could. He's cute. If he does nothing more than fuck your ex of your system, then he is so worth a hook-up.'

TWENTY-ONE

Cynthia Princeton opened the file on her desk and buzzed through to the intern.

'What time is Mr Duke getting here?'

'Ten thirty.'

'Excellent, just show him through when he arrives, will you? Thanks.'

She smiled to herself. Bless Luke, feigning illness he hadn't gone to Cornwall with her. She figured, if he was too scared to go for it when it was on a plate, he would certainly be no good to her in bed. No, she would maintain a professional relationship with this one. Probably for the best all round.

Persuading Emma to come instead, it had been lovely to chill out by the sea in Cornwall and have some mother-daughter time. Plus with all the headspace she had down there, she had found a loophole which with luck would get her client off his rape charge with ease.

TWENTY-TWO

Noms was combing Jack's hair through with nit treatment in the kitchen when Gracie returned from the common.

'Auntie G, tell her to stop.' He screwed up his face in annoyance.

'Here.' Gracie took the comb. 'Let me do it more gently for you.' She winked at Noms. Boris leapt up at her knees.

'Enjoy your run with the posh commoners?' Naomi washed her hands.

Gracie smiled. 'Hmm. It was a very short jog actually. Maya and I bunked off and had a chat for most of it.'

'Well, you look better for it. It's nice to see some colour in your cheeks.'

'Right, that's it, mister, you just need to rinse it off now.' Gracie kissed Jack on the cheek and put the comb straight in the bin.

'Yeah, get in the bath, Jack, it's run. I'll be up in a sec.' The young lad dutifully did as he was told.

'You wouldn't think they'd get them at private school, would you?'

'I didn't know *he* paid for that as well?'

'He doesn't give me extra. I kept some of the money aside for Jack's education.'

'Have you heard from *him* lately?' It was funny that between them they didn't even say the actor's name, as if the secret would be out to the world if they did.

'No, he emails me if he's on location, but rarely. It's easier that way. For Jack's sake more than anything, really. If it got out, it would be scandalous even now, I think.'

'Talking of scandal, I met someone today.' Gracie smiled coyly.

Noms's eyes and mouth widened. 'Whoa, Gracie Davies, now that's thrown me completely.'

'Well, I say I met someone, a landscaper at the common gave me his card, said he wanted to know where my trainers were from.'

'Yeah, right.' Noms grinned. 'More like he wanted to know how he can get in your knickers.'

'Exactly. Coffee-shop Maya said it was obvious that he fancied me.'

'I'm proud of you, Gracie, I mean, you only kicked Lewis into touch days ago.'

'I know that. But do you know how good it was to feel that first flush of attraction from somebody else? It felt bloody good, Noms. And I *am* going to message him.' Gracie held her head high.

'Hello, is this really my little sister standing in front of me? The shy, retiring one, who wouldn't normally say boo to a goose?'

'It's the new me, Noms. Losing the babies and now Lewis... I'm not taking any shit anymore. I'm going to have some fun. Take control. No more tears.'

'I commend that fully, but be careful, eh?' Noms squeezed her sister's shoulder. 'I know I'm all about you getting back on the saddle but maybe heal those wounds first. I know you couldn't cope with even a single grain of salt going into them at the moment.'

'It's fine. He seems sweet. A bit of a lad, but a genuinely nice bloke. And it is what it is.'

TWENTY-THREE

Maya checked her phone. If she was quick she could fit the doctor in. He usually came on a Monday, but had texted earlier to see if he could come tonight instead as his wife was away. He was easy too. She didn't even have to get naked. Just prance around in the requested red lacy underwear and black thigh-length boots and whip him how he liked it. He would get excited, go the bathroom, finish himself off then leave. A perfect client, in fact.

She wondered what the professor would think if he knew that she masqueraded as a cleaner and barista to pay her taxes but really earned most of her money as a sex worker. Knowing him, he probably wouldn't bat an eye. She was always very safe with her punters, insisting they use a condom, so there was no danger to him or her of contracting any STDs. And anyway, she felt that too much time had passed to tell him now.

She worked hard for the specified hours on the minimum wage and still was able to look respectable with her tax credits and her rent paid. Her mother would be proud. How did anyone survive living in London with a 'normal' job, anyway?

But she loved it here in the UK and especially London.

There was just so much to do and now she was able to save, she was on her way to achieving her dream of training as a beautician and opening her own salon.

She never ever took risks; she knew she was safe. Her four regulars had been coming for months now. She was so used to their quirky fetishes and fantasies, she could almost pre-record the noises and expressions she used to keep them all happy. However, despite it being such easy money, she looked forward to the day when she could swap playing with cocks for cutting off locks.

The professor acknowledged the doctor with a smile as they crossed on the stairs up to Maya's flat. Strange, he usually saw him on a Monday – at least he would get the red undies treatment tonight.

'Professor! You're early for once, that's not like you.' She was breathless, having rushed around tidying the bedroom for fear of evidence of another man.

He pulled back her cream silky robe.

'Ooh, red on a Thursday, now there's a treat for the professor.' He felt a stirring as he noticed her pert little nipples poking through the lace. 'You seem breathless, little bird.'

'It must be the effect you have on me, Professor.'

TWENTY-FOUR

Ed smiled warmly as he saw Gracie's red Puma pull into the Wimbledon car park, where they had agreed to meet. He had thought she might chicken out and was pleased she'd stuck to her word. He jumped out of his van as she approached.

'Hey, you look lovely.' He kissed her on the cheek.

'Well, you know, it's not every day you get asked on a date by a handsome landscaper.' She self-consciously pulled her jumper down over her jeans.

'Oh, it's a date, is it?'

Gracie reddened. 'Err... well... I... err.'

'I'm joking with you, Gracie. Now what do you fancy doing? I thought maybe a quick jog around the common for starters?'

'Yeah, right.'

'Pub, then?'

They found a quiet table in the corner of a quaint Wimbledon pub.

'Cheers.' Ed raised his glass to her, took a slurp then wiped the froth of Guinness from his top lip.

Gracie liked his boyish looks and confident demeanour. She noticed he'd tidied his goatee and had had his hair cut, too.

She had spent ages deciding what to wear. She'd never had to think about it with Lewis. The comfortableness of a long-term relationship had its benefits. Noms had said that jeans and a plain jumper with a V-neck to show off her cleavage slightly were perfect for a first 'meeting'.

'So you make a habit of picking up women on the job, do you?' Gracie smirked.

'None as pretty as you.'

Gracie wrinkled her nose. 'Ew, excuse me whilst I'm sick into my glass.'

Ed laughed. 'There are, however, many rich wives who are bored with their lives, so I'm sure I could pick one up every day if I wanted to. Nothing to do with the way I look, just that they'd all fancy a bit of rough, I reckon.'

'Ooh, you've made me feel so special now.' Gracie's sarcasm was evident.

'You're cute. You also looked a bit sad. Felt like I could make you smile.'

Gracie blushed. 'If you don't mind me asking, how old are you, Ed?'

'I'll be however old you want me to be.' He laughed. 'How old do you reckon I am?'

'I hate it when people say that, I don't want to offend.'

'Gracie, do I look like a man who is easily offended?'

'OK. I reckon you're twenty-eight.'

'Thirty-two, actually.'

'You must have had an easy paper round.' Gracie took a sip of wine.

'Ha! I know I shouldn't ask a lady her age, but I'm going to.'

'Thirty-eight.'

'Nice. Always have had a thing for an older woman. All that experience and a lovely womanly body. Can't bear a stick, me.

What's the point of teasing a Twiglet when you can stroke a warm, curvaceous peach.'

'Don't get too carried away, Mr Duke, we are only having a drink.'

'And there I was thinking I had finally found my duchess.' Ed winked at her and she felt her tummy go a bit funny. 'So how come someone as lovely as you is single?'

'It's a long, sad story that I really don't want to go in to now.' Gracie sighed.

Ed took Gracie's hand across the table. 'I'm a good listener.' His eyes met hers.

'Oh. I was living with someone for quite a while, but we split recently.'

'How recently?'

'Like, very recently.'

'Wow, so I'm rebound doors, then, am I?'

'You can be whatever you like.' Gracie smiled smugly.

'Touché!'

'How about you? Can't imagine a hot man like you has been single long?'

'A few months. But I don't want to talk about me.'

'So are you looking to settle down, have kids?' Gracie inwardly cringed as the words flew out of her mouth. She had just met the bloke, but she knew this was a question she'd have to ask. If someone wanted kids, she couldn't be with them. Her life situation suddenly hit home and she felt a wave of sadness sweep through her.

'Why, do you fancy practising?' Ed laughed loudly. 'Seriously, I think so. But I'm realistic about life. Who knows what it's going to bring you, eh? How about you, do you want children?'

Gracie shot up. 'Blimey, look at us talking all grown up. My round. Another one of those?'

Another hour flew by with no further mention of kids or marriage. Ed made Gracie laugh. She needed to laugh.

'Right, I'd better go. I can't have another wine or I won't be able to drive.' Gracie felt quite giddy as it was.

'You could always have a soft drink, Gracie?' Ed urged.

'No, it's been really lovely but...' Gracie went to stand up.

But what? What was wrong with her? She was having a lovely time with a great bloke and she wanted to end the evening. But she was newly single. This wasn't the right time. And he wanted kids. She would get hurt. No more salt in the wounds, Noms had said. Noms was, for once, right.

'No, it's fine, Gracie. A woman's prerogative and all that,' Ed said respectfully.

As he was getting up to help her with her jacket, Gracie noticed him glance at a young, tarty-looking blonde as she walked into the bar. The girl glared at him. Ed seemed to freeze, then almost pushed Gracie through the door.

He was visibly shaken when they got outside.

'Are you OK, Ed?' Gracie looked genuinely concerned.

'Yeah, yeah, of course.'

'Who was that girl?'

'She just reminded me of someone, that's all.'

Gracie had kept things from him, so who was she to question further?

'I've had fun, thanks, Ed.' She went to kiss him on the cheek and he pulled away. He could see the disappointment on her face and it pained him inside.

'You're a great girl, Gracie. I'll see you around, soon, I hope.' He seemed jumpy.

Within seconds he had sped off to the car park, leaving an open-mouth Gracie standing on the pavement. That was it, she had blown it already. He thought she wasn't interested. And was it just paranoia that made her imagine that girl was giving her funny looks? Oh God. Being single was going to be so much harder than she thought.

TWENTY-FIVE

Noms opened the door to a shattered Gracie.

'Baby sis, what on earth's the matter? I had a gut feeling he might be a wrong'un.'

'It's not him, it's me. I like him. He's cute and funny and seems kind but...' She let out a massive sigh.

Noms sat her down at the kitchen table and put the kettle on. She took her sister's hand and squeezed it.

'Maybe it was a bit too early?'

'Maybe.' Gracie sighed again. 'He said he wasn't sure but I know he wants kids. How am I ever going to find anybody who wants me, Noms? I'm not a proper woman anymore.' Gracie's eyes filled with tears.

'Oh, darling. You'll be surprised how many men out there don't want kids, or have kids already...' The kettle bubbled furiously. 'So you told him, then – that you can't, I mean?'

'Of course not.' Gracie tutted. 'He'd have run a mile, I expect.'

Noms looked pained. 'Oh, sis, I guarantee someone will fall in love with you, for you.'

Gracie rolled her eyes. 'Miss Naomi Davies, ever the optimist.'

'I mean, Lewis accepted it, didn't he?'

Gracie threw her hands up in the air. 'And then went and slept with someone else. Bad example, Noms.'

'That had nothing to do with the fact you can't have kids. He was more than ready to adopt when you were.'

Gracie whined. 'I don't want to talk about Lewis.'

Naomi stood up to make the tea. 'Are you sure you don't? I'm quite surprised how little you've said about him.'

'It makes me burn inside.' Her voice became a whisper. 'I hate him.' Gracie sighed deeply.

Noms looked pained. 'Oh, Grace.'

'It's fine. I'll get over everything; it'll just take a bit of time.' Her voice wobbled. 'I may have mucked things up with Ed, but, you're right – I'm sure there's someone else out there who'll show me attention.'

'You need to concentrate on yourself first.' Noms placed two mugs of steaming tea down in front of them.

Gracie shook her head. 'You sound like bloody Professor Princeton.'

'Maybe you should see him again? He helped you, didn't he?'

'Yes, I guess so, but I really can't afford him at the moment. We're still paying off the IVF, remember, and I want to get that over with. Until I've cleared it, it keeps me bonded to Lewis.'

'How much do you owe?'

'A thousandish each now, I think. We put it on a loan. All that bloody money and for what? Heartache and a broken relationship.'

'You got to feel how it was to be pregnant, Gracie. Some women don't even get that far.'

Gracie put her hand to her stomach. 'Always a silver lining,' Gracie spat sarcastically.

'Sorry, sorry, that was a silly thing to say.' Noms looked pained.

'Yes, it was – that is no comfort to me yet. And if I'm honest, I didn't actually enjoy feeling so bloody sick all of the time.'

Naomi took a sip of her tea. 'Have you thought any more about what you are going to do workwise?'

'With Rob agreeing for me to work flexible hours, I would be silly not to hang in there for a bit. Especially as *she*'s not there anymore.'

'Yeah, that was a blessing in disguise, her leaving. Or, from what you've said about Rob, I bet he fired her. He's got a soft spot for you, I reckon.'

'Don't be silly, Noms, and anyway he's been happily married for years.' Gracie laughed it off.

'Anyway, dear sister. You've got to do what makes you happy.'

'You say that but we don't all have the luxury of a sugar daddy, sadly.'

Noms stuck her tongue out childishly.

Gracie's phone beeped in her bag. Hoping it was Ed she reached for it quickly. Her face soon fell.

'What's wrong, Grace?'

Grace turned the screen round to show her sister.

How do I love thee? Let me count the ways. I love thee to the depth and breadth and height. My soul can reach, when feeling out of sight. Please talk to me, Gracie. I miss you. Lewis xxx

'It's from the Elizabeth Barrett Browning poem. The one I always said I'd like him to read out when we got married.'

Noms stuck out her bottom lip. 'Aw, bless him.'

Gracie huffed. 'Noms! You can't say that.'

'I know. I know. But he is sorry, and he did genuinely make a mistake, and you do fit together so bloody well.'

'Not that bloody well or I'd have been able to have kids with him. I really do think that. I think that if a couple are compatible then they can have children easily.'

'I think that's just your skewed opinion at the moment, Gracie.'

Gracie huffed. 'You were slagging off Lewis the other day. Why the change of heart all of a sudden?'

'I just want what's best for you, sis, that's all.'

'But he's *not* the best for me. I don't want Lewis. Not now, not ever. He cheated on me. It makes me feel sick every time I think of him with *her*. And her sitting opposite me the next day, and touching my face when she put my make-up on. It makes my skin crawl.' Her voice cracked. 'But most of all it makes me so, so sad, Noms. I can't cope with all this. I thought losing the babies was hard – but this hurts, it really hurts.' Gracie's face screwed up in anguish. 'I loved him so much.'

Jack appeared weary-eyed at the kitchen door.

Noms gently put her hand on the top of his head. 'What are you doing out of bed, matey? Come on, back up those stairs, you've got school tomorrow.'

'I heard your voices.' He ran and put his face in Gracie's lap, then looked up at her.

'Auntie Grace. You can be my mummy whenever you like, if you want to, that is.'

Gracie bit her lip, stroked his hair and smiled through her tears. Even the ever-strong Noms had to turn away and sniff at this expression of love in its purest form.

TWENTY-SIX

Gracie woke up to the sun streaming through her curtains. The house seemed very quiet. She checked her watch. Blimey, ten o'clock. She didn't usually sleep in. After tossing and turning all night, she felt awful too. She'd dreamt of walking down the aisle with Lewis and then not being able to go through with the wedding. Then she'd been with Ed, who had taken her for a ride on his quad bike and she'd squealed with delight like a child, until she'd fallen off and he'd ridden off and left her on the ground. She wondered what Professor Princeton would make of that one.

She eased herself up and went to the bathroom, sighing as she saw her red-eyed reflection. On the plus side, her cheek-bones were becoming more evident. She was definitely eating less than normal as she felt so out of sorts. She heard Boris whimper from his crate in the room next door.

'Come on, boy, I'll get ready and we'll go for a walk.' The sweet little terrier scampered in and licked her hand. She had enjoyed her week off, but it was Friday already and she'd be back to the grind on Monday. She showered, pulled her running gear on, and checked herself in the mirror. Her tummy had definitely reduced slightly. She couldn't be single *and* a lard-arse. Now the weight had started coming off she would stick to her regime. Maybe allowing herself just one flapjack a week for a treat, to make it all slightly more tolerable. Oh, and wine, she would still have a few wines, of course.

Ed had said he liked curves and she was sure he wasn't the only man on the planet who did. So as long as she toned up she'd be fine. She had never been really skinny, anyway. Curvy and firm. That's what she would aspire to. Perfect.

She walked downstairs to the kitchen and put the kettle on. Thinking of Ed, she applied some mascara and covered her blotchy face with some foundation. Whether he wanted to see her again or not, she couldn't bump into him looking a complete minger, now could she?

As she was zipping up her make-up bag, she saw a note from Noms to say that she was taking Jack to school and then was off to buy some fabrics for her bag making. Beside it was an envelope addressed to G with a kiss. When Gracie opened it, she found a cheque for £2,500 and a note:

No arguments, you are to clear your IVF debt, book some sessions with the prof and the rest is for you to spend unwisely, dear sis. PS. I love you x

Bless her dear darling sister. She knew the interest she earned from Jack's dad's money kept her completely solvent, but still this was a big deal. This thin piece of paper represented freedom from the debt which was a constant reminder of the lost twins, plus complete freedom from Lewis. She would have no need to contact him at all now. She would settle their joint loan and move on.

Boris yapped at her knees. 'We'll go in a minute, darling,

promise. Look, here's a treat.' Boris sat in the corner, happy for a minute to eat the biscuit she'd given him.

Gracie made some tea and scrolled through the photos in her phone, ticking every one of Lewis. Her finger hovered over the delete button, but she couldn't quite bring herself to press it. She sighed deeply and popped her phone back into her rucksack.

'Come on, Boris, let's go burn some fat.'

TWENTY-SEVEN

Maya put out her cigarette and jumped into Gracie's car.

'Thanks for giving me a lift, Gracie. I really couldn't be arsed to cycle today. Hello, Boris.'

Boris barked and put his paws on the back of the seat.

'No worries, good to have the company.'

They parked up at the common and started a steady jog.

'So, how did the date go with Eddie boy, then? And more importantly how big *is* his cock?'

'Maya Bakova, you are possibly the rudest girl I have ever met.'

'Possibly?' Maya laughed. 'Anyway, tell me. I have to know.'

'We had a drink in The Goose, that was it. I left early. He seemed a bit twitchy. Not even a kiss goodbye.'

'And any word since?'

'Nothing, so I obviously blew it.'

'Shame you didn't at least blow it, Gracie. You could do with some action.'

'I'm not that fussed, to be honest.'

'Don't lie; it's obvious you fancy Ed.'

They sat on their customary bench allowing Maya to have a

cigarette and Gracie to admire the daffodils. She wasn't sure whether to be pleased or not when she heard the familiar sound of a quad bike approaching. She wondered if Ed had some sort of personal CCTV device as he always seemed to appear when they were sitting down.

'Hey.' Gracie smiled shyly as Ed turned off the engine and got off the bike.

'Hey.'

'It's good to see...' Gracie noticed how fit he looked in his tight red T-shirt and black cargo pants.

Ed cut Gracie short. 'Look, I'm so sorry about rushing off the other night, and then I lost my bloody phone, so I couldn't get in touch.'

'Yeah, right,' Maya uttered under her breath.

'Yes, right.' Ed sounded annoyed at Maya's comment. 'Got it back this morning. How about I make it up to you and we go out for dinner tomorrow night? My treat.'

'I... err...' Gracie screwed up her face.

Maya stepped in. 'She'd love to, Ed.'

He looked to Gracie for confirmation.

She smiled. 'OK. Sure, that'll be lovely.'

'I could pick you up at seven thirty? Text me your address. Do you like Thai food?'

'Love it.' Gracie smiled broadly. 'Thank you.'

'Great, I'll book a table.'

Gracie and Maya headed to the common café, where Keen Kate was sitting outside sipping on a skinny latte. Gracie noticed her beautifully manicured nails and expensive running gear. Maya headed inside to get their drinks.

'Too fast for you, were we?' Kate smiled, but Gracie thought there was a sadness behind her eyes.

'Something like that.' Gracie sniggered. 'You OK today? Are you on your own?'

'Yes, I'm OK. A bit tired, that's all. Just fancied getting out the house, having a coffee, you know.'

Maybe she was human after all, Gracie thought.

'Your name's Gracie, isn't it?'

'Yes, that's right.'

'Margot mentioned that you arrange events?'

Gracie screwed her face up. 'Margot... remind me.'

'Long red hair, she was near the back when you did run with us.'

'That's right and yes, events is what I do for a living.'

'I was wondering – well, hoping really – that you might be able to help me with something.'

'Go on.' Gracie was intrigued.

'I've just taken over part-ownership of this place. We've got a function room behind the café and I think it would be ideal for parties, christenings and things like that. It's not my forte but I would love to get an events business off the ground. I'm spreading the word to see if anyone wants to partner up.'

Gracie felt a little thrill of excitement go through her. 'Wow. That's a surprise... and I am working at the moment, but do you know what? A new challenge is maybe just what I need.'

'I mean, it can be on a part-time basis if that's better for you? I was thinking of some kind of arrangement where the other person takes a fifty per cent profit cut from anything they arrange personally. What do you think?'

'Loving the sound of it.' Gracie felt her mind already whirring with possibilities. 'Can I take a look at the room?'

'Of course. I've got an appointment shortly, but I could meet you here in the morning, at say eleven to show you and discuss everything further?'

Gracie checked her work diary quickly. 'That would be great. It will give me a chance to think things through, too. Thanks so much, Kate. I'll see you in the morning.'

Just then, Maya reappeared with two Diet Cokes.

'What was that all about?'

'A new work proposition, using the function room behind here for events.'

'That sounds right up your street. If there are toilets, goodness knows what you and young Edward could get up to in there, as well.'

Gracie laughed and shook her head. 'You're insatiable, girl. Right, let's get these down us, I've got therapy later, then might whizz out and get a new dress for my night with Mr Duke.'

'Therapy?'

'Yes, I used to see a guy at the university. He saw private therapy clients as well as teaching. I thought I'd see him again – it might release a few more demons.'

Maya took a big gulp of Coke. 'I know a professor who's a counsellor, as it happens. He's not called Scott, is he? Tall, willowy, handsome in an older man kind of way.'

'Yes, that's right. Scott Princeton. How do you know him?'

'Oh, I think one of my friends used to go to him, that's all. Very good, I hear, especially with women.'

'Well, he's certainly helped me. So compassionate. And I hadn't really thought about him being handsome before you just mentioned it... Imagine, handsome, clever and compassionate. Maybe that's the sort of man I should be looking for. Rather than a gardener who says he lost his phone.'

'Maybe,' Maya said nervously. 'But those academic types are usually useless at normal life and have no common sense.'

'You're right. I'll stick with young Ed for now. He'll do.'

Maya was disturbed by how relieved she felt.

'Shag him tonight, Gracie. You need to move on, I reckon.'

'No, it's too soon?' Gracie shook her head.

'Like you said to me before – you're not going to marry the guy, so no rules apply.'

Gracie saw Ed arrive and wave at her from across the car park. He really was very gorgeous. Damn Lewis, she had to try and move on. Maya was right, maybe it was time to break her sex drought. And there were certainly worse people she could break it with than the hottie in front of her.

TWENTY-EIGHT

Gracie placed some daffodils in a vase and put a box of Noms's favourite chocolates next to them. The relief of being debt free was immense. She knew she had to tell Lewis the good news, but not today, in fact, not this weekend. It would feel too weird contacting him before her dinner date with Ed.

She showered, dressed and headed off to the university campus.

* * *

Scott Princeton greeted her with a smile. He was pleased that Gracie was back. He liked her and felt that for once he had been able to help a client. The money, of course, was also handy. He'd had a chance to check out the *Racing Post* and a horse called Piscean sounded a dead cert. He would have a bet later, then go and see Maya. He hadn't seen her for a week and really could do with some sex.

As Gracie came in, he noticed that her walk was not as laboured, her shoulders were higher, and she had lost a bit of weight. She was coming through the worst, he thought.

She lay on the chaise and shut her eyes as usual.

'How are you doing, Gracie?'

'I'm OK. Actually, no, who am I trying to kid? I'm not OK, but I'm better than I was. I still can't forgive Lewis in my head. But my sister's given me some money to clear the final loan we had for IVF payments, his half included. I'm going to pay that off, so I can't hate him that much.'

'How do you feel about paying this off? Quite final, isn't it?' Scott quietly turned to today's racing page.

'Yes, it is. I'm looking at that as a positive, though. Time for a new start.'

'That's good, Gracie. Does Lewis know about this?'

'No. Not yet.' She sighed deeply.

'Why's that, do you think?' Scott wrote his bet on a betting slip.

'I haven't really had time to tell him yet. But I've got a date tomorrow night. Dinner, in fact. With a guy I met on Wimbledon Common.'

'Ooh, OK. Tell me more.'

'His name's Ed Duke. He jokes about me being his duchess.' She laughed, something she hadn't done in this room very much before, if ever.

'We went out last week and I got a bit upset as he said he probably wanted children. I don't think it showed but I wanted to leave. I felt that it was unfair to stay – why would he even consider me if I couldn't have children? But then it was weird when we said goodbye. He saw some girl in the pub then he left very quickly. I went to kiss him, but he didn't kiss me back.' She took a deep breath. 'And then he didn't call or text me. I bumped into him today and he said he had lost his phone. We arranged a second date, so it's all OK now.'

A question niggled in Scott's mind. Where had he heard the name Ed Duke before?

'So why were you upset?'

'I guess it's the realisation that my choice of men is going to be limited now that I can't have children. I'm struggling with where I fit in. The pattern is that people meet, fall in love, have a family, have grandchildren, die. I'm bouncing around in my no-womb state without any of that focus or structure to my life. Do you see what I mean?'

'Shit,' Scott said.

'Do you think it's as bad as that?' Gracie opened her eyes suddenly.

'Not at all, I'm sorry. I just spilt my coffee.'

Scott hadn't spilt his coffee at all. He'd remembered why the name Ed Duke was familiar. He didn't think Gracie's new boyfriend had been lying about his phone. Cynthia had taken the phone of the guy she was representing in a rape case to go through the text messages that the prosecution had had access to, so that she was ready for everything they were going to throw at her. He felt terrible. Clearly, he could say nothing to Gracie – ethically his wife shouldn't have told him. But here in front of him was the sweetest girl – and she could be about to date somebody currently accused of rape.

'So, do you understand how I'm feeling?' Gracie prompted.

Scott's mind was all over the place. 'I do, Gracie. As to the issue of structure, it is tough, I agree. Maybe a career change is what you need, some sort of new focus to occupy you? Or a new hobby? Concentrate on you rather than a new man. For now, maybe reconsider your date.'

'Oh. I was looking forward to it.' Gracie screwed up her face in confusion. The professor had never advised her on what do with her life to this degree before.

'Do you believe he lost his phone?'

'Yes. I don't think he's a player. I believed him.'

'Well, maybe don't rush into sleeping with him. Protect yourself. I mean, it is only weeks since you left Lewis. You are still grieving for that relationship.' Scott did his best to stay on the same level.

'Maya – my mate from Marcy's café – thinks if you fall off one horse, you should get on another.'

'Maya?' Scott's voice had gone up an octave.

Gracie sat up and swung her legs so that she was now sitting on the chaise. Scott discreetly put a textbook over the racing paper.

'Yes, have I not mentioned her before? We exercise together. She really makes me laugh. And she thinks I should have sex with the gardener tomorrow night.'

'No! You mustn't.' He was aware that he sounded far too stern and wasn't maintaining his usual professional detachment.

It didn't seem as though Maya had divulged any secrets about their dalliance. Or had she? He wondered if his lover knew that Gracie was coming to him. And of course, he couldn't mention Gracie to Maya as he had to honour his client's confidentiality. It was getting more and more complicated by the minute. He would need a stiff drink when this was over.

'You've never told me what to do or not do before,' Gracie said boldly.

Scott tried to steer back to a professional footing.

'I'm sorry, Gracie. I just want you to protect yourself. I was worried that you're still fragile. You need someone with a lot of love to make you feel special. Not a short-term sexual relationship.'

'You're probably right, but I do like Ed. Having sex is important for me now. I need to break away fully from Lewis and I think this will help.'

'I disagree but I'm not here to tell you what to do. Please be safe.'

'Of course, I will use a condom,' There was a pause. 'I actually can't believe we are having this conversation!' Gracie was wide-eyed. 'I'm nearly bloody forty.'

'I didn't mean safe in that way, Gracie. Just look after *yourself*.' Scott's voice wavered.

Gracie smiled. 'Another good thing happened today.'

'Go on.' Scott now had a look of fear on his face. 'There's more?'

'I met a woman – one of the runners at the club – who has asked if I would consider arranging events in the function room behind the café at the common.'

'Brilliant! Like I said earlier, a new challenge would do you good. Could you keep your current job running, too?'

'Maybe, I guess it depends on how much I can make with this new venture. I'm meeting Kate – she's the café lady – tomorrow morning to discuss details. I'm excited about it.'

'That's really great, Gracie. So it's a big day tomorrow, then?'

'Yes. Potentially a new job and a new knob.' Gracie laughed out loud. 'That was so rude, sorry!'

The professor hid his surprise. Gracie was usually so reserved. She'd obviously been spending too much time with Maya.

She got up from the chaise.

'If you did want to come along next week, I have Monday evening at seven? I think the sooner I see you the better.'

Gracie nodded. 'I will need a chat by then, with all that's going on. I forgot to tell you – Lewis sent me a poem he knows I love.'

'Interesting that it wasn't at the front of your mind, don't you think?'

'Yes, I guess so.' Her face dropped slightly. She handed the professor his cash. 'Right, I'd better go.'

'Good luck with everything and see you next week.'

As the door shut behind her, Scott hoped that she hadn't picked up on the fact that he had completely slipped out of professional mode and had been talking to her in a way he may have spoken to his own daughter.

TWENTY-NINE

'Hi, there.' Kate was just unlocking the door to the function room when Gracie pitched up.

It was a bright April morning and for the first time in ages Gracie was in a buoyant mood. As she followed Kate in, Gracie thought they must be about the same age. Kate had a perfect, tiny figure, long straight dark hair and an elfin-shaped face. But she looked as tired and strained this morning as she had the day before. When Kate reached up to open a window, Gracie noticed her wince.

'Let me help. Are you OK?' These simple kind words were too much for Kate. She swiftly brushed tears away with the back of her hand.

'It's nothing, really.'

'You sit down.' Gracie ushered Kate to a couple of chairs that were not stacked up with the others in the corner of the wooden function room. 'I'll go and get us a coffee. And none of this skinny latte rubbish, I think you need some nourishment.'

Kate was looking at her phone when Gracie came back with the hot drinks in hand.

'Right, down to business.' Kate was all official now. 'I'm Kate Johnson by the way, and it's Gracie *Davies*, isn't it?'

'Yes, that's right. And are you sure you don't want a chat? I'm a good listener, you know.' Gracie smiled warmly.

'Like I said, it's nothing really.' She took a noisy intake of breath. 'I had a miscarriage two weeks ago. I was only ten weeks pregnant, so I know it doesn't really count.'

Tears rushed to both of their eyes.

'Stop right there, lady. Doesn't count? Of course it counts. Ten whole weeks is a quarter of a pregnancy.' Gracie tutted and gave Kate a sad smile. 'I'm so sorry.'

'Oh, Gracie, not everyone understands that! My husband thinks I should just get on with it. I'm finding it hard. We had been trying for six months, too. I only have Alice and I'm thirty-nine, so have to be realistic. Time is not on my side.' Tears started to run down her cheeks.

Gracie reached for a pack of tissues in her bag and handed one over. 'Bless you. I do totally understand.'

'Do you have children, Gracie?' Kate sniffed.

'The million-dollar and completely heartbreaking question for me. And my standard answer: no, sadly, I don't.' Gracie reached for a tissue and blew her nose.

'You don't have to tell me anything if you don't want to.' Kate took a tentative sip of her coffee through the lid.

'I need to tell you.' Gracie took a deep breath. 'It may help us both. I lost twins, you see, seven months ago now. I was five months pregnant.' Gracie looked up to keep her own tears from falling.

Kate began to cry again. 'Oh, you poor girl.'

'It gets worse. I then had to have a hysterectomy. It's shit. I'm sad. I miss what could have been. Last month, my boyfriend cheated on me. That's it in a nutshell, I'm afraid.'

'I am so, so sorry, Gracie. How the hell do you ever get over that?'

'I just keep putting one foot in front of the other, I guess.' Gracie sighed.

'I think you're amazingly strong. My little miscarriage is not even worth fretting over.'

'Don't let me ever hear you saying that again, Kate Johnson. You've still suffered a loss; you are grieving. Five weeks, five months, it makes no difference. You have still lost that life you were going to bring into the world. It's a huge thing for a woman to go through physically and mentally – heartbreaking, in fact.'

'I wish everyone understood like you do. It's like it's a taboo subject. Stiff upper lip and all that. And then when you do start talking about it, so many women come out of the woodwork, having had miscarriages too.'

'One in four pregnancies ends in miscarriage. I bet you didn't know that?' Gracie felt back in control.

'No, I didn't. That's incredible.' Kate sniffed then took another sip of coffee.

'I'm the guru on losing-baby facts,' Gracie added. 'I wallowed in misery and self-pity while I was recovering from the hysterectomy.'

'I can't even imagine. You poor thing.'

Gracie had held it together for once. She definitely did feel stronger and, at last, that she had a real purpose. She took a slurp of her milky coffee, and put her hand on Kate's. 'You, my new friend, have just given me a great idea.'

'Really?'

'Yes. I know we need to talk business, but this room already has its first club booked.'

'It has?' Kate looked sceptical.

'I am going to set up a support group. We owe it to our lost babies, at least. Their little energies are still flying around causing mischief, I'm sure. We need to acknowledge that.'

Gracie was excited now.

'We can have tea and coffee – or vodka and gin, if required.

Eat cake and chat about losing babies and how we're all feeling. It may sound macabre but it's very necessary, I think. A women's group with a difference. If it's OK with you, we could keep it under the SW19 Club banner. We could combine it with exercise classes, too? They're so important for mental health. I wanted to cling on to my baby weight but it's not the way forward.'

Kate looked animated. 'Yes, and we can still do other stuff, like bring small companies in to sell nice gifts, maybe offer talks from experts or people who've been through similar experiences.'

'Yes, yes, yes!' Gracie was on a roll; she could really see this working. 'We can charge a token amount for the tea and coffee and then, if people want to come in – my sister, for example, makes and sells amazing handbags – they can pay a fee for renting a table.'

'It sounds bloody perfect, Gracie. It's a brilliant idea.' Kate's eyes were shining.

'We can run it weekly. Maybe alternate an afternoon with an early evening, then we are catering for working mums, too.'

'You're so thoughtful, Gracie.'

'It's not all about ladies who lunch, you know, Kate.' Gracie gave her a wry smile.

'I know. I've been very blessed not having to work, but blessed *and* bored to be honest. Can I help you set this up?'

'Of course you can!' Gracie enthused. 'Hopefully, it will help you get through this dark time. And I know it's a cliché, and you are still feeling raw, but time *is* a healer.'

Kate smiled. 'Gracie, you are a complete star.'

Gracie grinned, then said, 'Do you know, I thought you were uptight and unapproachable when I first met you.'

'I probably am. I need someone like you to get my feet back on the ground. Let's talk turkey, so to speak. I would love to make this whole project work for us both.' Kate lifted her coffee cup and put it next to Gracie's. 'Cheers to the new and reformed SW19 Club.'

Gracie smiled widely. 'Cheers, partner.'

THIRTY

Scott passed a grey-bearded fellow carrying a rucksack with a lemon logo on the stairs to Maya's flat. He recognised the logo from one of Gracie's T-shirts. Another visitor. He hoped Maya wasn't going to be too tired to fuck him now.

She opened the door wearing just a mac and thigh-high boots. He could feel a stirring already.

'It's been too long, Professor.' Maya led him by his tie to the bedroom and expertly took it off. 'Now get naked and put that blindfold on. I have a special treat for you.'

Seeing him lying there naked aroused Maya greatly.

Her four paying tricks were just that – tricks. No emotion. Just bodies and cold, hard cash.

There was something else about the professor. His body wasn't particularly great, just normal. His cock was big – always a bonus – but it was him that she liked. His company. His intelligence. His flippancy and, weirdly, his lack of emotional depth.

The sex was sweaty, hard and furious. Her need for him was great after a week apart.

. . .

Maya lay back on the bed, completely sated, and took a hard drag on a cigarette.

'Filthy bloody habit.' Scott opened the window.

'And I'm guessing you're married. It's not a perfect world, Professor.'

The way she only called him 'Professor' was another huge turn on for him.

Scott lay back on the bed. 'And there is a no such thing as a perfect person, I'm afraid. You guess right and I'm not going to start saying my wife doesn't understand me, because unfortunately for her, she does. And you can take that how you will.'

It was even strange for Scott to hear words of reality in this usual place of pure play. An unfazed Maya wiggled to face him on the bed. 'I know one of your therapy clients.'

'Really?' Scott was interested to see what she was going to say.

'Gracie. Gracie Davies.'

'Ah, right. Did you tell her you were fucking me?'

'Of course not! For God's sake, Professor, who do you think I am? I am discreet. I know you have a reputation to think about.'

'What do you think she'd say if she knew we were?'

'She'd probably be jealous.'

The professor was wide-eyed. 'Really?'

'I'm not going to flatter your ego if that's what you want, but she speaks very highly of you.'

'Well, that's good, and thanks for being discreet, little bird.' Scott kissed her forehead.

'It's a good job I don't sing like one, isn't it? I could get you into all sorts of trouble.' She bit his nipple gently.

He groaned. 'Any excuse to pull my whip on that cute little arse of yours.'

'Promises, promises.' Maya smiled seductively.

Scott could feel himself getting hard again already. Most women would have flown off the handle at his marriage confession, but not Maya. They were similar in more ways than he cared to dwell on. She was a temporary distraction and he was under no illusion that she would tire of him one day. There was no fool like an old fool and he would just enjoy her and this whilst it lasted.

As he started to kiss her, he could feel her melt in to him. He caressed her nipples and rubbed his big hands gently over her tiny back. On easing his fingers slowly into her and hearing her moan, he realised he had maybe become a little too accustomed to her sweet little sex noises.

'I want you,' she said between gasps. 'Inside me right now.'

Scott gently eased his throbbing member into his young lover. He could feel how wet she was and her heightened pleasure turned him on even more.

And then it happened. In an almost inaudible whisper '*I love you*' escaped from Maya's mouth. She had no control. It came right from the middle of her heart. Those three little words just spilt out. She coughed as if to disperse them. She had shocked herself. She had never ever said 'I love you' to a man before. And since she had said it without any thought, it must be true. She was in trouble now.

Scott continued to push deeper into her. He seemed oblivious, though her pleasure was marred by what she had said.

Had he heard her? She hoped not. It would ruin everything, she was sure. In her mind, they were sex buddies, that was it. Emotion would just get in the way of whatever this was.

The professor came with force; Maya came with preoccupation.

'That was amazing,' Scott exhaled deeply. He propped himself up on one arm. 'You really are very beautiful.'

'You're not so bad yourself, Professor.'

'But I have to go, I'm afraid.'

'That's fine. Don't leave it so long next time.'

Scott went to the bathroom and showered. She loved him? Yes, it had been said in a whisper but there was no doubting what he had heard. How very flattering, and how very complicated.

Maybe there shouldn't be a next time – not for a while anyway.

Maybe it was time for a new distraction.

THIRTY-ONE

Naomi was sneaking a peek out of her bedroom window when the taxi pulled up outside.

'Bye, sis,' Gracie called up the stairs.

'Have fun. Don't do anything I wouldn't do,' Noms shouted back.

'Ha. Don't give me that much scope. Bye.'

Gracie was laughing as she shut the door. A grinning Ed held the taxi door open for her.

'You look amazing, Gracie.'

She felt amazing. She'd dried her hair straight and with her slight weight loss felt slim enough to wear a little black dress that accentuated her curves. Finished off with heels, coral lipstick and freshly painted nails she felt confident. And she felt sexy.

The handsome landscaper handed her a bunch of pink roses wrapped in pink tissue paper.

'Ed, that's so sweet, thank you.'

'Thought we'd go to the Thai, down by the river in Putney.'

'Lovely. I went there for a work meal once. The food is amazing.'

. . .

Over their meal, conversation flowed, laughter bubbled, wine was drunk. Time passed quickly.

'Anything else to drink?' Ed smiled with his eyes as he asked.

She hiccupped. 'I'm a little drunk already.'

'Not too drunk to forget you've been on a date with a handsome younger man, I hope?' He leant down and retrieved his napkin from the floor.

'God, no, I'm not at the stage of not remembering stuff, don't worry.' Gracie grinned broadly.

'That's a relief. I want this to be a special night. A special night for a special lady.'

'It's been great, I haven't eaten such good food in ages and the company's not that bad either.' Gracie meant it. It had felt natural being in Ed's company and there was no denying she really did fancy him. 'Coffee would be good,' Gracie added.

Ed reached for his wallet. 'How about we go back to mine for a coffee?'

'For coffee or for coffee?' Gracie winked.

'Depends how lucky you're feeling.' Ed laughed as she play-hit his hand across the table.

Back at Ed's Clapham apartment, Gracie noticed the photos above the fireplace. 'So, you're a skier?'

'More a snowboarder. How about you?'

'Never been, actually.'

'Oh, you should, it's such a fun holiday.'

'Is that your brother?' She pointed to a photo of another handsome smiley man with a girl on his arm.

'No, that's my flatmate, Greg. He's gone to Paris with his girlfriend this weekend. Rumour has it he's going to propose.'

'That's so sweet.'

'Another one bites the dust, I say.' Ed laughed.

Gracie smiled. 'You're so wrong.'

'But oh so lovable.' Ed took her by the hands. 'Anyway, sexy lady, I've been waiting to do this all night.'

He gently tilted Gracie's head and kissed her lightly. When she pushed into him he gave her a full-on passionate toe-curler of a snog.

They came up for air.

'I feel dizzy,' Gracie giggled.

'So, do you want a coffee, tea, me...' Ed grazed her lips again.

'Just you.' Gracie leant up to kiss him again. She put her hand to his crotch and the slight bulge that greeted her made her feel horny.

'Let's have a coffee first, hey, Gracie?'

For a moment Gracie felt a little rejected. 'Hello, is this really the hot-blooded landscaper who was going to have his wicked way with me?'

'I just want you to be comfortable with this, that's all. You've had a lot going on.'

He sat on the sofa and patted the seat next to him. 'Come here.'

She leant in to kiss him again. 'I am comfortable.' She looked right into his almond-shaped brown eyes. 'Really, I am.'

'So, if I wanted to make love to you, you would say yes?'

'Ed, you're being weird. Just kiss me.'

Gracie moved herself to lie along the sofa and pulled Ed towards her. She spoke very slowly and deliberately. 'Ed Duke, I want... to do... despicable... things to your body...'

He grinned. 'As long as you are sure, who am I to argue?'

The foreplay was tender and oh so good. Ed's body was taut and strong and Gracie could almost have cried at how complimentary he was about her.

'Have you got condoms?' Gracie said breathlessly.

Ed rifled on the floor for his wallet. 'Here. You do it.'

As she was hurriedly ripping off the wrapper, Ed suddenly got up.

'Shit, I'm so sorry, Gracie, must be the drink.' He ran to the bathroom.

Gracie sat up. What was going on? He was gone for what seemed like ages, then he appeared in his boxers and came to join her at the sofa. He hugged her tightly.

'That didn't go quite as planned, did it? How embarrassing.'

'Hey, it's fine. Don't be silly.' Gracie felt awful. He obviously didn't fancy her at all. 'I think I may just head home.'

'It's 1 a.m., Gracie. Are you sure? We could go to bed and cuddle, then see what comes up in the morning, maybe?' He kissed her on the forehead.

'No, I'd really like to go home, it's fine. I'll get an Uber.'

Ed smiled weakly. 'I know this is so cliché, but it's not you, it really is me. And I'm so sorry if I've made you feel uncomfortable.'

Gracie reached for her phone and booked a car.

Ed brushed her lips with his at the door. 'Make sure you text me when you get in, yeah?'

Gracie got in the car and rested her head back on the seat. Yes, things like that did happen, but it still seemed odd. If the drink had affected him, then fine, but the fact she had seen his huge erection in the mirror when he ran to the bathroom made it all the more strange. She wasn't that unsexy, was she? It didn't make sense. He really had seemed to like her. Maybe she should have stayed but her feelings of rejection had made her want to run. She was just thinking that she hoped that she hadn't left Ed feeling bad about the situation when the driver braked too hard and jolted her out of her thoughts.

Remembering she had run out of her favourite tea bags and

skimmed milk, she asked the driver to pull into a garage. And that was when she saw him.

Lewis.

Staggering out of the garage with a full carrier bag of hangover supplies, Gracie guessed by the look of him. He was smashed! Hiswhole face lit up when he saw her. 'My Gracie... My Gracie with the special hair!'

She put her hand to the back of her head and realised she had a bad case of 'rolling round on sofa' hair. Shit!

He put his hand on her arm. 'I miss you, Gigi,' he slurred. 'I miss you so much.'

She thought she was going to cry. 'Look, I do need to talk to you, but not now. I'll ring you this week, I promise.'

She scurried back to her Uber shaking. He had looked so sad, then so happy when he saw her. Her heart was beating too fast. Maybe she did still love him?

That was the trouble with the head and the heart, Gracie thought. How could you just switch love off? One day everything seems perfect, and the next day they cheat and you have to hate them. The heart doesn't understand, as it's the head telling you what to feel. Gracie's thoughts were confusing her. The sooner she got home and into bed the better.

A text from Ed flashed up.

You home yet babe? x

Then another.

I still love you Gigi X

THIRTY-TWO

'Come into the meeting room and take a letter, Miss Davies.' Rob Warhurst laughed as he minced by Gracie's desk and beckoned her into an empty office. He shut the door behind her.

'How are you?'

'Great, thanks. Been doing lots of exercising and thinking.'

'I was going to say you are looking trimmer. In fact, you look great. Probably not supposed to say that in this day and age, but I just did. And how are you feeling about everything now?'

'Confused. Lewis realises he's made a dreadful mistake, but I think it's my time now. I feel that I need a fresh start on life.'

'Please don't say what I fear you are going to?'

Gracie made a face. 'Oh, Rob, this is so hard. You've been so bloody brilliant about everything, but I have got the chance to do something where I can make more of myself, for myself.'

'Go on.'

'There's a function room behind the Windmill Café on Wimbledon Common and the woman who part owns it says I can make it my own. Just give her a commission of whatever I earn on events.'

Rob frowned. 'Will you make enough money doing it, though, Gracie?'

'I don't know: it's a completely new venture. We need to start marketing it pretty sharpish. I realise I'll have to work out my notice.'

'Let me think... How about this as a proposition?' Rob Warhurst scratched his beard. 'You stay on the payroll and work as on-site event support instead of being an events manager. I'll probably need you around eight days a month, but at least then you'll have a steady base income coming in. Julia in production has expressed an interest in events, so can take on your full-time position.' He banged his hand down on the table. 'Sorted!'

Gracie couldn't believe it. 'I could kiss you, Rob Warhurst, that's perfect!'

'Could you? Could you really?' Rob looked serious, then lunged towards her and placed a scratchy, coffee-breathed kiss on her lips.

Gracie jumped up. 'Whoa, where did that come from?'

'Shit! I'm sorry, Gracie.' Rob looked mortified and put his head in his hands. 'Mrs Warhurst isn't only gadget-worn, she appears to be *me*-worn, too. We haven't had sex for weeks.'

'Oh, Rob. I think you're great, but one, you are married and two, you are my boss. Not forgetting, of course, that I have just split from my boyfriend and don't know where my head is at the moment.' Gracie blew out a noisy breath and ran her hands through her hair. 'Maybe it's not a good idea that I stay here?'

'Don't say that. I love having you around. You are a breath of fresh air.'

Gracie thought for a moment but she knew what she had to do. 'No. I've made my decision. I'll work the week out and then I move on. My sister has cleared my debts and I'm living at hers rent free until I sort myself out, so I'll be fine financially for a bit.'

Rob exhaled loudly as Gracie went on. 'I'm sorry, Rob. I

really do appreciate all you've done for me, but the time is right, especially since this has happened. I would feel awkward now.'

'What a prat. I need to sort myself out. Look, don't even worry about your notice. I'll pay you to the end of the month. Go and be happy, Gracie Davies. I know you will be successful in whatever you put your mind to.'

Feeling slightly grossed-out at what had just happened, Gracie faked a smile and got up to leave. 'Let's have a catch-up in a few weeks, eh? And thanks again for being such a great boss. Maybe take Mrs Warhurst away on holiday somewhere nice? But be sure not to take one single gadget with you.'

Rob laughed. 'We'll sort it out, I'm sure.'

'You will.' Gracie got up and walked towards the door.

'And Gracie? Don't ever lose sight of what an amazing person you are.'

Tears pricked her eyes.

'It's been a blast, eh, Rob? And when life gives you lemons, what do we do?'

'Grab tequila and salt!' they shouted in unison and laughed.

THIRTY-THREE

Gracie's hand shook with excitement as she turned the key to the Windmill Café hall. To her relief, there had been no sign of Ed's van in the car park; she hoped it was one of his weekdays off. Today was about moving forward with her life, not about men.

She put her bag and laptop down on the side and looked around her. It was a decent space and the kitchen and toilet areas were modern and clean. There was even a little office and she smiled to see that Kate had put a printer in for her already. It really was perfect. Her very own event space that she could fill however she wanted. For the first time in ages, she felt happy and liberated. She knew that Kate would let her have free rein; it was like having her own business but without the worry of all the overheads. Quite perfect, in fact.

As she popped around to the café and grabbed herself a cup of tea and a banana, she made a mental note to buy supplies for the kitchen so she could cut out the expense of buying teas and coffees from the counter every time.

Cutting down on the flapjacks and doing more exercise was certainly doing the trick. To her losing weight had never been complex. It was the first push to want to do it that was hard. And if she cut out the crap and moved more it was a guaranteed route to success. Not a hard concept to grasp. Maybe she should market that, too, and blow all the faddy diets out of the water. Although, saying that it seemed that everyone was turning to weight loss injections now!

It was great that the weather was starting to get better. She wouldn't need to use the heating here for the time being and she could make use of the outdoor space at the café, too.

She took her tea into the office with her laptop. Then, deep in thought, tapped her nails on the table. Her main target audience were the array of women who frequented the common. Opening the computer, she began to create a list of ideas that she and Kate could discuss on top of the SW19 Club.

- Children's birthday parties – maybe themed – goody bags (anything to save mum time)
- Easter party – hire a big Easter bunny/arrange an egg hunt on the common
- Christmas party – Father Christmas – sleigh rides
- Yoga classes
- Slimming club
- Running club
- Craft days
- After-school club

Gracie rubbed the back of her neck. What needed most thought though, *was* the SW19 Club. How could she market it without it sounding too macabre? Maybe she should have a brainstorm with Kate? Her mind began to whir. For women who have lost babies? No. For those of you who have lost a child? *Lost?* Not a good word but the whole point was getting people to face up to and discuss their sadness, so maybe 'lost' was all right.

Perhaps she was being too thoughtful about this? Did it really matter how she marketed it? Then the idea came to her: 'Yes! Yes! Yes!'

A movement behind her made her jump out of her skin.

'God, Ed, have you not heard of knocking before? You scared the bloody life out of me.'

'I'm sorry. The door was open. I saw your car and...' Ed's face fell at Gracie's reaction.

She took in his toned tanned legs and softened slightly. 'It's fine. Next time, give me a bit of warning, though. Sneaking up on me like that is not funny.'

He went to tickle her and she pushed him away. 'Hey, Gracie. Don't be like that. It's a shame I couldn't make you scream out like that the other night, eh? So bloody embarrassing – the old fella gets a mind of his own after a few pints.' He pointed down to his European-style long khaki shorts and gave a half smile to gauge her reaction. It wasn't a good one.

Gracie said nothing, just shuffled on the spot.

'It's OK, Ed. We had fun and not everyone is going to have a connection in this world, or that "ol' devil called love" would be even more complicated than it is already.'

Ed was looking at her curiously. He beckoned her towards him.

'Come here,' he said gently. She felt confused. He put his muscly arms around her and hugged her to him. 'Gracie Davies, hands up – I confess I fancy the pants off you. And the other night...'

'Coo... eee!' Kate's timing was rubbish. They broke their embrace before she could spot them. 'Oh, hi, Ed.'

'Hey. Rumour has it there's a new venture afoot and I, of course, didn't want to miss out on the common gossip.' Ed smiled warmly.

'Oh, right?' Kate clocked his tanned legs. Gracie was still

reeling from how Ed's hug had made her feel. Fact: hugs were an amazing invention.

'I'd better get on. Catch up later.' He winked at Gracie and sped off.

'Gracie? Is there something you should be telling me?' Kate gave a knowing look.

She shrugged. 'I went on a date with him the other night, that's all. I don't think it's going anywhere.'

'He seems nice. Maybe you should just go on another one. He's cute and it sounds like you could do with some fun.'

'I'll see. I want this to be my focus now. Not pesky men.'

'You're funny, Gracie. "Pesky", I love that word.'

'Yes, so underused. I also just had a eureka moment about how we could market our new club. How about the strapline – *The SW19 Club – Miscarriage Matters*.'

Kate's eyes shone. 'Well done, you! That's perfect. I think we should create some flyers ourselves, put one on the café noticeboard and leave some on the tables, too. And I can ask the mums at my Alice's school to spread the word.'

'Shall we advertise the first one for next week?'

'Yes, let's get on with it. One of my friends is an author – I know she'd happily come along and sign books – and I know someone who sells a great make-up range. Do you think your sister might come along with her handbags?'

'We can make it a social ladies' event. If people want to talk about what they've been through, then all the better.'

'How much should we charge, do you think?' Kate screwed up her face.

'I think £10 each is reasonable,' Gracie enthused. 'With free tea, coffee and biscuits. I mean, it's not going to make us much, but it's a start and there is so much scope here to think of more money-making schemes.'

'Baby steps and all that.' Kate laughed. 'Excuse the terrible pun.'

Gracie grasped her arms to herself. 'This is so exciting.'

'Yes, it is. I'm glad I met you, Gracie. I think we both needed this.'

'Ditto and, yes, I think you're right.'

'I'd better get going.' Kate grabbed her bag. 'Little Flossy is booked into Poncy Paws at midday for her grooming session.'

Gracie smiled to herself at the confirmation that the women of Wimbledon Common were far from common. But women they were, and now she could try to help some of them and maybe even herself along the way.

Before she could concentrate on her new beginnings, there was one important call she needed to make. She reached for her phone and scrolled for Lewis's number.

THIRTY-FOUR

Gracie had barely taken off her jacket when Scott Princeton began his interrogation.

'So how did the date go?'

She had chosen not to lie down today and sat in a chair across from him. She clearly felt strong enough not to have to shut her eyes. The old adage that time was a good healer was true.

'It was OK. Great dinner, and Ed is good company. He makes me laugh.'

'And how did the night progress?'

'I went back to his, but I didn't stay over.'

Scott sat back in his plush leather chair, visibly relieved.

'Did you want to?'

'Being honest, I did. And I felt so damn happy that I wanted sex, too.'

'But you didn't stay?'

'I was going to, but then Ed was a bit strange and now I'm confused and not feeling very good about myself.'

'Strange in what way?'

Gracie shuffled in her seat. 'I feel weird telling you this.'

'Gracie, it's fine.' Scott's tone was soft and low.

'Well, we were kissing and stuff, but then he jumped up and I could see... well, I could see that he was excited.'

'Go on.'

'And then, he was gone for ages. When he came back he just apologised for things not going as planned and said that it was really embarrassing.'

'And how did that make you feel?'

'Like shit, to be honest. I felt confused as to why he didn't want me. Maybe he had felt my muffin top, which I know *is* getting smaller.'

Scott wished he could tell her that Ed might have been terrified of getting involved after being accused of rape, but it was not his place to. He hoped the lad would explain and then she could make her own decision.

'Gracie, don't be silly. He obviously likes you. And can I just tell you that if men know they are going to be getting sex, the last thing they will be thinking of is a muffin top.' He grimaced. 'Sorry for crossing the line there, but it's true.'

'Oh. Well, that's good to hear from the horse's mouth, so to speak.'

Scott nodded. 'We are fickle creatures, us men. Just think of the three Fs. Feed us, fuck us and let us watch football and we are happy.'

Gracie laughed. 'And you thought you'd crossed the line before.'

Scott coughed to centre himself. 'Maybe Ed got a bit scared that things were going too fast. If he really likes you, it could be that.'

'Really? I can't see that myself.'

'You're a lovely and attractive woman, he'd be silly not to. You've got to start believing in yourself.'

'Then, to make things even more confusing, I bumped into Lewis at the petrol station on the way home. I can't hate him. In fact, it was nice to see his familiar face. I was mortified that he commented on my hair. He never comments on my hair.' Gracie gave a sad smile.

'That was nice, then.'

'No, it wasn't, Scott, he was commenting on how "special" it looked – I'd been rolling around on the sofa with another man.'

'He couldn't have known that, and anyway it'll do him good to think you're out having a life and not stuck in moping.'

Gracie stuck out her bottom lip. 'I got home and he sent me a text saying that he loved me.'

'And how did that make you feel?'

'Sad. It made me feel sad. Ed sent one checking that I'd got home safely, which was sweet.' She blew out a huge breath. 'Maybe it is a bit early to be starting something fresh, even just for sex?'

Scott's face showed palpable relief. 'Only you can make that decision, Gracie, no one else.'

'I'm seeing Lewis later, to tell him face to face about the loan being paid off. It's a final goodbye.'

'You could call and tell him, if that would be easier.'

'No, I need to see him. I can't leave it the way we did. It's definitely over: he's hurt me too much. But for some reason, I need to say goodbye to him properly.'

'That's good, Gracie. It's good to finalise endings. Leave things hanging and you will never get over them. Like with the twins.'

'What do you mean?'

'It will take time to deal with getting over such a terrible loss. You must grieve for them. It was a terrible shock to both your mind and body. It's something that changes a person.'

'And you think I don't know that?' Gracie bit her lip. 'Not everyone thinks like that. Lewis thinks I should move on. They've gone. I didn't meet them.' Gracie's eyes filled with tears.

'You shouldn't dismiss the loss. I can't imagine the gamut of emotions that you went through and still go through. Just because a life – two lives, in your case – isn't visible to the rest of the world, doesn't make it any less significant.'

Gracie had tears running down her cheeks. 'I said that to Kate but thank you. Thank you so much for reiterating it.' Her voice went childlike. 'They were my babies.'

Scott cleared his throat again and handed her the tissue box.

'You're doing the right thing by talking to me.'

Gracie nodded, then blew her nose loudly. 'I'm hoping setting up my own support group will help me, too.'

'I'm sure it will. Be kind to yourself, though, Gracie. It's all right being Mother Teresa, but you are important, too. Make sure you put your own life jacket on first, eh.'

Gracie took a sip of water. 'It's like letting go of a white heat inside me. It's hard to explain. Knowing that I will never, ever be able to have a child of my own is a terrifying thought and I can't change that, not ever. This is my lot. Just me: Gracie Davies.'

'Gracie Davies looks all right to me, you know. And you will find love again. If you want to. You just need to build up that self-belief again. We are all stronger than we think.'

She sighed. 'I'd better go. I want to look my best for Lewis, despite everything.'

'That's good. Feel confident, say what you've got to say, and leave as cleanly as you can with your head high. What happened wasn't your fault. A dreadful case of circumstances led to him cheating. Emotions were all over the place for both of you.'

'Are you saying that I should give him another chance?'

'I'm not saying anything, Gracie. I'm not here to tell you what to do. Although I do apologise that I may have done that last week.'

Gracie stood up and handed over five ten-pound notes. 'It's

OK. I know you have my best interests at heart. Thanks again.' She paused. 'You do help me see things more clearly.'

'Thank you and, like I've said before, that's my job.' Scott smiled as he stood up and gently touched Gracie's arm. 'Grief is an insurmountable emotion. It sneaks up and bites you when you're least expecting it. The sooner you get as much of the beast out in the open, the less chance it has to catch you unawares. Think of it as a big lion.'

'I shall try and roar as much as I can' – Gracie managed a smile – 'right at Lewis.' She laughed. 'Actually, I meant to tell you something else about Ed.'

Scott checked his watch. 'That's fine, we've still got five minutes.' They both sat down again.

Gracie cleared her throat. 'Well, after the hard-on, leave-me-alone incident, he came into the event hut and gave me the most massive hug. It made me tingle all over. So now I'm totally confused.'

'Maybe he isn't right for you at the moment, if he's confusing you.'

'We'll see.' Gracie stood up. 'Same time next week?'

'I've left my diary at home so I'll text you to confirm, but that should be fine.'

* * *

Scott Princeton ran his hands through his thinning hair and sat back in his chair. He wanted sex. He wanted Maya. He would block out the fact that she had said she loved him. His phone rang, making him jump.

'Scott, it's Cyn. I've got a meeting in Manchester tomorrow. I'm on the train now and I'm going to stay overnight. Emma's staying at Josh's so there's no need to worry about her. I was thinking, shall we have dinner together tomorrow for a change?'

'Yes, let's. I'll book the usual. Safe trip, old girl.'

Never one for procrastination and with an all-night free pass, Scott scrolled down to the M's in his phone.

He didn't want complication, but his 'little bird' knew just how to turn him on and while she was happy, too, who was he to complain?

THIRTY-FIVE

Lewis was feeling sicker than the night that Gracie had caught him out. There was just so much he wanted to say to her and he knew this was his last chance not to fuck things up.

He regretted every single moment of the infidelity. He could barely remember the sex, as he had been so drunk. He had not seen Annalize since, thankfully. He hated to think of the hurt it must have caused Gracie having to face her at work. That was if she had gone back to work. He hated that he didn't know what his lover of seven years was doing. Seeing her the other night with her hair all over the place had given him sleepless nights, imagining that she was seeing someone else. He had been drunk again then, so maybe he had just imagined it. It had become far too habitual, his drinking, since losing the babies. And even worse since Gracie had left. He should address it, but now wasn't the right time. He needed to escape from reality.

He had chosen a little Greek restaurant in Wimbledon that he knew would be easy for Gracie to walk to from her sister's. He hoped then she would be able to relax and have a glass of wine or two without the worry of the car.

He found a seat outside, bought a pint and sat in the spring evening sun. It had been a lovely day. Somehow everything seemed better when the sun was out. He wouldn't let himself think that this could be the last time he would see his beautiful girl. No, it couldn't be. He would be positive; he had played this night out for days now. It had to go his way or he didn't know what on earth he would do with his life.

'Hey.' Gracie smiled and slid into the seat next to him. She looked gorgeous, in a flowery shift dress and wedges. Her lipstick matched the pink in her dress, and she was glowing from walking in the sun from Naomi's.

'You look amazing, Gigi.' A lump formed in Lewis's throat and he was frightened he might cry.

'You're probably wondering why I'm here,' Gracie said.

'I didn't think it was for you to declare your undying love for me.' Wondering why on earth he had said something so bloody stupid, he took a noisy slurp of beer.

'I've got amazing news for us both, actually. Noms gave me a cheque to pay off all our IVF debt.'

Lewis's eyes shone. 'Wow. Are you sure?'

'Of course I'm sure. She had a massive order in for some bags and wanted to share the joy.'

Lewis – along with the rest of the world – had no idea about the real source of Naomi's money.

'Blimey. It's great she's doing so well. I can't believe this, to be honest. That's two grand!' Lewis raised his voice.

'I know. I cried. It's amazing, isn't it?' Gracie smiled.

'Are you really sure, Gracie? I mean, I earn a lot more than you. I can keep paying my half. Do you not need the money?'

Gracie shook her head, her mood tightening. 'Give it a rest, Lewis. The amount of times you threw the debt in my face when I was with you. I'll be happy to clear it. And it'll mean that there's nothing keeping us together. It'll be a clean start for us both.'

'That's what I'm worried about,' Lewis said softly. He summoned the waiter over so that Gracie could order a drink.

'This isn't a social evening, Lewis. I wanted to tell you this news face to face. And...' she shuffled slightly in her chair. 'And... I wanted to say goodbye properly, I guess.' A lump rose in her throat.

'You could easily have done that over the phone.' He noticed the look on her face and quickly put his hand on hers. 'But I can't tell you how pleased I am that you didn't. I miss you so much, Gracie, it hurts.'

She pulled her hand away as the waiter delivered her wine. 'You should have thought of that before you betrayed me, shouldn't you?'

'I'm sorry. It didn't mean anything. What can I do to make you believe me?'

Gracie took a massive slurp of wine and spoke carefully. 'It may not have meant anything to you, Lewis, but to me it meant a bloody lot.'

She took another slug of her drink.

'Do you want another one?'

'Getting me drunk won't help,' Gracie replied curtly.

Lewis knew this was his last chance. He needed her to know how much he cared. 'I love you, Gracie. I will always love you. You are beautiful, funny, kind, sexy, clever. The list goes on. You light my fire, ring my bell, clatter my letterbox! And I don't know what to do to make you forgive me.'

Gracie blinked quickly to stop tears from forming in her eyes. Why couldn't men say these things when they were with you every day!

'I've moved on, Lewis.'

'So you *are* seeing someone else?'

'I'm not, but it would be none of your business if I were. I have been on a date, yes.'

'What, when? The other night when I saw you?' Lewis's voice shook.

Gracie grimaced. 'I don't want to discuss it with you. It's not your business anymore.'

'So you are, then?' He slammed his hand down on the table causing other diners to stare.

'Oh, Lewis. Shut up, you're causing a scene now.'

'Are you still working for Rob? You can answer that surely?'

'What you mean is, is your precious "perfect one" still there?' Gracie reeled once again at the injustice. How could she ever bear living with the thought of them sleeping together? She had made the right decision in moving on from Lewis, and from that memory.

'Gracie, that wasn't what I meant. I would just hate for you to feel hurt every day.'

'Don't flatter yourself, Lewis, because I don't even care about that anymore.'

What had happened to her 'letting go with love' mantra that she had so wanted to guide her tonight? Her emotion was completely taking over her head.

Lewis leant forward taking Gracie's hands in his, and looked into her eyes. 'How are you feeling about the babies now?'

Gracie pulled her hands away from his and bit down on her lip. She couldn't stop the tears. 'You didn't care about that when I was with you. Why bring it up now?'

'You are so wrong. You went into yourself. I couldn't get close. I cried myself to sleep, too, you know. I think everyone forgets that they were mine as well. I lost them, too.'

Gracie's face crumpled. She clumsily got up out of her chair and started to run. She couldn't face confronting this, couldn't share her hurt with the one person who had always understood her the most. It was like sticking a knife into an open wound and twisting it.

Lewis threw some cash down on the table and ran after her. The other diners in the restaurant, now totally invested in the drama, couldn't help but stare after them as they sped up the street. Catching up with a now red-faced Gracie, he swung her round.

'Just go, Lewis. Go home,' Gracie screamed into his face.

He didn't even flinch. 'I'm not leaving you like this.'

'You left me like this before and didn't care.' Pulling away from him, Gracie began to cry.

'Of course I cared, it was just – it was a bloody awful time, Gracie. I made a huge mistake but it wasn't because I didn't love you. I guess I felt I had lost you already.'

Part of her wanted to grab him, hug him to her, to go back. But something held her back. She couldn't, not now. And then the words popped out: 'I don't love you anymore, Lewis.'

'I don't believe that, not for one minute,' Lewis replied, calmly now. 'I can tell by the way you just screamed at me.'

And then, as if she was on the set of some kind of Hollywood romcom movie, Lewis was down on one knee in front of her.

Gracie whined. 'What are you doing? Please just let me go home.'

A taxi tooted encouragement. A couple across the road stopped to see what was going on.

Lewis pulled a red box from out of his back pocket. Gracie could barely take it in. This was the moment she had been waiting for her whole life: and here she was in the middle of a busy street in Wimbledon on a Monday night being proposed to by a man she clearly did still love – but who she could no longer trust.

'Gracie Mae Davies, I love you. I've always loved you. From your beautiful wavy hair to your funny bent little toe. And most of all I adore the scar that runs across your sexy soft belly. You are the most amazing woman I have ever met and I want, more than anything in the whole world, for you to be my wife.'

THIRTY-SIX

The professor passed the doctor on the stairs, comforted by the fact that the routine was as normal, and it would be red underwear tonight. The flat door was open. He didn't dare go in, in case any of Maya's flatmates were there. Then he saw a note on the door greeting him:

S. Wait in bedroom, I'll be ready in ten. M x

The red underwear had been kicked under the bed. Scott could see a stray bra strap sticking out. Maya must be making a special effort: that wasn't good, wasn't good at all.

Scott lay down awkwardly on the bed, not entirely sure that he liked this new form of welcome. Much easier to be pushed on the bed, have his clothes ripped off and to get down to business. At last, Maya appeared in a silky dressing gown which gaped open just enough to show tasteful, but sexy, white lace underwear and, set on her feet, a pair of very high white stilettos. She put a slender leg up on the bed, so that it rested on his thigh.

. . .

'Get undressed.' Maya could see his cock already rising in his jeans and became wet at the thought of putting it in her mouth. She had hugged herself in delight when the professor had called her, reassured that he hadn't heard what she had whispered the last time or, if he had, that he was not put off by it. It was a win-win situation in her eyes. Tonight she was going to fuck him so hard that he would never ever let her go.

'Little bird, you are just so demanding.'

'Just how you like it, Professor. Now, I've been a very bad girl today and I think you should punish me.' She whacked the black leather horse whip against her palm.

'You had better bend over then, you little whore.'

Maya got on all fours, seductively allowing the professor to get a full view of her perfect pert arse in her white lacy thong.

By the time the deed had been done, they were both sweating furiously. Maya was so overcome by her orgasms that she'd had to lie still as her body experienced little 'aftershocks' of pleasure. Eventually, she got up, opened the sash window and lit a cigarette. The professor watched her as she went, hungry for more of her already.

'Fuck, that was good. I'm going to miss that toned little arse of yours.'

Maya spun around. 'What do you mean? Where are you going?'

'We both know that this isn't going to last, Maya. There's a big age gap between us. You have your whole life ahead of you. You may want kids. I don't.'

'We can go on and do this for a few years yet. I'm young. I don't want to settle down. I don't want not to see you.' She tried to keep the panic from her voice. But Scott must have been able to hear it anyway.

'I just want you to know the score. This is sex, right? I enjoy your company but we can never be a couple.'

Maya laughed. 'Of course we can't, and of course I know it's just sex. I'm not stupid.' She felt like she was going to cry. She took a deep breath then rushed out her lie. 'I'm sorry to have to rush you off, but I'm meeting some friends for a drink soon.'

'But I can stay for at least another couple of hours.' Scott's brow furrowed in confusion.

'That's a shame, but I really must get ready.'

When he left, Maya leant against the bedroom door and let herself slide to the floor, her legs splayed in front of her. She was crying. She rarely cried. Bugger emotions. Bugger the bloody professor! She got up slowly and reached for her phone. Being hurt wasn't on her agenda. She was going to have to wean herself off him, like a dirty cigarette. Scrolling down till she found his number, she hovered her index finger above it for a second and then, with a look of anguish, pressed delete.

THIRTY-SEVEN

Gracie felt like she was watching herself in slow motion. She tried to regain her balance, but at the speed she was running, there was no chance of stopping her fall. She yelped in pain as she hit the pavement with force and she lay there, for a second, praying she had not broken anything and that nobody had seen her.

That would teach her for running away from her emotions. What was Lewis thinking of? How could she say yes to marrying him? Why did he even think she might say yes? He had said that he loved her hysterectomy scar. She had so wanted him to love that scar. God, she was confused.

A woman in her mid-forties, with cropped hair dyed a bright red, helped her to her feet. Her voice was soft and comforting: 'Come on, let me help you up, you poor thing. Now, where are you hurting?'

Gracie lifted her damaged leg off the ground, like a flamingo. Her right elbow and left knee were badly cut.

'Here...' The woman led her to a wall nearby. She picked up Gracie's bag, which had flown to the edge of the pavement, and put it by her side. 'Now, let me take a look at you.'

Gracie was mute as the kind lady continued. 'I've just come off my A&E shift. I thought I was done for the night. I'm Ali, by the way.'

'Gracie, Gracie Davies. And I'm sorry.'

'No need to be sorry. You're lucky I was in the right place at the time. Although it looks bloody awful and hurts like hell, I think a clean-up with an antiseptic wipe and a dressing will sort you out.'

Gracie panicked. 'I don't want to go to hospital.'

'No, you don't need hospital for this. I'm getting the bus so it's not ideal for me to take you back to mine to dress it. Are you far from home? Is there someone you can ring?'

Gracie reached for her phone and saw that she had three missed calls from Lewis. He was minutes away from her. Maybe she should just call him? Suddenly a red van screeched to a halt in front of them, passenger window already down.

'Gracie? Oh my God, what have you done? Are you OK?' Leaving the van running, Ed leapt out.

'There's nothing broken, apart from her pride. Just a graze that needs a clean. I had best be on my way. I need to catch this bus.' Ali put her hand on Gracie's shoulder.

'Thank you, thank you so much,' Gracie said softly. She fished in her handbag and handed Ali a flyer. 'My details are on here. It would be lovely if you could send me yours. I'm setting up a club. I'll send you details, so maybe you could share it at your hospital?'

'Sure. OK. Now take care, hey? And slow down. Running away isn't ever the answer, you know.'

'Fuck, babe.' Ed noticed Gracie's bleeding limbs. 'Come on, get in the van. I'll patch you up.'

* * *

Gracie sat awkwardly on the edge of Ed's bath.

'Ouch.' She was trying so hard to be brave.

'I'm sorry, beautiful girl, but we need to get it clean.' Ed dabbed gently at her elbow with an antiseptic wipe. 'What were you doing anyway? I thought you hated running and I wouldn't call this exercise gear.'

Gracie shut her eyes for a second. 'It's too complicated.'

'Gracie, we're both grown-ups. Not much fazes me, really.'

'If you really must know, my ex just asked me to marry him.' Her face screwed up as the antiseptic wipe touched her elbow. 'Ouch!'

'Sorry, sorry! The ex you just split from, right? Literally weeks ago?'

Gracie sighed deeply. 'I said it was complicated.'

'You don't have to tell me anything else,' Ed soothed.

'It's about time I opened up to people. I'm going to get it out really quickly. I'm sure it's boring to other people.'

'Take your time, it's OK,' Ed carried on, dabbing gently.

Gracie's breath hitched. 'I struggled to have kids; we had IVF; I got pregnant... with twins.' Her voice wobbled at the word 'twins'.

Ed was visibly upset. But now she'd started, she had to finish.

Tears filled her eyes. 'Obviously, I lost them and, with a following hysterectomy, my ability to have children, too.'

'You poor love.' Ed kissed her forehead.

'And that's when we started to grow apart. I went into myself. I didn't lose my baby weight, didn't feel attractive. Lewis went off me. He slept with someone else... a woman who used to sit opposite me at work.' Her voice tailed off and she exhaled deeply.

'What a twat.' Ed shook his head.

Gracie winced at this comment. 'He was hurting, too.'

'Gracie, don't make excuses for him. Love is love. I can't believe he didn't see what was in front of him. You've been through hell. How could he not wrap you up and protect you? And look at him now, tail between his legs thinking he can just get you back, now that he's ready.'

Gracie bit her lip. 'I'm so confused.'

'I'm not surprised you are. I can't think of anything more traumatic for a woman to go through, especially as you're so young. Losing the babies would throw most people, without your tosser of a boyfriend being a complete and utter dick. You're strong, Gracie, and you should never doubt yourself.'

'Really?' Her voice quivered.

'Really.' Ed bent to kiss her. She closed her eyes. It felt so lovely. He had said all the right things. Maybe he did care. Maybe he was just nervous the other night. They kissed gently, slowly, lovingly.

Standing up, Ed laughed. 'My back is killing.'

Gracie stood up and winced again.

'Keep those bandages on for a couple of days, I would.'

'Yes, Doctor Duke.' Gracie smiled.

He raised an eyebrow. 'Now there's a thought. Doctors and nurses. Haven't played that in years.'

Gracie laughed. 'Yeah, right. Maybe not tonight, though, eh? As much as I'd like you to administer an injection, Doctor Duke, I think I need to go home to my own bed.'

* * *

Ed pulled up in his van up outside Naomi's place and turned off the engine. He was torn about whether or not to tell his beautiful passenger about his current terrifying predicament. She had opened up to him about something so delicate and he was sure she would be supportive. But it didn't seem fair to add to her troubles tonight. No, there would be a right time, he was sure.

He took off his seatbelt and leant over to kiss her. Then

cupping her face gently in both of his hands, he looked right at her.

'No more running, eh, Gracie?' He rubbed his nose gently with hers. 'Unless it's to me.'

THIRTY-EIGHT

Naomi was drinking hot chocolate and sewing sequins onto a pink bag when Gracie pushed open the kitchen door. She noticed her sister's bandaged arm where the blood had started to seep through.

'Blimey, Grace, what have you done?'

Gracie lifted her leg to reveal a further bandage. 'Oh, Noms, what a night.'

'You poor thing. What happened?'

'I was running from Lewis. I fell.'

Noms furrowed her brow. 'Running, why on earth? I was just going to text you. Thought you may have changed your mind and gone back with him, but obviously not!'

Gracie felt tears rushing to her eyes. 'He proposed to me in the middle of the bloody high street!'

'What the hell... No!' Noms was wide-eyed.

Gracie sighed deeply. 'I know, it was crazy. Can you believe it?'

'Fuck. Oh my god! You obviously said "no"?'

'I said nothing. I just ran away, like a madwoman, then I fell in the street and this really lovely woman picked me up. Then

Ed turned up and... Noms, what am I doing? I feel so confused about everything and everything hurts.' Gracie's face contorted in anguish.

'Ssh.' Noms got up and held her sister to her. Gracie was shaking.

'It was just so bizarre, like everything I've always wanted from Lewis but at so the wrong time. Ed was my knight in shining armour. He was so lovely.'

'Ssh. It's going to be OK, it's all going to be OK, darling.' Noms rocked her gently, as if she were Jack after a nightmare.

'Ed kissed me. I told him about the babies and he still kissed me.' Gracie began to cry. 'How lovely is that.'

'And why wouldn't he.' Noms soothed.

'He seemed to really give a shit,' Gracie cried.

'I'm sure he does, darling.'

Gracie sniffed loudly. 'And Lewis still loves me.'

Noms stroked her sister's hair. 'I know. I know, darling.'

'And I still love him.' Gracie took a big blubbery breath. 'But I don't want to be with him. I can't even look at him without thinking about her. I can't do it.'

'You don't have to do it, baby sister. You don't have to do anything you don't want to.'

'But I really felt close to Ed, then, too. What's wrong with me?' Gracie let out another sob.

'Nothing, nothing is wrong with you.' Noms continued to soothe.

Gracie pulled away and sat down at the kitchen table. Noms put the kettle on. 'Let's have a cuppa, eh?' Gracie nodded. 'And let's get some paracetamol in you, too. It will take the edge off the pain.'

Gracie's face screwed in anguish. 'If only there was something you could take to get rid of emotional pain.'

Noms smiled. 'There is – it's called gin.'

Gracie smiled weakly back as Noms searched her messy

drawer for the painkillers. 'We'll get you through this, darling girl, we will.' She handed over the tablets.

'It's as if I move a step forward then take two back.' Gracie blew her nose noisily.

'And these bloody men don't help,' Noms stated. 'Maybe you should go on holiday. In fact, why don't *we* go away somewhere hot? My treat. It's half term next week.'

'Noms, you can't keep spending money on me.'

'Who says I can't?'

Gracie groaned. 'But what about Miscarriage Matters?'

'Gracie Davies matters more.' Noms put two teabags in their favourite mugs, and poured on boiling water. 'You're just creating obstacles now.'

Gracie sighed. 'I don't want to let Kate down.'

'Kate will understand,' Noms replied gently. 'You can start the marketing this week for dates when we get back. You need to put a distance between what has happened and a new start, I reckon. I don't know why the both of you didn't go away after the hysterectomy.'

'Because we couldn't afford it then, but I guess you're right.' Gracie felt tempted. The thought of some hot sun on her face. Escaping into a book, forgetting everything *would* be blissful.

Noms took the milk from the fridge. 'I know I'm right, and Jack will love having you around. He gets a bit bored when it's just the two of us.'

'What am I going to do about Lewis?'

'Lewis is a grown up, Gracie. If he does love you and you him, love will win. Let him wait. Let him worry. He's all you've known for the past seven years and a lot of that time has been tainted with sadness. It will do him good, too, to take stock and think about what he's done.'

Gracie blew her nose loudly again. 'Do you think that maybe he doesn't really want to spend the rest of his life with me, then? Just feels sorry for what happened.'

'I don't know, Gracie. And right now you're not ready to take him back, whatever the situation. As time goes on you'll either get over him or realise you want to forgive him, but not yet. I know you so well. You've lost trust.'

Noms placed their drinks down on the table and sat down.

'Yes, I have.' Gracie sighed again. 'Not so long ago, I felt our relationship was so... so clean, in a way. It was so comforting to have to know one hundred per cent that neither of us had ever been unfaithful.' Gracie adjusted the bandage on her arm. 'I do really like Ed, though, you know.'

'Well, that's great. But don't jump into anything just because he's showing you attention. Maybe get to know him a little better first.'

'When did you become so wise?' Gracie became animated. 'I want to see him before we go away.'

Noms laughed. 'So *we* are going, then?'

'Looks that way.' Gracie grinned and took a drink of tea.

'And yes, give Ed a chance. From what you've said tonight, he does seem like a decent bloke, but just be mindful, OK?'

Gracie took a deep, more measured breath. 'Yes, I saw him differently tonight. He's a charmer but he has a good heart. He was so kind after me telling him I couldn't have kids.'

'I think you need to stop making that such a big deal, Grace. You've just met the bloke. Start playing it a bit cool. If Lewis isn't the one, then there will be plenty more Eds, I expect.'

'Don't say that. I don't want to be constantly on the search for men.'

'You know what I mean.'

'I don't, actually, Noms. Not everyone is going to be buried in a Y-shaped coffin like you.'

Noms laughed. 'Uncalled for, but very true. Saying that, when's the last time I had sex? Bloody ages ago. I'm off men. Properly off men. I actually felt quite attracted to one of the women at the WI meeting the other day.'

Gracie's eyes widened. 'No!'

'I did. I sat there while she was fingering one of my bags, and looked at her lips, full and pouty, and imagined what it would be like to kiss them.'

'You never fail to amaze me, dear sister.' Gracie shook her head.

Noms laughed. 'And don't knock it till you've tried it, I say.'

A now grinning Gracie drained her mug, then yawned loudly. 'I'm so tired.'

'I bet you are. You've probably got a bit of shock after that fall. You obviously went down with quite a force.'

'I'm a tough cookie, me.' Gracie looked down to her leg to check the wound. Blood had stopped oozing through the bandage.

'That's what you want the world to believe, Gracie Mae, but you can't kid a kidder.'

Gracie's voice lilted. 'So, where shall we go on holiday, then? I'm quite excited at the thought of it now.'

Noms grinned. 'So am I! I actually got an email from Jack's dad last week. He said I could take Jack to his house in St Lucia whenever I wanted to. He's filming in Barcelona at the moment so only his staff would be there.'

Gracie's eyes widened. 'That would be amazing. He's not usually so forthcoming, is he?'

'I know, I haven't even heard from him for ages. I'm not sure, though. What if there are photos in the house and Jack realises who it belongs to and tells his school friends or something?'

'Who's the one creating obstacles now?'

Noms stuck her tongue out at her sister. 'Smart arse.'

'Just tell him to get everything taken down that might shout "film star". I think you worry too much. If anything were to get out, you can always say that you're a friend of his. And Jack won't realise anything, he's too young.'

'Yes, I'm being too paranoid, I guess.'

Gracie became animated. 'And imagine how amazing his place will be, Noms. And wow, St Lucia. I've always wanted to go there.'

'OK, OK. I'll sleep on it. Now, get to bed, you. Hope you're not too sore in the morning.'

'Thanks and sweet dreams about your new fancy woman.' Gracie giggled childishly as she ran up the stairs.

With a shake of her head, Noms washed up the tea mugs.

THIRTY-NINE

'Of course I don't mind that you're going on holiday.' Kate sipped on a skinny latte outside the Windmill Café. Boris, keen to get off his lead and out on the common, whimpered impatiently.

'I don't want you to think I'm not taking this venture seriously, because this will mean pushing the first event back.'

'It's fine,' Kate soothed. 'It's probably much better to do it after half-term anyway as a lot of people will be away.'

'Actually yes, you're right.' Gracie leant down to pat the impatient pooch. *Soon, Boris, soon.* 'Where's Flossy today anyway?'

'I popped her in doggy daycare – wanted to be hands free today, so to speak.'

Gracie laughed. 'She has a better life than all of us!'

Kate grinned. 'So where are you going, then, Gracie?'

'I'm not sure yet, my sister's booking somewhere today. We'll be leaving tomorrow hopefully.' Noms, in her paranoia, had thought it best not to announce their destination to anyone.

'Wherever you are going, I'm well jel,' Kate laughed. 'We need to sort somewhere for our summer holiday or everything will be booked up, and the thought of having Alice at home for eight weeks without any distraction is too much to bear. She's such a live wire.'

'It will do you good to get away, too. Don't they say that twenty per cent of babies are made on holiday? Can't you do something this half term, too?'

'I always wonder who "says" these things. But Kevin is a bit reticent between the sheets lately – he's far too stressed with work.'

'All the more reason, then. You've got to get on it like a car bonnet if you want another baby!'

Kate laughed. 'What?'

'It's one of Ed's expressions, don't even go there.'

'Talk of the devil.' Kate nudged Gracie's arm.

Ed sauntered over to their table. A fixed grin on his face. 'How's the injured soldier today, then?' Gracie was surprised to find her heart doing a little leap.

So much better, thanks. The bandages are off already – look.' Gracie lifted her arm to show a light graze on her elbow.

'My expert medical skills, see.' He winked at Gracie. 'Ladies, if you need a first aider for your events, Doctor Duke is your man, the kiss of life, my speciality.'

They all laughed.

Gracie got up. 'Have you got a sec, Ed?'

'For you, I have a clock full.' They walked towards the café door, Boris in tow.

'Sorry I've been a bit elusive the past few days,' Gracie said, shyly.

'It's cool. You let me know you were OK, that was all I asked. I thought you might need some time after what had happened with your ex.'

This man is getting better and better, Gracie thought. 'I also wanted to let you know I'm going on holiday.'

'That's great. Will do you good.'

'With my sister, and my nephew, of course,' Gracie offered.

'Nice. But if you do need someone to carry your suitcase...' Smiling, he gently squeezed her shoulder. 'So where you off to?'

Gracie smiled. 'Now, here's a thing, I don't know yet, Noms is booking today, so it's all very exciting. Leaving tomorrow, if all goes to plan.'

'Blimey, you don't mess around, girl. And how long do I have to miss your beautiful face for?'

'Nine days, I expect, to fit with Jack.'

'So you're saying you don't want your injection administered for nine whole days, Miss Davies? How will I cope? Or, I should say, how will you?'

Gracie took a deep breath and spoke quickly. 'I was hoping we may be able to go out tonight?'

Ed closed his eyes and sighed. 'This is so annoying but I, I err... promised my flatmate I'd take him to the airport this evening.' He tutted. 'How annoying. Maybe I could come to you afterwards, say nine thirty-ish?'

Gracie thought for a minute. 'That will work well, actually. I can get packed first.'

'Cool, that's a date, then. How about when you know what time your flight is and, if it fits then... err. If you want to, that is, you could stay over.'

'I'd like that.' Gracie felt she could get used to this endearing new Ed. 'Right. I'd better walk young Muttley here. I owe him a few miles – he's going to hate us for putting him in kennels while we are away.'

'And I'd better do some work. Can't wait to see you later.' He patted her bum gently.

Kate smirked as Gracie walked back over to her with a yapping Boris.

'I thought you said you two weren't going anywhere? Doesn't look that way to me.'

Gracie laughed. 'I'm seeing him later.'

Kate raised her eyebrows. 'You could do a lot worse. He seems like fun.'

Gracie nodded. 'Time will tell. My holiday will clear the cache, so to speak. Do you need anything from me before I go?'

'Not at all. Go and have an amazing time and I'll see you when you're back. If there is anything pressing I do need an answer on, I'll email you.'

'Sure. I can pick up emails easily from my phone, and Kate... thanks for everything. You don't realise how much you've helped me.'

Gracie noticed Kate welling up. 'We are a team, now.'

Gracie put her hand on hers. 'Now, you get that family holiday booked yourself and get shagging, girl. I need a baby to cuddle.'

Leaving Kate with a kiss on the cheek, she realised that she was feeling an emotion she hadn't felt in a long time – happiness.

FORTY

'Auntie Grace!' Jack ran into Gracie's arms, nearly knocking her over. 'We're going on holiday! I can go snorkelling and everything and play in the pool and eat as much ice cream as I want. I'm so excited! We are going to have so much fun. Mummy says we're going on a big plane, early in the morning.'

Noms appeared fresh from the shower with a towel wrapped around her head.

'Six a.m. flight. Sorry, Grace.'

Gracie grinned. 'You know I love early flights. It makes it seem like we're really going on an adventure.'

'The taxi's coming at three thirty.' Noms groaned.

Gracie laughed. 'You'd better get to bed now, then.'

'No, we'll be fine, I've booked us all dinner at Fregos on the corner for seven. We'll be home and in bed by nine. And all the better if Jack is tired on the plane: hopefully he will sleep and not fidget.'

'You two might be in bed by nine, but Ed is coming to pick me up after he's dropped his mate at the airport.' Gracie did a little dance.

'You go, girl! Start the holiday with a bang and all that.'

'Let's hope so.' Gracie smiled. 'I really do want to see him before we go.'

'Then you must, my pretty little sister. Do you fancy dinner with us first, though?'

Gracie smirked. 'Yes, I expect I will need to keep my energy up.'

Noms and Gracie swung Jack's hands high as he walked in between them. It was busy in Wimbledon Village. Pubs and restaurants with outdoor seating areas were already filling up, with punters enjoying the warmth of the May evening sunshine. Jack was reeling off exactly what he was going to do as soon as they reached the villa when Gracie saw something out of the corner of her eye that made her heart freeze.

It was Ed.

Ed, not only looking particularly handsome, dressed in shirt and tie, but also talking animatedly to an attractive older blonde woman. In fact, he was having dinner with the attractive older blonde woman! The pair of them sat, bold as brass, in the window of an Italian restaurant.

Noms glanced at Gracie and saw the look of horror on her face, but before she had a chance to say, 'Quick, let's walk on,' Ed had spotted her.

He came running out of the restaurant at full pelt. 'Gracie, it really isn't...'

Noms walked ahead with Jack, but stopped within earshot of the conversation.

Gracie felt furious with herself for trusting him, for thinking he might be interested in her alone. 'So much for driving to the airport.' She could feel tears threatening. 'I thought you were decent – that you really gave a shit.'

'Gracie, you don't realise how much of a shit I give. It's not what it seems. But... I can't tell you any more than that. You have to trust me.'

'For God's sake, Ed. I don't need to hear any more. It's blatantly obvious. A shirt and tie, too – good effort.' She started to walk off and he spun her around.

'I've been wrongly accused of rape, Gracie. That woman is my barrister.'

FORTY-ONE

Noms had plied Gracie with a large gin and sleeping pills at the start of the flight, knowing that she hadn't slept a wink before they left. She woke up groggily and looked over to her sister, bleary-eyed.

'All right, chicken?' Noms said, lovingly. Jack was sprawled, sleeping half on her lap, half on his seat.

Gracie came to a bit more, and nodded.

'Did you speak to him after you went to bed?' Noms asked.

'No. He texted, pleading to let him come over, so that he could explain properly, but I didn't want to hear it. I said I'd see him when I got back. I just can't get my head round it. I mean, who has dinner with their barrister?'

'Maybe it was the only time they could meet. Barristers work silly hours. And she was old enough to be his mother.'

'And what if he has raped somebody? I could have been in real danger!'

Noms looked as confused as Gracie felt. 'He doesn't look like a rapist.'

'That's possibly the most stupid thing you've ever come out

with, Noms. They don't come with an *I am a rapist* tattoo on their foreheads.'

'Well, it proves one thing.' Noms took a slurp of her orange juice and buttered her white roll.

'What's that?'

'That he really does care about you. Or he wouldn't have told you about the rape charge that lightly. He also knew how much it would hurt you if he was with another woman. He cared enough to put himself on the line.'

'I guess – and it could explain why he couldn't go through with sleeping with me that first night.'

'Yes, he's probably shit scared. I bet that's it. Innocent until proved guilty, Grace.'

'No smoke without fire, Noms,' Gracie sighed.

'Grace, that's a really small-minded response. We don't know the facts, yet. Personally, I would text him when we land.'

'And say what, exactly? *There, there, you've been accused of rape, I'll stand by you.*'

'I'm not sure, but imagine what he is going through,' Noms replied matter-of-factly.

'I'm not sure I want any sort of involvement. It's scary stuff, Noms.' Gracie wished she knew the right thing to do.

Noms sighed. 'It is a really hard one. Maybe when you know more you can make a judgement yourself. Now, come on, eat something – you must be starving.'

FORTY-TWO

Cynthia Princeton drained her mineral water with fresh lime. She had been working hard all day and would much prefer a glass of wine, but she knew she needed a clear head. She liked Ed Duke and wanted to do her best for him.

She had been mid-sentence when Ed had charged out of the restaurant. He came back completely flustered.

'Oh God, I think I've just completely blown it with someone I really like.'

'Ed, come on. Don't sweat the small stuff. This is serious. You can sort your love life out when we've got you off this charge. Let's go through it one more time. Tell me again what happened. I think I may have got something, but I need you to repeat everything to make sure I haven't missed anything.'

Ed groaned. 'I need a beer.'

'You can have a beer when we're done. Now come on, concentrate, this is your future we're saving here.'

Ed sat back in his seat and took a deep breath. 'OK. So she had been at the club, and told me she couldn't get home. She was going to stay at her friend's but she didn't have enough money for a cab. I offered to let her share mine. I felt sorry for her. We got to her friend's and she knocked and called the friend, but no answer. I stupidly said she could stay in my spare room.'

'Did you want to sleep with her at this stage?'

'No, not at all, when I first saw her I thought she was pretty but far too young and tarty for me.' He put his hand to his head. 'If I'd been sober I would have just walked away, I know it.'

'So, go on,' Cynthia Princeton urged.

'I was just dropping off to sleep – I might have been asleep. But then I woke up to find her in bed with me, playing with my, you know...'

'Your cock, Ed.'

He was quite astounded at the barrister's frankness. He nodded. 'It felt good... I had sex with her.'

'At any time did she say "no" to you?'

'Quite the opposite, she came on to me. I was half asleep and obviously still a bit drunk, but I even remember saying something like, "Are you sure, because you've had a drink and you might regret it in the morning?"'

'And can you remember what she said to that?'

'This is embarrassing... She said something about giving me the best blow job I'd ever had in my life. I'm a man, Cynthia. Obviously, a weak one, sex was on a plate and I took it. But there was not one moment I would have hurt her, had sex against her will. I have the utmost respect for women. This is just a bloody living nightmare.'

'OK, you wake up to find her gone and fifty pounds stolen from your wallet. Tell me again exactly what she said when she called. Actually, how did she get your number?'

'I didn't give it to her, but I do have business cards in my wallet. The bitch probably took one when she took the money.'

'You can't be saying words like that in court, Ed.'

'I know, I'm not that stupid.' Ed's face contorted in anguish.

'Do you think I have a chance of getting off with this? I swear I did nothing wrong.'

'I do, but you have to listen to everything I say,' Cynthia replied firmly.

Ed shuffled slightly in his seat. He just wanted this nightmare to be over. He also couldn't bear to see how upset Gracie had looked. The last thing he wanted was for her to go off on holiday unhappy and thinking the complete worst of him, when he couldn't be any more innocent.

'Ed, concentrate now, please.' Cythia could see his mind wandering. 'Carry on with what happened again, please.'

'So she, Trudi, called late the night after. Woke me up. And said that, if I didn't meet her on the corner of Duncan Street in an hour with a thousand pounds, she would say I had raped her. I told her not to be so stupid, that we had had fully consensual sex and I hung up. I had to be up early for work, so I went back to sleep and thought nothing of it. The next thing I know, first thing in the morning, the police are at my door. I mean, what has she got to gain from this?'

'I really don't know, Ed. This sounds like a scam to get money out of you. I have heard of a case like this before. And I bet a lot of men do pay up, just in case, especially if they were drunk.'

'I wish I bloody had now.'

'And take the chance of her crying rape anyway, with a grand in her hand? If it was just your word against hers, then the Crown Prosecution Service might have thrown it out of court. But a bouncer from the club has made a statement which incriminates you, saying that you were making crude remarks about Trudi to him. Is there anything else you can think of – anything else at all that may help your cause?'

'I don't think so, nobody else saw us together, apart from the cabbie. I don't get it with the bouncer. I just got in the cab with the girl. I didn't make one crude remark, I'm sure I didn't. I'm a joker but... In fact, I remember now... I steadied her and helped her in. I didn't say anything that might have suggested I would even have sex with her. I was just being a bloody gentleman.'

'OK.' Cynthia nodded. 'We can hopefully get the cab driver as a witness. He can say that nothing untoward went on in the cab.'

'Yes! And we did try and get into her friend's house, that's in my favour, surely.'

'It is helpful, but the alleged crime was committed behind closed doors.' Cynthia shut her file. 'OK, that's enough for now, Ed. I'll do my best for you, but if there is anything else at all that you think of, however small, then call me.'

'Of course. Thank you so much, Cynthia.'

Ed drained his beer, and swiftly ordered another one. He had learnt a very expensive lesson with this woman. He was thirty-two, a grown-up. It really was time he started thinking about his future. This nightmare would hopefully be over soon and he could get on with his normal life.

FORTY-THREE

Gracie felt like she was on the set of a Hollywood movie. It was day eight of their nine-day holiday in paradise and she still thought she was dreaming. It would be such a wrench to go back to the normality of London life.

Lying next to Noms, on a huge white sunbed with a retractable hood, holding a cocktail that their waiter (yes, their personal pool waiter) had just brought to her, she sighed and lay back, her face to the sun. Jack was flailing around on a lilo with his armbands and a snorkel on. St Lucia had been more special than she could ever have imagined. So green, so tropical, the beaches beautiful and the happy people just so wonderful.

The villa was out of this world. Set high up in the quietest part of the island, it was a white-walled haven of expensive artefacts and extreme comfort. They had ventured out to the nearest beach a few times, and to a street market one night, but most of the time they chose to stay at the villa. It was hard to do anything else when they had a personal chef to cook all of their meals, all the entertainment and space they could wish for and, in the evening, could put Jack to bed at a reasonable hour and sit up drinking and chatting for as long as they liked, undisturbed.

Jack's dad had done as Naomi had asked and there were no photos anywhere. He had obviously also briefed the staff to look after them exceptionally well. No expense had been spared for his only son.

Gracie stretched out on her double sunbed and sighed contentedly.

'Maybe you should consider making another play for him, Noms.'

Noms laughed. 'He's dating Risella, the new supermodel on the block, now. Not sure I'd have a look-in, and I actually wouldn't want to, not now.'

Gracie laughed. 'He was obviously attracted to you once.'

'Yes, at a drug-induced private beach party I managed to crash in Croatia. I didn't even know who he was until he told me the morning after.'

'And I guess you've done all right out of him, so why complicate life? But on the other hand...'

'Gracie, I have all the perks of dating an international film star, without any angst. Why change that.'

'What are you laughing at, Auntie Grace?' Jack appeared dripping wet next to her and took a glug of lemonade.

'Just your mummy and what a funny lady she is.'

'Can we go to the beach now, perlease?'

Gracie inwardly groaned; she was so comfy and was just about to start reading her much-anticipated new Milly Johnson romcom.

Noms sat up. 'You stay put. I'll take him for a bit, it'll be a bit cooler down there now and it's easy with the jeep in the garage.'

'Yeah! I need a poo, though, first.' Jack peeled off his trunks and kicked them under the sunbed.

'Nice one, son, thanks for sharing. Go on, then, I'll wait for you around the front.' He charged off at full pelt. 'Grab clean beach towels from my bedroom on your way out,' she shouted after him.

Gracie heard her phone beep.

'Ed, again?' Noms wrapped her sarong around her.

'Yep.'

'What's he saying, this time?'

'Just confirming when we're back.' Gracie had agreed to see him again. She didn't know what to think or what she wanted, but she knew she liked him enough to at least hear him out. 'He did offer to pick us up from the airport, but I'm going to meet him the day after. I need to be on good form.'

'Good plan. And any more from Lewis?' Gracie sat up and rested on her elbows.

'Not a thing since I ran away from his proposal. I feel so bad, Noms.'

'You need to stop beating yourself up. He took a chance, you weren't ready.' Noms sat up straighter and looked serious. 'OK, let me pose this question. If one of them was to walk around the corner of the villa right this second, who would you rather it be?'

Gracie didn't have a chance to relay a response as walking towards them – in loose khaki three-quarter-length trousers, a white linen shirt and dark glasses – was not Ed, not Lewis, and not Dustin the pool waiter but – even more delicious in the flesh – Hollywood superstar and absent father of one, Leo Grant.

FORTY-FOUR

Maya clicked her front door shut, walked slowly to the bathroom and started to run a bath. She checked her phone – two days without contact from the professor, but that wasn't unusual. She had deleted his number but had remembered the last three digits of it. She was trying her best to move on and, if he contacted her, well, she would have to try and be strong. It was silly, really, she thought. It wasn't that they were having a relationship or anything. Just an affair. A sex-fuelled, intermittent affair. But she was still reeling from how she could have been so silly to let feelings get in the way of bloody good regular sex with benefits.

She'd just lost another punter, too. She didn't know his real name – he'd always wanted to be known as Mr Grey, she assumed because of his grey beard since he was far removed from the handsome *Fifty Shades* character. Today had only been his third visit. His ruse originally had been that he wanted some tips on how to liven up his marital sex. Now he said he felt ready to go back into his relationship. She had nearly told him she was a sex-worker, not a bloody counsellor. But most of her tricks were only with her because they were caught in loveless, sexless relationships. They were not after kinky fetish – apart from the whipping doctor. They liked the chat, as well as the physical release.

She got into the bath and tipped her head back under the hot water. She was just giving it a final rinse, when she heard her phone ringing in the bedroom. Leaping up, she threw a towel round herself and ran to get it. She swore loudly when it rang off, but then smiled broadly as a text came through.

Does my little bird fancy a big cock tonight?

Aroused already, the professor's number was saved promptly back into her phone.

Why was it that love was just so much easier to fall into than out of?

FORTY-FIVE

'Now this is a surprise,' Noms uttered as the handsome actor swaggered towards them.

'Hey, doll. A good one, I hope.' Leo Grant's words came in a slow Texan drawl. It was like he hadn't seen the mother of his child in six days, not six years.

Despite her apparent nonchalance, Gracie could tell that Noms would be feeling slightly sick. The rich actor didn't do surprises. Gracie had wondered why the offer of the villa had been made in the first place, after all the years of anonymity and separation.

Gracie stood up, pulled her sarong around her, then lay down again and assumed the thin stomach position. She wasn't sure what she should say to someone she had seen in so many films. She felt like she knew him already.

Leo smiled. 'I'm sorry. I thought you were leaving this morning. I must have got your dates wrong. Have the crew been looking after you OK?'

Gracie remained mute and nodded.

'It's been great. We can't thank you enough,' Noms said. 'This is my sister, Grace. I told you she was coming, right?'

'How goes it, Grace?'

Gracie smiled and held her hand out to shake his. Oh my God, she had just touched the hand of one of her favourite actors and she couldn't tell a single soul about it.

Noms gestured to the house. 'Jack's inside. But... I really do think he is still too young to know who you are.'

Leo Grant cocked his head to the side. 'Don't you think maybe it's time he did, Naomi?'

'No!' Noms fired off, then softened slightly. 'I'm sorry, I think it's best we keep things as they are, for all of our sakes. When he's older he'll understand better. And he'll be more able to cope with your fame.'

'Yeah, yeah. I guess. It would be amazing to meet the little fella, though.'

Gracie was drawn to the actor's slow, deliberate drawl.

'Anyway, I'm just off to the beach with him.' Noms jumped up, itching to get away from the situation. 'Are you hanging around here for a bit?'

'Yeah. I've got a break in filming, so I'm here for a week. I've got guests coming over in the morning.'

Gracie sat up. 'I'll come with you, Noms.'

Kingston, the butler, came out of the house and indicated that the actor's room was ready. The handsome one turned to Gracie. 'Don't go just because of me, honey. I need a sleep anyway. It's been a long day. Catch you alls later.' And he walked with a sexy strut into the villa.

'I can see why you did it, dear sister.' Gracie loosened her sarong.

Noms's expression was pained. 'Oh, Grace. I don't want him even to see Jack. This is awful. I bet he's set this up.' She sighed heavily. 'I should have known.'

'He sounded pretty genuine, to be honest, and it'll be fine.

Look, why don't you take Jack now. I'll get showered then join you for dinner on the beach at Mangos later. It will be perfect, we can all watch the sunset on our last night here. We can stay out late so our boy is sleepy and pop him in his bed. It's an early flight tomorrow, he won't even see him.'

'How romantic, just me, you and Jack,' Noms laughed.

'When you could be under the Caribbean stars with a Hollywood star.' Gracie sprayed suntan lotion on her legs.

Noms screwed up her nose. 'I don't see him like that now, it's so weird.'

'Extremely weird and sorry, but I could eat him for breakfast, lunch and tea!'

'Gracie Davies!'

Gracie laughed. 'In my dreams. Anyway, I don't do sloppy seconds.'

Naomi screwed up her face. 'Ew. See you in a while, little sis. And don't ever say I don't make your life just that little bit more exciting.'

* * *

Gracie read a few chapters of her new book, then slipped it down next to her as she drifted off into a wonderful sun-induced slumber.

She was woken an hour later by the sound of her favourite song, 'Happy' by Pharrell Williams, blasting out of the poolside sound system. As she came to, a glass of champagne was being placed rather clumsily on the table next to her by a freshly showered and edible-smelling Leo Grant.

Sitting up with a start, she grabbed her sunglasses and put them on.

'I love this tune, man.' Leo began to dance, and, feeling uncomfortable watching, Gracie stood up, her sarong draped low on her hips, her flowery bikini top showing off her buxom chest. Swimming every day had toned her waist and her tan gave her a radiant glow. Despite having a slight red mark on her cheek from sleeping, she looked naturally beautiful.

She sipped from her glass of champagne and began to move to the music, too.

'I'm having this track at my funeral,' Leo shouted over the music. 'And I want everyone to be wearing bright colours and dancing in the aisles. It's just one of those songs.'

Kingston came out and topped up their glasses.

Gracie laughed as the handsome actor took her by the hand and swung her round.

'Forgive me if I'm speaking out of turn, but it's so refreshing to see a proper womanly body for a change. I get bored of all these long, skinny women.'

Gracie found Leo's Texan drawl hypnotic. 'But you're dating a supermodel, aren't you, so you can't say that.'

'Risella, you mean? She's OK, but she's Miss Right Now, that's all.' He downed more champagne. 'Good job my PR's not here, me saying that out loud, but something tells me I can trust you, Grace, or you wouldn't be here at all.'

'I'm like the Bermuda Triangle of secrets, me.' Gracie grinned as the track ended and Aretha Franklin's beautiful voice started to sing '(You Make Me Feel Like) A Natural Woman'. 'Oh wow, I love this song.'

'Me too. So good. Let's sit.' Leo led her by the hand to the covered verandah where a huge citrus candle was burning and rose petals had been sprinkled on the circular wooden table.

She would wake up in a minute, Gracie thought. This was just all so surreal.

'Are you the sister who was in hospital last year? Naomi mentioned it in an email.'

Bless him for remembering, Gracie thought as she nodded.

'Nothing serious, I hope?'

She felt she had nothing to lose being truthful with this man. Their worlds were so far apart.

'It was quite serious, actually. I had to have a hysterectomy.'

'That's shit, man. Do you have any children?'

'No, I was pregnant and lost twins and that led me to losing my womb.'

'That's so sad. I'm sorry, Grace. Shit happens to the nicest people.'

Gracie tried to smile but her emotions welled up.

'Hey,' Leo said tenderly as a tear escaped from her eyes. He wiped it away with his little finger. 'You're so sweet, you make my teeth hurt.'

'You don't even know me,' was all Gracie could muster. And then it happened. Leo Alfredo Grant, handsome Hollywood actor, father to her beautiful nephew, leant forward and kissed her right on the lips.

She broke away. Her tears seemed to have decided to take on a life of their own. 'I'd better go and shower. Noms and Jack will be waiting for me.'

Leo stood up with her. 'Never hold back, Grace. Tears are words that have been trapped in your heart. I'm glad I could kiss at least a couple away.' And with that, he engulfed her in his muscly brown arms, pulled her tightly to his broad chest and gave her the biggest, longest, warmest embrace she had received in a long time. As Gracie melted into him, a feeling of complete peace enveloped her.

Then, suddenly feeling really awkward, she pulled away with a jolt. 'I really must shower,' she said, at a million miles an hour.

Leo nodded. '*You* really are a natural woman, Grace. And I'm so damn sorry for your loss. But I'm not sorry that Jack has you in his life. To be honest, I had my doubts that that free-spirited sister of yours would be a good mom, but she has surprised me. Now I've met you I feel even more secure about the whole situation. You'd have made a really good mom, Grace.'

'Thank you,' she replied softly, liking the way he called her Grace too.

'OK, get yourself ready. I'll get Kingston to drop you at the beach.' Gracie pushed open the door of the villa. Leo faltered slightly. 'Will I see you all later?'

Gracie smiled apologetically. 'Probably not... if you don't mind.'

He looked really disappointed. 'I get ya, Grace. And, I respect that.'

Gracie smirked. 'Oh and the "you're so sweet, you make my teeth hurt" line. I'm sure I've heard that said in a film before.'

Leo laughed. 'How about me having you at hello, then?'

'Oi,' Gracie laughed. 'How about you thinking of some original lines and I will go and shower.'

With a wry smile, Leo Grant drained his champagne glass.

Gracie smothered herself in fragrant shower gel. She had just been kissed by a Hollywood film star in a luxurious Caribbean setting, drinking champagne and dancing to her favourite song. He had even called her a natural woman!

She would tell Noms, of course. But she was sensible enough to realise that it was no more than a drunken peck on his part. From what she had heard from Noms, he wasn't a bad man. And the hug had been completely dreamy and was just what she needed.

It was uncanny how much Jack did look like him and it was a shame that Noms didn't want Leo to see him in the flesh. But she understood why. Leo would fall in love with the little chap, like most people did, and then it would get far too complicated.

As the soothing hot water soaked her body, she began to

think about home. And despite what had just happened with Leo Grant, if her big sis were to ask her now which man in her life she would like to walk around the corner, she would have to give a very convoluted answer. Ed, before his rape revelation. Lewis, before he was unfaithful.

The break had done her good, there was no doubt about that, but tomorrow they would be home. Back to normality. Back to reality.

It wasn't all bad though. Because she felt really excited about the SW19 Club coming to life. It offered a focus. A passion. Something that had been lacking in her life for far too long.

* * *

It was late when Noms, Gracie and a sleeping Jack returned to the villa. Somehow darkness seemed so much blacker and the stars so much brighter in the Caribbean. The sound of crickets was noisier than ever in the still of night, too. They had justified staying at Mangos far longer than they should have done by it being their last night. Noms, who was not a big drinker anymore, had driven them back.

'Ssh.' Noms put her finger to her lips as Gracie tripped drunkenly off the jeep step. 'We don't want to wake Mr Holly-wood or his number one son now, do we?' With a muted groan of effort, she leant in and lifted her sleeping child from the back seat.

'He'll keep out of our way,' Gracie replied knowingly.

'You know too much, little sister.'

Noms had laughed when Gracie had told her that Leo had kissed her. 'Unbelievable,' was all that she could say, but she was clearly relieved that Gracie had stopped him in his tracks. It would be a bit too complicated, having Jack's dad sleeping with his auntie.

* * *

Gracie woke in the middle of the night with a raging thirst. She staggered to the kitchen in her little shorts and vest to find a bleary-eyed Leo doing exactly the same thing. She had been so overcome by his kindness earlier that, seeing him standing there – a man wanting just one thing – she felt that she owed him it.

'Noms and Jack need never know,' she whispered. Leo nodded.

She put her finger to her lips to shush him and pushed the bedroom door open very, very quietly.

Her precious nephew was sprawled tummy down in his Bermuda shorts, sound asleep, with his cute little face to the side so that his daddy could see him perfectly.

Leo put his hand to his heart and bit his lip. Gracie left him alone for a second, before taking his hand and leading him back to the kitchen. This time, she wiped *his* tears with *her* fingers.

'I know it's so hard but in a few years you will be able to say all you want to him.'

Leo kissed her on the forehead. 'Thank you, amazing Grace. That one minute was the best gift anybody has ever given me.'

She lifted his hand to her lips, kissed it, poured herself a pint of water, and sleepily headed back to bed.

FORTY-SIX

Gracie felt more nervous about meeting Ed tonight than she had on their first date. He was cooking dinner for her at his place as they felt it would be easier for them to talk openly in private. She was knackered after the long flight and was slightly thrown by jet lag, so she was glad not to have to go anywhere more formal.

She recognised Ed's flatmate from his photograph when he opened the door – he was a handsome cheery guy who was just on his way out. At the bottom of the flat steps he turned around.

'He's a good man, Gracie.'

Gracie just nodded.

'I'm in here,' Ed shouted from the kitchen.

She greeted him with a kiss on the cheek. 'Wow, that smells good.'

'Chilli with sweet potatoes, my signature dish. Well, actually the only dish I don't have to look at a recipe for.' Gracie laughed. 'Wine?' Ed asked and carried on stirring his culinary delight.

'Yes, lovely, thanks.'

'White OK?'

'Great.'

He went to open the fridge, stopped and turned to her.

'Come here.' He put his arms around her loosely. 'You look amazing with a tan.'

Why couldn't this be it for the evening, being nice to each other, eating, drinking, maybe even making love? Gracie thought. But no, soon the small talk would have to stop and she would have to face the facts.

'You should see the white bits.'

Ed laughed. 'I should be so lucky, eh.' He sighed. 'I'm so sorry, Gracie, that what has happened, has happened. Let me get this served up and we can chat. Why don't you go through and make yourself comfortable.'

They ate and drunk in comfortable union, with Ed holding nothing back by explaining every single detail, just as he had done to Cynthia Princeton.

'Is this why you were funny with me the other night when you didn't sleep with me? I could tell you wanted to.'

'Yes. I fancy you so much, Gracie, but my head is so stuck with all this, that I just couldn't.'

'Look.' She put her hands on his across the table. 'There must be something we can do.'

Ed shuffled his feet slightly. 'Gracie, I really don't want you to get involved.'

He got up and kissed her.

She broke away and smiled. 'But I am already.'

She could see Ed was visibly moved by her comment. Her flirt switch had been activated by the wine. 'I just hope this bad boy is as hot between the sheets as his signature dish.'

Ed smiled. 'I am just so happy you're here. I thought I might lose you.'

'You've been honest with me and trust is a huge part of a relationship to me.'

Ed sighed. 'Gracie Davies. I think you're amazing.'

She stood up. 'And Edward Duke, I think it's time for dessert, don't you?'

FORTY-SEVEN

It was a glorious summer's morning, which allowed the whole front of the event hut to be opened up. Kate had set up tables, chairs and flowery parasols outside. The whole area looked really quaint and inviting.

The vibrant woman greeted Gracie with a smile and a kiss. 'Wow, you look amazing, girl. The break has certainly done you good.'

'You look pretty chirpy yourself and I had a fab time, thanks.'

Kate picked a piece of litter up from the grass. 'Where did you go in the end?'

'Noms has got a friend who has a villa in St Lucia, we went there. It was pure bliss.'

'Lucky you! I adore the Caribbean. We ended up going down to Cornwall for a week; the house was lovely but the weather was bloody awful.'

'Bad weather means lots more bed time, though, surely?' Gracie smirked.

'Really? With a petulant child on board? We only had sex once.'

'Well, it only takes one of those little swimmers, Kate.'

'I know.' Her face dropped. 'I just wish Kevin would enter them into a few more galas.'

Gracie smiled. 'Well, chin up, chicken, we have a new venture now to take your mind off all that. Saying that, I'm a bit nervous, actually.'

Kate put her arm on Gracie's. 'Aw, don't be. To be honest, I've no idea how many we will get coming along today. The Facebook page you set up has helped, but I've only been back a week myself and know I could have done more advertising.'

'This looks fantastic, though.' Gracie scanned the outside area. 'And I've got more flyers to dot around today too, the same ones I dropped in some places in the high street.'

'Good, good.' Kate retrieved her mobile from her pocket and checked for messages. 'That's somebody else who's coming from the school.'

'Great! I can obviously put a lot more time in moving forward and I think it was a genius idea to do a launch for the whole event business and not just start with Miscarriage Matters. This weather makes it perfect, too.'

Gracie went inside and noticed a sectioned-off area with a dressing-up box, toys and books. Kate followed her in. 'Brilliant, you've set up a play area. You've thought of everything.'

Kate flushed at the praise. 'Well, I thought a little investment now with toys, the parasols and all that would bolster interest. I've got jugs of lemonade and fizz in the fridge. The urn is on in the kitchen for teas and coffees. Mac from the café is firing up the BBQ at eleven.'

'Great, you've got it all covered, by the look of it. Noms will be down at ten to set up her bag stall and Ed said he'd connect my phone to the speakers when he's got a minute.'

'Good stuff. My make-up friend is coming at ten. Sally, that's my author friend, is busy today, but hopefully will make the next one. Talking of the lovely Ed, I don't suppose you have seen him since you've been back, have you?'

Gracie blushed slightly.

'Ah, so you have?' Kate smirked.

'So you have what?' Ed appeared with a big smile on his face. Gracie blushed some more. She couldn't deny that sex with him the other night had been amazing. He had been so gentle, but also so passionate. It was as if opening up to him about the babies and him being completely honest with her about his predicament had allowed her to feel so much closer to him. Meeting Leo had also given her an inner confidence. For the first time in ages she liked her body and wasn't shy of being naked. She still wasn't the size she'd like to be, by any means, but she was brown and toned and, most importantly, felt really well.

She had been nervous to make love to someone other than Lewis and, as she lay looking up at Ed's ceiling, she did fleetingly think of him. More because she had made the breakthrough of sleeping with somebody else, than the fact she was comparing the two.

'Just the man.' Gracie smiled. 'I need to set up the music.'

'Here, give me your phone, I'll get it sorted.'

Gracie handed her handset over and followed him into the hall. Within seconds he connected it up and soothing notes from London Grammar caught the breeze outside.

'God, you're good.' Gracie skimmed his bum with her hand.

'I know. Bloody brilliant.'

He ushered her into the kitchen area and edged her towards the wall. She put her hands under his shirt and felt instantly horny.

She laughed as he bent to kiss her.

He pushed himself gently against her and whispered, 'God, I so want to fuck you again.'

She laughed. 'I love it when you talk dirty but I'll need to check my diary. I'm a busy girl now, don't you know.'

'Well, don't take too long, or the women of Wimbledon Common will be forming an orderly queue later.'

Gracie mock-swiped his face.

'The other night was lovely.' Gracie blushed.

'I do my best, girl.' He kissed her on the forehead. 'Good luck today, I know it will be great. Give me a shout when you're done, maybe we can grab a drink.'

With that he headed out into the sunshine, jumped on his quad bike and shot off.

* * *

Gracie flew around making last-minute checks to ensure everything was perfect. She had created flyers to promote the party side of the venue, plus a smaller, more discreet flyer to promote Miscarriage Matters. She dotted them around on the picnic tables. There were clipboards and application forms on the side tables, in case anyone wanted to book an event today with a twenty per cent discount.

By midday, everything was ready. The smell of cooking from the BBQ, combined with the music and the sunshine, threw a distinct party vibe on the breeze.

Gracie poured two glasses of Prosecco and handed one to Kate.

'Ready?'

'As we'll ever be.'

They raised their glasses. 'Cheers to us.'

Despite a lot of the Wimbledon women being extremely wealthy, as Kate had guessed, the offer of a free glass of fizz at lunchtime would still draw them in.

'The rich are usually the tightest, you wait and see,' she had said to Gracie.

Gracie had replied, 'We are here to help anyone, from whatever circumstance, so it doesn't matter how much free fizz is quaffed.'

And quaff a lot of them did. By one o'clock the fizz had run out and Mac was sweating furiously from putting his fortieth chicken skewer on the BBQ. Gracie reckoned there were nearly seventy people milling around. She and Kate were absolutely delighted.

She had already taken a booking for a tenth birthday party in two weeks' time, and a yoga instructor wanted a weekly hour-long slot on a Tuesday morning. A few Miscarriage Matters flyers had also been taken from the piles on the edge of each table, so that was a start at least.

It wasn't until three o'clock that the crowd started to dwindle. People had made the most of the sunshine, sitting at the tables, chatting and enjoying the ambience. Noms was chuffed, as she had sold eight handbags and Kate's make-up friend had almost sold out of her revolutionary new 'magic' wrinkle cream.

Gracie had started to take the parasols down to store inside when a young girl, who Gracie guessed could be no more than eighteen, approached her. She had mousey shoulder-length hair, small rimless glasses and wore a flowing maxi dress with a big sunflower print.

'Excuse me.' Her voice was very quiet.

'Can I help?' Gracie replied kindly.

'Your club about the miscarriages?'

'Yes. You can talk to me about that.' Gracie stopped what she was doing. 'Here. Take a seat.' She patted the seat next to her.

'Well, I'm not sure this is appropriate at all, but I just wanted to talk to somebody really.'

'Go on.' Gracie could see the girl was overflowing with emotion.

'The thing is – and you may hate me for saying this – I really want to have a miscarriage.'

Gracie took in a big gulp of warm summer air.

'So you're pregnant, obviously? How many months?'

'Not even a month, well, I guess about a month. I've just missed my period and done a test. I can't have a baby. It's the wrong time. I go to university in September, it will just mess my life up. My parents will kill me. And I know what you're thinking.'

'Hey, no judgement here.' Gracie had seen the girl having a glass of fizz earlier. 'I'm listening. What's your name, by the way?'

'It's Lana. I bet you're thinking what's a bright girl who's off to get a degree doing not using a condom.'

'We've all made mistakes, Lana.'

'I just can't face the thought of having an abortion. If I were to just lose the baby naturally, then that would be OK. Then it wouldn't be my fault. I'm sorry. I should go. I can't believe I'm telling you this.'

'Don't be silly. This is what this club is going to be about; we should all be honest about how we are feeling, and not what we think we should be feeling. Every day I think should I have eaten this, drunk that? Not eaten this, not drunk that. Rested more. My world fell out of me with my babies, Lana. But I do understand how you must be feeling.'

'I'm so sorry that happened to you,' the young girl added. 'Do you disagree with abortion?'

'No, I don't. We have a right over our own bodies,' Gracie replied immediately. 'I do think that women need to take responsibility, but I'm no prude. I got drunk and had sex without a condom when I was your age. I have to say I was terrified for the whole week leading up to my period.'

'You must think I'm so awful.' Lana got up to leave.

'You sit right down, young lady. You have the right to make

a choice. You have your whole life ahead of you. There are always ways and means to manage with a child but it would be bloody hard at your age. How old are you?'

'Seventeen.'

'So, if you did have this baby, then by the time you get to my age, he or she would be twentyish! All wouldn't be lost. And at least you know you can get pregnant, a lot of women can't do that, you know.'

Gracie realised that her words would mean nothing to this young girl right at this moment, but she hoped that being balanced in her view would guide her to make the right decision, whatever that may be. She envied the bundle of cells growing inside her, but she did not envy her situation at all. At seventeen, she would have been very torn herself about what to do.

Lana sighed. 'Thank you.'

'I hope talking has helped a little bit. You should talk to your mum, she might surprise you. Granted, she may be angry at first but, do you know what, a mother's love will burn through that anger pretty damn quickly, I bet you.'

Gracie thought of her own mother, whose love probably wouldn't even smoulder a ten-denier stocking, and felt momentarily sad.

Kate walked over when Lana had left. 'That looked intense.'

'Yes, poor kid. She's pregnant and wants to miscarry.'

Kate put her hand to her heart. 'We are going to have to be strong ourselves doing this, aren't we?'

'We are, but how wonderful she felt safe enough to confide in me. We are going to do so much good, here, Kate. I suddenly feel I have a purpose.' Gracie welled up. Kate squeezed her hand tightly.

Gracie cleared her throat and her voice lightened. 'I think that went rather well, don't you?'

'It did. A big pat on the back for us both.' Kate grinned and headed off the kitchen.

A male voice interrupted Gracie's thoughts. 'And how could it not be a success with you at the helm.'

Gracie's voice shook. 'Lewis, what are you doing here?' He looked more handsome than she had remembered with his blue eyes matching his shirt. His tanned face, bringing out his bright smile. She also noticed the bags under his eyes and felt a sense of sadness enveloping him. Her heart began to beat at one hundred miles an hour.

'I saw a flyer in the post office with your name on it. I knew you were here. Gracie, I cannot stop thinking about you.'

A vision of him proposing flashed through her mind. Gracie gulped. 'I'm so sorry I ran away from you.'

At that moment Ed screeched up on his quad bike and walked over towards them.

He smacked her on the bottom. 'So many people! See, I told you you'd be brilliant. Celebrations later, I reckon.' He noticed Lewis. 'All right, mate?'

Feeling Lewis's pain, Gracie cringed. 'Ed, this is Lewis.'

'Ah, the infamous Lewis, no less?'

Wishing that the ground would swallow her up, Gracie slowly nodded.

Lewis's face was contorted. 'Didn't take you long, did it, Gracie? Well, fuck you. I'll leave you to... get on with it with your...' He looked Ed up and down. 'Your gardener.' He marched towards his car.

Gracie wanted the ground to swallow her up. Ed went to follow him but Gracie blocked his way.

'Ed, don't.' She felt a lump rise in her throat and ran to the toilet. Looking at herself in the mirror, she bit her lip. The realisation dawned. Yes, she was still angry with Lewis, but true love was a relentless bugger and, cheat or no cheat, they *had* been his babies, too.

FORTY-EIGHT

Professor Princeton wafted his Jo Malone spray around his office and swallowed a mouthful of coffee. He had five minutes before Gracie Davies arrived. He would call Maya again. He glanced at his *Racing Post* as her answerphone message spoke to him. This was getting strange, he thought, a whole month had passed and she hadn't picked up. He was so used to her being at his beck and call that he began to worry. What if one of her tricks had hurt her? He would hate to think of her in danger or hurt in any way.

He texted her, put his phone on silent and got his book out ready to take notes when Gracie arrived. He sat at his desk and drained the rest of his coffee. If he were honest, he was missing the young Czech girl. Sex aside, he liked her: her devil-may-care attitude, her flippancy; liked the fact that she had said that she loved him. *I mean, what man wouldn't, really?* Especially someone with as big an ego as him. It was never going to go anywhere. It couldn't. He was old enough to be her father. He would try her phone again when Gracie had gone. Maybe he would even pop by her place with some flowers. Women loved flowers. He would woo her back to his way of thinking. She would start taking his calls again, he was sure. He was starting to understand why all the women he saw with relationship problems found it hard to deal with men who didn't respond immediately to their texts or calls. Maya's treat 'em mean, keep 'em keen attitude was certainly working. He wasn't used to not being in control and realised he didn't like it. Didn't like it at all.

* * *

Gracie lay on the chaise longue. She had sat and talked with him on the chair before but realised it was easier for her to have her eyes closed. Lying down and not looking at the psychologist made her feel less vulnerable so that she could say more. This was definitely going to be her last session. Miscarriage Matters had become such a big part of her life now and the weekly sessions were getting busier and busier. She and Ed were dating officially; in fact, they were going for dinner that night. His rape case was going to court in two months' time. He was optimistic that he would be proven innocent.

'It's been an age, Gracie.'

'I know. I can't believe it's July already. I just felt the time was right to see you again.'

'I'm always here, you know that.'

Gracie felt soothed by Scott's words. 'I knew the miscarriage sessions would be a success. It's amazing how many women have appeared out of the woodwork who have suffered losses. It's been so cathartic for me to talk things through, too.'

'How are you feeling about that now?' Scott took a drink of water.

'I feel that talking about my experience has sort of cleansed me inside. I sometimes leave the hut and cry all the way home, but that in itself is helping me. I've also started doing deep yoga-type breathing from my stomach whenever I feel a bit stressed or panicky. It works so well to relieve the stress.' Gracie sighed deeply.

'All very positive.'

'I'm dating Ed, now, remember, the landscaper from the common?'

The professor nodded.

'Please don't judge – I can't believe I can say this so flippantly – but he's up on a rape charge. But there is no way he did it. He is so caring and gentle with me. Remember me telling you that he was a bit funny the first time we were going to have sex? Well, it all made sense once he told me about what had happened to him.'

'You are being very grown up about this, Gracie.'

'I'm communicating, we are communicating and it does make such a difference.'

'Good, good.' Scott glanced at his *Racing Post*. Rightly or wrongly, he had discussed the case with Cynthia over dinner one night and she had more or less said that if the lad was guilty she would eat her hat, so he had dropped all concern for Gracie on this front now.

'I also went on the most amazing holiday with my sister and nephew to the Caribbean. It really chilled me out.' Gracie was desperate to tell him about Leo Grant but her allegiance to her sister was too strong for her to give anything away even in the safety of a therapy session.

'That's excellent news. I always feel taking a holiday allows you to kick-start a new beginning.' Scott noticed a horse called Coconut Hooves and ringed it with this red pen.

'Yes, it has felt like that, with the new job and everything. Something else major happened since I last saw you, too.'

'Go on.'

'Closure with Lewis.'

'Really?'

'He proposed, you see,' Gracie said matter-of-factly.

'OK?' Scott nodded slowly. 'And closure, really?'

'Yes, it was in the street, not anywhere romantic, on Wimbledon High Street, actually.'

'And how did that make you feel?'

'Sad, weird, confused. Wishing he could have done it a year earlier in different circumstances.'

'Oh, for there to be a textbook of how life should really go, eh, Gracie?' Scott sighed.

'I know. It's so depressing. I ran. Ran as fast as I could. And fell over.'

'You ran?'

'Yes.'

'What were you running from, though, Gracie?'

'The situation, my feelings, I guess. I went to tell him about the IVF being paid off. I wasn't going to be cross. I wanted it to be nice, to say goodbye, hold my head up and walk away. But I thought about him with the woman he slept with and I felt so hurt again that I just couldn't stop myself. Why couldn't I just hold my head up high? Walk away with respect, instead of going on like some mad fishwife?'

'There are no rights or wrongs, Gracie. We would all love to be able to deal with situations in the "correct way" but when strong feelings are involved that's not always easy. I think it's good to show the emotion. Hold it in and it manifests itself in other ways, not always good ones.'

'He was being really caring about the babies. I couldn't cope. I wanted him to have been like that when it happened.'

'What couldn't you cope with?'

'Him expressing his emotions to me, I guess. Knowing that because he cheated I can't cave in. It's too little, too late, though. And although he is the person closest to me, and he went through it with me, it feels he's now the furthest away.'

'Was there not one part of you that wanted to say yes to his proposal, Gracie?' Scott probed.

Gracie turned her head to the wall.

'It wouldn't be right. Not after what's happened.' Scott didn't push as Gracie continued. 'I haven't seen or heard from him for ages now. He turned up at the event hut and saw me with Ed, and he stropped off. He's such a proud man, I know that that's it for us now.'

'What, he ran off just like you did in the high street?'

'Yes, closure.'

'And are you glad of that... that closure?'

'In a way, yes. It's been months now since his indiscretion. We both need to move on. I've moved on. I'm seeing Ed, aren't I?'

'Do you see you and Ed as a long-term relationship, then?'

'Initially I did but, as time is moving on, I don't know. He is lovely and does seem to care genuinely for me. And we go to nice restaurants, have great sex and we do laugh.'

'What is the but?' Scott paused. 'Do you love him?'

'I love being with him and, for now, that's enough for me.'

'Are you sure?'

Gracie tutted. 'Professor Princeton, I don't know. I feel confused again, now. Too many bloody questions.'

Scott suppressed a smile. 'That is kind of what you pay me for.'

Gracie harrumphed. 'I haven't been with him long enough. And to be really honest I'm frightened of getting hurt again. Ed gives me fun company, good sex and I don't feel alone. Isn't that the basis of a good relationship, anyway? It's all a bit different from with Lewis, though.'

'Why's that?'

'Because Lewis was my mate, my baby maker.'

'And you were in love with him?'

'Oh God, yes, you know that, but now I have to think differently about men and the relationships I have.'

'Why?'

'Because I can't have children. I don't need a mate – I need a lover and a partner who is going to want to be with just me. No family required. It's almost liberating because I don't have to follow the traditional route that people go through. I can go for any age, a free spirit, poor or rich.'

'But surely you could fall in love with any of those people, regardless of whether you can have children or not. Lgracove decides, not you, Gracie.'

'But we make choices to cement our paths, surely?'

'Yes, of course, but if you open up your heart you could fall in love with anybody. But what you are saying is brilliant. You have no constrictions now. You can fall in love with anyone you want. The romantic in me says that should be the case anyway. Look around you, Gracie, the world isn't full of perfection. There are not many perfect relationships. Kids or no kids. Everybody has their own story to tell.'

'I guess the reason I'm being non-committal at the moment about Ed is that he is just thirty-two. As much as he says he hasn't even thought about kids yet, I'm sure he will and then I'll be cast aside.'

'Not if he thinks about adopting them with you. You're a great girl. You're fun, you're pretty. Love outweighs a lot of things. Ed would be a fool not to keep you very close.'

'That's so sweet of you to say. We're going on holiday to Cornwall soon, I'm really excited.'

'Well, that's commitment right there. But Gracie, please do pitch your self-esteem higher from now on. Believe you are amazing, because you are. And if Ed's urge to have children is stronger than his feelings for you, well, it'll be his loss.' He cleared his throat. 'It's time for my next client, I'm afraid.'

Gracie sat on the edge of the chaise.

'Thank you for today. I know everything will be all right. It has to be.'

'We don't know that but everything will be as it will be.

You're doing well. Look how far you've come. You've got a job you love, where you are helping people and helping yourself, and a new man to boot.'

'I know. I just need to find some peace within.'

'Just keep working on you and you will. And just text me if you want another session – you know where I am.' Scott shuffled some papers on his desk. 'I meant to ask, have you seen your friend lately? You know, Maya, the girl you were exercising with?'

'Actually, not for a while, I've been so busy with the new venture. Why do you ask?' Gracie looked at him quizzically.

'Oh, she seemed like she was good for you.'

Gracie laughed. 'Yes. Maybe not such a good moral influence, but I really must call her.'

'You do that.'

* * *

When they'd said goodbye, Scott sat back at his desk. Four long weeks since he'd been able to get hold of Maya. Four long weeks to realise it wasn't actually the sex he was missing – it was her.

FORTY-NINE

Another Wednesday, another successful Miscarriage Matters. Gracie was just clearing away the empty tea and coffee cups when she heard a knock at the hut door.

'Oh, sorry, I didn't realise you would have finished up this early.' It was the young girl she had met on the launch day.

'Hello. Lana, isn't it? Come on in, it's fine. I'm just clearing up.'

'I had a miscarriage,' the girl said, devoid of all emotion. Her ponytailed hair and knee-length floral dress made her look even younger than her seventeen years.

'Oh, darling. Sit down.' Gracie ushered her to one of the round tables and chairs. 'Tea?'

'No, no. I don't want to keep you.'

'It's fine. Let me put the kettle on.'

Gracie left her for a moment then came back and put the hot steaming tea in front of her.

'Sugar?'

'I'd like to say I'm sweet enough but that's obviously not the case.' The young girl weakly smiled. 'I've been drinking, smoking, praying I'd lose this baby. I couldn't tell my mum, even though you suggested it. And then last week, there were spots of blood and then the most terrible pain I've ever experienced. It made me scream. I've never seen so much blood. It was awful.'

Gracie knew that pain all too well. 'You poor thing.'

'No, I don't need sympathy. I'm not even sure what I feel. I was so adamant I didn't want this baby and now I know I'm not having it... well...' She began to cry. 'I feel kind of empty. It was almost as if my body knew that I wanted to get rid of it. Do you think a body is that clever?'

'No. I think if a baby wants to hang on in there then it will regardless of what you throw at it. But don't feel guilty, Lana.' Gracie put her hand gently on the girl's hand.

'I feel more guilty that you went through the same thing, but you wanted to have them, and I'm talking to you about it.'

'That's why I'm here.' Gracie handed her a tissue. 'And I'm very flattered that you came back to me.'

'I feel like I can tell you anything. More than I can tell my mum.' Gracie realised that at thirty-eight she was old enough to be this girl's mother. 'You were so kind to me before. You really made me sit up and think. To be honest, I had arranged to have an abortion. My friend was taking me next week actually. I also feel guilty that I had such terrible thoughts.'

'Lana, you were justified to. You have your whole life ahead of you now. It's just a lesson in life. From now on, protect yourself until you're ready. OK?'

Lana nodded. 'And getting my education is so important to me. I want to be with someone I love when I have children, too, in the right situation.'

'Go to university, have the time of your life.' Gracie smiled. 'The memory of this will fade. Did you go to the doctor after it had happened?'

'Yes, he checked me over and everything appears to be back to normal.'

'Good, that's a relief.' Gracie smiled warmly.

'I'd better go.' Lana stood up. 'But thank you. Thank you so much for listening. You really did help me before and now. You'd have made a great mum, you know.'

As Gracie waved her off she felt a bolt of sadness. People telling her she'd make a great mum burnt like a red hot poker straight into her heart. She then thought of Lana saying that she found her easier to talk to than her mum. Maybe, just maybe she had found her calling, just in a different way than she had ever planned.

FIFTY

Ed was tooting a horn outside as Gracie charged around throwing last-minute things into her bag. This was the first time she had been away with a man for ages and she couldn't help feeling a bit nervous.

'Calm down, little sis.' Noms threw her a bottle of water out of the fridge. 'Enjoy it. A week away by the sea with shaggin' aplenty on offer. What's not to like?'

'What's shagging?' Jack piped up.

Noms and Gracie cringed and ignored him. Ed knocked on the door impatiently.

She flung it open and grinned broadly. 'I'm ready, sorry.'

'Wow.' Gracie was wide-eyed. 'This is cool.'

The luxury apartment was right on the Fowey quayside with a magnificent sea view from every room and a large balcony. Seagulls shouted their approval of the sunny evening.

Gracie ran around checking over the apartment before,

finally, jumping on the bed. 'This is so comfy. You're going to be in trouble, young man.'

Ed laughed. 'Let's hope so.'

Gracie made her way to the bathroom. 'I need to get freshened up after that journey. Shall we go out for dinner then? I'm starving.'

'Actually, I've arranged to meet a surfing mate of mine, to discuss tactics.'

'Oh, you never said.' Gracie hoped her disappointment didn't show in her voice.

'I won't be long. You get yourself bathed and I'll meet you in The Galleon, just over there. Say nine?' He pointed to the pub from the balcony.

Soon after, Gracie lay back in the soothing bubbles. She was happy to be away but she was slightly perturbed that Ed hadn't mentioned anything about meeting his mates on their break. It was hard not to feel disappointed. She'd imagined them arriving, settling in and then, perhaps, having a quick bit of fun before a candlelit dinner.

She made the most of the wonderful bathroom and poured herself a glass of wine from the bottle left as a welcome, taking it out to the balcony. The view – busy with yachts, rowers and water taxis – was magnificent. By the time nine o'clock came, she felt a bit squiffy. She put on her favourite summer dress and wedges and made her way to the pub.

Inside she looked around, but Ed was nowhere to be seen. She rang him. No answer. She ordered herself a glass of wine and texted him from a seat in the beer garden. A guy in his twenties smiled at her. 'The signal is pretty shit down in these parts, you're sometimes better off with smoke signals.'

Despite the beautiful sunset, by nine forty-five she could feel a slight anger rising. The signal may be bad but Ed knew where she was. Just as she was about to march back to the apartment, he appeared chatting to a guy with shoulder-length hair and two really pretty women, one blonde, one dark, who both looked in their mid-twenties.

He came over to Gracie and kissed her.

'I'm so sorry, beautiful. I ended up drinking and had to leave the van in Newquay and it's taken an age to get a taxi.'

'You could have called.' *Keep it together*, Gracie's inner voice said. *This is the first night of your holiday you don't want to ruin it.* 'And why Newquay?'

'Skye lives there. Skye, meet my friend Gracie.'

'Hi.' Gracie could have spat feathers.

'And this is Glyn, a uni mate, and his girlfriend, Leah.'

'Hi.' Gracie smiled as sweetly as an angry woman could.

'Another wine?'

'Actually, no thanks. I'll leave you all to it. I'm a bit tired after the journey.' Gracie knew if she stayed it wouldn't be a pretty ending and she didn't want to embarrass herself.

'Oh, OK. Suit yourself. I did try to call but the signal is shite down here.' Ed turned back to his friends. Gracie marched to the next pub. More alcohol was required. She bought a bottle of wine to take back to the flat. It was an amazing summer evening, still warm in the darkness, with a gentle breeze. From the balcony, she could hear the pub crowd talking animatedly and laughing. At eleven o'clock she took herself to bed for fear of throwing the now-empty bottle of wine at them.

Feigning sleep, she could see from her mobile phone that it wasn't until 2 a.m. that Ed slipped into the bed beside her. When she heard whispers from outside their room, she couldn't keep her anger in any longer.

'What the fuck are you playing at, Ed?'

'What do you mean?'

'Don't act the innocent. Is everyone staying over? Who's that girl anyway?'

'Who? Skye, you mean? She's just a mate of Glyn's. Don't tell me you're jealous. Don't be ridiculous, Gracie.'

'I can't believe you've asked people to stay.'

'Just Glyn and Leah; Skye had to get home and feed her dog. Glyn's boat is here. I thought we could all have a little day trip tomorrow.'

'Ed, I thought this was going to be our holiday.'

'Take a chill pill, Gracie. We've got a whole week to have some fun and they are great people to hang out with.'

'Why didn't you mention this before?' Gracie huffed.

'I didn't think. Glyn's back at work on Monday, anyway. It's just for the weekend.'

'I'm more hurt that you were so damn late, and introduced me as your "friend", to be honest. Why did you do that?'

'Well, you are my friend.'

'Well, that's my bad, assuming I am your girlfriend then, isn't it?' She wriggled herself to the edge of the bed and pulled the duvet around her so that he couldn't touch her. Not that he even noticed. Within seconds he was snoring as loudly as Gracie's heart was beating in anger.

The seagull cries accentuated Gracie's hangover as she marched to the cliff top as soon as she woke up. Her disappointment had not subsided. She found a place where she had some signal, then phoned Noms.

'Come home, Grace, sod him. He's acted like a twat.'

'I know he has, but maybe I need to loosen up a bit? I mean, they are his friends.'

Noms tutted. 'And some random girl in her twenties. I'd have gone mental, too.'

'I think I should be the bigger person, take back brunch supplies and see what the day has in store. They were all drunk and it really is beautiful down here, you know. I've just had a cup of tea in the Fowey Hall Hotel. It has breathtaking views and the waiter told me that Toad Hall was based on the building.'

'Sounds lush. But if he treats you any less than perfect from now on, he'll have me to answer to.'

Gracie laughed. 'A fate worse than death. At least the perfectly bodied Skye isn't here now, she went home. She's a mate of Glyn's girlfriend, so I don't know why on earth I got jealous. I can't even blame it on my hormones anymore.'

As Gracie headed back towards the flat she was greeted with a 'Hey' from the outside area of the restaurant which was directly below their apartment, and saw that Ed was there with Glyn and Leah. 'I thought it might be good to have brunch here, seeing as it's so close to our place and I knew I wouldn't miss you coming past.'

Glyn and Leah smiled widely. Gracie sat down and put her bags of supplies next to her and ordered a cup of tea. If she couldn't beat them, she might as well join them.

Brunch was amazing. The restaurant made its own bread and the smoked salmon and scrambled eggs were to die for. Leah and Glyn made the effort to get to know her and Ed was his usual self. It wasn't until they wandered round to the harbour that her heart sank, because there, in tiny denim shorts and a cropped top, was the Amazonian Skye.

Gracie picked up on Ed's delight and tried to keep calm. 'I didn't know you were coming.'

Skye smiled. 'How could a girl resist on a day like this?'

* * *

Gracie hadn't realised quite how short her sea legs were until she started being sick over the side of the boat. The sea wasn't even that rough, but the rocking motion was just enough to upset her equilibrium. Leah was an angel, bringing her tissues and water. Ed, a self-professed sick phobic, couldn't get within two feet of her so stayed up the front of the boat with Glyn and the long one.

Glyn insisted that he take her back to shore. Gracie, getting greener by the minute, just nodded in agreement.

Ed helped her onto dry land. 'Do you want me to come back to the apartment with you?'

'No, you go back out there. I'm fine. Sorry to be such a lightweight.'

Gracie lay on top of the covers with the curtains blowing a delicious sea breeze over her. Her mind was suddenly full of doubt. Of course she had wanted Ed to come back with her and see if she was all right. Maybe he just wasn't the person she had hoped he was. Maybe she had been swept away by the initial spark of attraction. Maybe it had been too early to get involved so soon after Lewis. Maybe a man at thirty-two wasn't a grown up yet. Maybe this had all been a terrible mistake.

It was getting dark when she woke up and she couldn't believe how long she had slept for. She felt much better. And she was relieved to see a note next to her on the pillow, telling her that 'the crew' were all in The Galleon and asking her to join them if she was feeling up to it.

Taking her time to get ready, she put on the dress she knew Ed liked her in and took special care with her make-up. Serene Skye may have legs up to her armpits and ten years on her, but Ed had invited her here, Ed wanted to be with her, nobody else. What had Professor Princeton said about self-esteem? She really had to think more of herself. Just because Lewis cheated on her, it didn't mean that every man would.

It was 10 p.m. by the time she was ready. She could hear a

band playing in The Galleon as she walked across the quayside. She smiled. She loved live music – it was going to be a great night. She walked into the heaving bar and looked around for Ed and the others. Leah was at the bar with Glyn.

'Hey, Gracie, you look a bit better now, how you feeling?'

'So much better for being on terra firma. Thanks for your help earlier.'

'Drink?'

'I'll just have a Diet Coke, please, where's Ed?'

'Outside on the terrace. See you out there in a minute.'

Gracie wandered outside. There was barely any space to stand. At first she couldn't see Ed anywhere. But then she spotted his large shoulders, very close to skinny Skye's. They were flirting animatedly and, as he noticed her approach, she saw him freeze. He leapt up as she got near.

'Gracie! How you feeling, darling? Can I get you a drink?' He was slurring his words.

Skye looked discomfited. 'We thought you'd conked out for the night.'

'You mean you wish I had.' Gracie couldn't help letting her feelings show.

'What?' Skye looked confused.

'Gracie, don't be silly. What's wrong?' Ed put his arm around her.

'I'm going to the toilet,' Gracie huffed.

'Gracie, what is it? We were just talking.'

'You were flirting your arse off.'

Ed gave a sheepish smile. 'Well, she's a pretty girl.'

Whoosh! A red mist covered the pub.

'I don't bloody believe you, Ed Duke. First you have the audacity to invite friends to join *our* holiday without even telling me. You let me go back from the boat on my own and left me all day. And then I come here and you're practically licking the face of somebody ten years younger, who undoubtedly can still have children.'

Ed held Gracie with both arms now.

'Hey, stop it. You know how much I think of you.'

'Do I? Do I really? I hardly know you, Ed. And my gut is telling me this isn't the way I deserve to be treated.'

'Don't be irrational. It's all cool.'

Skye appeared from outside. She was obviously drunk.

'Chill out, sister, we're just having fun.'

Gracie thought she was going to internally combust. Rather than cause a scene, she scurried down the alleyway from the pub and into the street. She marched to the Town Quay, sat on a bench and took a massive deep breath. It was windy now but somehow the extreme of the weather made her feel better. The high tide was sending waves sloshing noisily against the moored boats. She sat until she could stand the cold no longer, then looked over to The Galleon. The outside areas were almost deserted now and she could hear whoops of delight as the band starting playing up again.

Maybe she had overreacted? They had only been talking, for goodness' sake. But a cheated heart is a paranoid one and she trusted her instincts. She had sensed their attraction from the start and as for saying 'she's a pretty girl' – what a bastard! And where was he now? A man who cared would have followed her out. It was all suddenly very clear, Edward Duke wasn't the man for her.

If she had had her own car there, she would have left. She reached for her phone. She had to call Noms. She would calm her, tell her what to do, tell her everything would be all right. There was a message on her answerphone. She struggled to hear what it said over the noise of the wind, but when she found a sheltered spot and could, she put her hand to her heart.

'Gigi, it's me, Lewis. I've had an accident, in the car. Don't

worry, nothing too serious, just had to have an op to reset my arm as it's broken. But... but I just wanted you to know that you were the first person I thought of when I came to. And I know you're seeing someone now, but I wanted you to know... His voice cracked... *that I still miss you... I miss you so much.'*

FIFTY-ONE

Gracie sat drinking tea with Noms at the kitchen table. Boris was sleeping soundly at their feet. Jack was at a friend's house.

'Feeling better?' Noms enquired lovingly.

'Do you think I overreacted?' Gracie groaned.

'He was just talking to the girl, but I'm with you on the gut-feeling thing. Has he contacted you since he asked where you'd gone?'

'Yes. He said that he was sorry he had made me feel that way and to get on the train back down there, but that was it. I can't believe he's staying down there on his own. The "friends"' – Gracie made her fingers into inverted commas – 'were only around for the weekend, supposedly.'

'He might come back early, you don't know,' Naomi said lightly.

'Maybe, but he does love his windsurfing, and he hasn't had a holiday for ages because he was waiting for his court date.'

'Well, you can cut him some slack for that then, poor bastard. He must be under such stress.'

'I know. But it wasn't just the girl thing, it was everything. I don't think he's the man for me, Noms. I need someone who cares a little bit more. Someone a bit more thoughtful.' Gracie sighed loudly.

'We both know men don't think like us, though, Grace. He probably won't even realise why you're upset.'

'Well, that's no excuse. He should have taken my feelings into consideration – and more importantly, I didn't like the way it made me feel.'

'OK, I get that.' Noms got up and opened a packet of chocolate digestives.

Gracie took the one offered. 'If somebody can upset me after such a short time together, well then, I can't see a future in it. A good relationship is about being happy, not about feeling hurt and sad. And if I'm totally honest, the rape thing... well, that's also been on my mind.'

'I didn't think you doubted him for one minute about that.' Noms wiped crumbs from her mouth with her hand.

'I didn't – I don't, but the fact that it's going to trial, well something untoward could have happened, is my thinking.'

'Oh, I don't know, Grace. Truthfully, though, it has been worrying me a bit, too.'

'He was so kind when I fell over, and in bed he has been nothing but gentle with me. He's not a bad person, I know that. But I saw a different side to him this weekend.'

'Well, maybe see what happens when he comes back.'

'I don't think he'll want to see me. Men can't deal with irrational women at the best of times.'

'We are all irrational, my sweet little sister. If he likes you enough, he'll be back. They all come back in the end. They realise how good they really had it. The amount of times I've had exes knocking on my door.'

'And they think we're complicated! Shit!'

'What's the matter, Grace?' Noms looked concerned.

'I forgot to tell you. Lewis has been in hospital. He had a car accident and broke his arm.'

'Oh, that's no good.'

'He left me the sweetest message saying that he still missed me.'

'Of course he still misses you. Who wouldn't. Did you respond?'

'I sent a text wishing him a quick recovery. Do you know what, though? Sitting looking out to sea when Ed upset me, I realised just how much Lewis and I did have. How deep our love and relationship was. He's not bad man either, Noms.'

'I know that. I've known him as long as you. I miss him in a way, too. Seven years is a long time.'

'I'm thinking about meeting him. Just for a coffee, a chat.'

'Do you think that's wise? I mean, last time you met him for a chat the poor bloke ended up on his knees in the street proposing to you. You have to be fair.'

'It's probably not wise at all. But I don't know if I can let go of him completely. Maybe we can just be friends for now, at least.'

'I think that will be hard. You should think seriously about it. Maybe take some time out from men. Listen to the professor and get Gracie Davies back on track.'

'Maybe.' She stood up and stretched. 'I'm so tired after that train journey, I'm going to go and have a lie-down.'

Gracie lay on her bed deep in thought. If somebody asked her now who she would like to walk around the corner, she knew exactly who it would be.

FIFTY-TWO

'At least it's your left arm.' Gracie greeted Lewis in the coffee shop with a smile. 'Can I sign the cast?'

'Gracie, that's what we used to do when we were ten.'

She laughed. 'Time to grow up, Ms Davies?'

Lewis looked serious. 'No, it's not. Don't ever change, Gracie Davies. I love you just the way you are. What are we doing laughing together, anyway? Last time I saw you, you were busy with your gardener friend.'

Gracie knew she needed to be honest; she couldn't risk getting his hopes up. 'I... err. I guess I miss you, too, Lewis, but I'm not ready for anything more than just seeing you like this... for a chat...'

'As friends, you mean?'

Gracie nodded.

'I've got enough friends, Gracie. It wouldn't work. Seeing you with the Neanderthal on the common the other week just about finished me off. Are you still seeing him?'

'I don't know.'

'What do you mean you don't know? Actually, I don't want to know. How's the event business going these days?'

'Brilliantly. It really does make me happy. I should have done something on my own years ago. Of course it helps that I have a free roof to sleep under. Not so much pressure to have to do well.'

'I would have supported you, once we'd paid off the IVF, you know that. I mean, I was going to have to when the babies came anyway.'

The mention of 'the babies' made Gracie take a deep breath.

Lewis looked pained. 'How are you feeling about it all now – our loss, I mean?'

'If I'm honest, I don't think I'll ever get over it, but it is easing. I don't wake up every day now thinking about what could have been. I do struggle with the thought of never being able to get pregnant again, though.' Gracie sighed.

Lewis put his hand on hers. 'I know. I would always have adopted with you.' He paused. 'I still would.'

Gracie shook her head. 'Don't say that. I'm so confused at the moment about everything.'

Lewis welled up. 'It's fine. It's just amazing to see you, smell you, talk to you. I never thought I could miss anyone this much.'

Gracie gulped. 'Oh, Lewis. Why did you do what you did?'

'Let's not down this road again.' He sighed deeply. 'I can't say any more than I am deeply sorry and I will never do it again. I just wish you could forgive me.'

Gracie's voice wobbled. 'So I take it you haven't met anyone else, then?'

Lewis snapped. 'Of course I haven't. Every time I close my eyes, there is only one woman in front of me.'

As Gracie began to believe in him again, she noticed him second glance at the counter, then go white as a sheet.

'What's wrong, Lewis, are you in pain?'

'No, no, it's nothing. Come on, let's go. This side door leads out to Retford Street, doesn't it?'

As Gracie stared to see what had created his reaction, she felt bile slowly rising in her throat. For there at the café counter, adorned in designer maternity wear and ordering a decaff skinny latte, was an obviously pregnant Annalize.

Gracie decided to flee rather than fight. Keeping her head down, she charged out of the café onto the street; Lewis threw money on the table and followed swiftly.

He grabbed her by both arms – she was now completely uncontrollable.

'No, no, no! How could you have kept this from me? Fuck off away from me.' She pushed him back and he winced in pain as she caught his bad arm.

'You have to believe me, Gracie! This is as much of a shock to me as you... And who's to say it's my baby anyway?'

Gracie hailed a taxi and scrambled in.

'I hate you, Lewis. I hate you more than I ever thought I could.'

FIFTY-THREE

Gracie fell through the front door, sobbing. Boris half opened one eye from his kitchen bed and went straight back to sleep. She went to the drinks cupboard, poured herself a large gin and slugged it down neat.

She knew exactly what four months pregnant looked like and it looked like Annalize. It had to be Lewis's. No wonder he'd gone white as a sheet. No wonder he was being so nice to her. He *had* to have known. All of this proposal shit must have been a complete ruse, a filthy, guilty ruse.

She poured herself another gin and reached for the tonic this time, sending a glass smashing onto the ceramic tiles. Boris ran to the sanctuary of the living room. Noms appeared with her hair sticking up and looking slightly flushed.

'What's all the noise about, Grace? What on earth's happened?'

Through snotty sobs she told Noms what she had seen.

Noms looked sympathetic but said, 'It's doubtful it's Lewis's. You're just being paranoid.'

'Paranoid? I've just seen the girl Lewis shagged four months ago and she's pregnant. I don't think there is anything that could happen that could be worse. Can you?' Gracie had never felt so angry. 'I'm going to kill him. I honestly want to kill him.'

'Is everything all right?' A woman appeared in the kitchen wearing Noms's dressing gown.

'What are you doing here?' Gracie recognised the redhead as the woman who'd come to her rescue in the street.

'Oh, hello. How are you? Your injuries?'

'Err... hello, Ali. All healed, thanks.' The surprise of this new development slightly sobered her madness.

'You know each other?' Noms was wide-eyed. Gracie thought back to Ali's kindness in the street when she had fallen over.

'Not as well as you two do now, I guess.' Gracie shook her head in disbelief at the scenario unfolding.

Before Gracie had had a chance to explain to Noms how they knew each other, there was a knock at the door.

'If it's Lewis, I don't want to talk to him.' Gracie rushed past Noms and a now open-mouthed Ali.

It was Noms's turn to look surprised. For standing in front of her – in all his handsome glory – was none other than Leo Grant.

She opened the door a small crack so Ali didn't see him and lowered her voice. 'What the hell are you doing here?'

'I'm filming in London and...' He clocked the horror on Noms's face. 'Is it not a good time, sweet cheeks?' He handed her a card. 'My UK cell. Look, I shouldn't have turned up unannounced, I know, but I've thought about it long and hard and I have a right to meet Jack.'

'He's not here.' Noms was furious. 'He's at a friend's overnight, thank goodness. What about our agreement? I can't believe you've got the audacity to turn up at my home!'

Leo noticed her dishevelled appearance. 'Ah, and you've got a visitor, I get it.' He winked and clicked his teeth.

Noms took a deep breath. 'Look, Leo. I appreciate we need to talk, just not today, eh? I'll call you, I promise.'

'OK, OK. I get it. Is Grace still living with you?'

'Yes, she's just had a terrible shock, though.'

'Gee, that poor girl. Get her to call me on my cell. I'm in town all week if she fancies a chat. I'm a good listener, she knows that.'

With that, he pulled his cap down to meet his sunglasses and sauntered back to his chauffeur-driven Mercedes.

'Who was that?' Ali enquired as she made her way back up the stairs.

'Just Ed, a guy Grace was seeing – is seeing. Actually, I've no idea what's going on anymore.'

'Oh, Ed, yes. Tall, handsome, goatee beard, drives a red van?'

'This is just too much for me. You know *him* too? So much for a discreet afternoon dalliance.'

'I'll get dressed and go. I think your sister needs you more than me right now.'

'Yeah, OK.' Noms smiled. 'It's been great. Let's do it again, if you fancy?'

'Sure.' Ali grinned. 'Let me know when you're about and I can work around my shifts.'

'Will do. And I promise it's not always like being on the set of Eastenders here.'

Ali let herself out as Noms knocked on Gracie's bedroom door. She was face down on the bed.

'Grace, come on.' She gently pulled her sister up and into her arms. 'Let's be rational for one minute.'

'Rational, bloody rational. My ex-boyfriend has got the girl he slept with pregnant! He is going to have a baby. We can't have babies. And you tell me to be fucking rational.'

'Did you ask him if he knew if it was his?'

'He declared he had no idea,' Gracie replied pitifully. 'I just ran, like I always do when I have to face confrontation. If it is his I'm moving away, I can't be near them.'

'Oh, baby girl, don't be so dramatic.'

'It's bad enough knowing that slag has managed to get pregnant in her forties. Miss Bloody Perfect. Managed to get everything she ever wanted.'

'I thought you said she never wanted kids?'

'Well, she obviously changed her mind. I hate her as much as I hate Lewis.'

'I know, I know. Look, do you want me to speak to Lewis? I can be calmer.'

'No! Part of me doesn't want to know. I don't think I can bear it. I don't know how I'd ever move on from it, if it is his. But it must be, Noms. Oh God.' She stood up and started pacing the floor.

Noms was ever the pacifier. 'If it is his, Lewis might not even know, she might not have told him. Actually, she obviously hasn't told him. Lewis would have had to let you know. He is honest and decent enough, I'm sure. And she could have been sleeping with a plethora of men, you just don't know.'

'Hahaha,' Gracie laughed falsely. 'Honest and decent, yeah, right. Why hasn't he called me then, Noms? Probably hatching a plan with *her* as we speak to get their stories straight.'

'Grace, stop it. Call him now and see what he has to say.'

'No. I can't bear it. It almost feels better that there is a chance it's not his. If I knew for sure then it would be worse than this.'

'So, this is what you are going to do instead of lying here moping and wailing.'

Gracie sniffed. 'What?'

Noms handed her Leo's business card. 'You are going to ring Leo and say you want to go out for dinner with him.'

'Leo? Why, is he in London?'

'He was at the door half an hour ago. I'm furious with him. I need to talk to him, too, but you go and be treated. I know you like him. It'll do your ego the power of good.'

Gracie shook her head. 'No. I don't think I can face it.'

'Get in the bath, get your glad rags on and just go. It will make you look at life as a bigger picture. You don't have to stay out late. Just be treated. You deserve it.'

'So... you and Ali, eh?' Gracie managed a smile.

'She's really nice.'

'And?'

'And nothing, dear sister.' She looked away. 'I meant to ask you if you'd heard from Ed again.'

'Yes, he messaged me. He's staying down in Cornwall for a few more days and said he'd like to talk on his return.'

'You've got a lot of talking to do, girl. Now get ready. You're on the "A" list this evening.'

'I can't. Leo Grant can wait. I mean, look at the state of my eyes. I want to run away somewhere and never come back. Oh, Noms, when is this nightmare going to end?'

'Ssh, now.' Noms held her sister to her. 'I'll run a bath for you.'

FIFTY-FOUR

Lewis sat in his flat with his head in his hands. His mind was racing. He winced as he saw Gracie's name flash up on his phone screen, not once, but twice. He couldn't talk to her yet. What on earth could he say to make her feel better? He had no answers. She would just end up screaming at him. He felt a dark smear of guilt wash over him like sticky tar.

Gracie had always said that when someone loves you even the way they say your name is different. She always said she thought her name was safe in his mouth. But it hadn't been, had it? He had betrayed her at her lowest and now this was too big a monster for him to comprehend.

The worst thing was there was nothing he could say to her to make it better. He thought back to the night he spent with Annalize: the drink-fuelled night of flirting and lust. He racked his brains; had they used a condom? He couldn't remember much. If he hadn't, how bloody foolish was he? Then suddenly he remembered laughing at the red dot on her bedroom ceiling and asking her what it was for. 'It's so I never forget to take my pill,' she had said. He cringed at the memory. Why had he not had some self-control that night?

But pill or no pill, the girl was obviously pregnant. Surely if it was his she would have told him? The worst thing was that he wanted to know. And if the child was his, didn't he have a right to know?'

But he was caught between a rock and a hard place here. If he were to have a biological child of his own, as much as he felt guilty admitting it, he would be over the moon.

But if he decided to confront Annalize to ask her, then he would have to tell Gracie that he was doing so, because he could never go behind her back again. And then if she was pregnant with his child, well, Gracie would be destroyed, and they could never be together again, anyway. Because just seeing Annalize pregnant had sent her over the edge, let alone knowing if it was his.

He poured himself a large whisky and gazed at the photo of him and Gracie on the windowsill. He pushed open the door to 'the nursery'. Although he knew that he should start selling things off, he still hadn't got round to doing it. Looking at it now, he understood how hard it must have been for Gracie to let go. He'd been such a bully telling her to get over things. He didn't deserve to get her back.

He leant back against the cold wall and slid down it. Looking at the two empty beds for an answer he said aloud, 'What the hell am I going to do?'

FIFTY-FIVE

Maya kicked off her high heels, peeled off her stockings and ran a bath. Although the money was so good, she was beginning to tire of pandering to men's dirty fantasies. She took a deep breath and looked at the picture of the Mayfair beauty salon she had pinned to the fridge. This was her goal. She had to keep going for just one more year before she had enough savings to pay for a full-time beauty course.

It had been good to chat with Gracie earlier. With the hours she worked in the café and seeing her clients, she hadn't had time to make many friends. And she liked Gracie. As her mother would say, she was beautiful within and without. She was also more than pleased that Gracie had said that the professor had mentioned her. He obviously was bothered about what she was doing. It had been the hardest thing to not contact him for the past few weeks. More than once she had turned her phone off and gone out for a walk, so as to not be tempted to reply to his many texts. They had started off with his usual sex talk, but after a week of silence from her, he began getting concerned for her well-being. The weaning-off process wasn't really working. She missed him. But if she were to reach her goal she couldn't be falling in love with a married man. It would be too complicated. Her mother had also told her not to let an attraction be a distraction. She would carry on ignoring him until he went away.

She got out of the bath, slung on an old white dressing gown, lay on the bed and lit a cigarette. She was just about to open her favourite magazine when the doorbell rang. One of her flatmates tapped on her door. 'Maya, visitor.'

Visitor? She never got unexpected visitors. Butting her fag, she pulled on shorts and a T-shirt that she had cast on the floor the previous night and opened her bedroom door.

'Professor? What the...' She was conscious of her unmade-up face and her wet hair sticking to her face.

'Can I come in?'

'I'm not dressed.'

'When has that ever bothered you before, little bird?' He stepped in and shut the door behind him. Seeing Maya's natural beauty, without her war paint and sexy outfits, he thought she looked vulnerable and endearing. He felt a sudden surge of love for her.

He pulled her towards him and hugged her tightly for what seemed like an age.

'I've missed you.'

'You've missed my body, you mean.'

'Of course I have, but also your flippancy, your attitude, your Maya-isms. Where have you been?'

'Nowhere and everywhere.'

'That's my girl. As secretive as ever.'

'I got bored of you.' Maya lit another cigarette. 'It's time to find another professor.'

Scott laughed. 'There's only one of me, I can assure you.'

'What do you want, Professor?'

'Like I said, I've missed you.'

Maya hurriedly brushed her tangled wet locks and smudged on some lip gloss.

'You look beautiful without it, you know, and I'm only going to kiss it off.'

He tilted her chin up towards him and kissed her softly and passionately. Maya felt like she was in a dream. She hadn't been kissed like that for a long, long time. She never kissed her clients and, when she had kissed the professor in the past, they had been deep, urgent, tongue-filled kisses enhanced with sexual urgency.

'Do it again,' she demanded, when he eventually allowed her to come up for air. He pushed her back on the bed and kissed her again. He put his hand up under her T-shirt and began gently fondling her pert little breasts. He lifted her arms and pulled off her top then undid her shorts and tenderly pushed his fingers inside her, making her gasp. She reached for his now bulging cock and he pushed her hand away.

Once he could feel her wetness, he removed her shorts and panties and pulled her legs round so she was on the edge of the bed. Crouching down he began to lick and tease her, until her body was arching in pleasure.

'Stop, I'm going to come already,' Maya panted. Scott groaned in pleasure himself as he could feel his little bird tense and then let everything go with one huge moan.

She lay back on the bed. 'Wow. That was bloody amazing.' She reached again for his erection. He moved her hand to his thigh.

'No. Today is about you.'

'But you know I love your cock in my mouth.'

Scott kissed her on the lips, biting her bottom lip as he moved away.

'Maya, I heard what you said the other week.'

'I don't know what you mean?' Though she knew exactly what he meant.

'When you came just now, I wanted to say the same back to you. But I'd never tell you that or say it out loud, of course.'

'Of course you wouldn't.' Maya felt a warmth flow right through her body.

'You'll have to give up one of your part-time jobs, though. I've never really liked that red underwear, to be honest.'

Oh God, Maya thought, he knew and hadn't said a word.

'I haven't been enjoying it lately – so that would be fine by me.'

'Good. Good.' The professor looked down at Maya's perfect naked body. 'Turn over, let me see that dragon of yours.' He fingered her tattoo, then gently massaged her back from top to bottom. She shivered.

'Let's get you warm, shall we?' He undressed quickly and held himself above her on his forearms. 'I honestly have never wanted to fuck somebody so much in my whole life. I will rephrase that – Maya Bakova, I want to make love to you.'

Maya had never experienced such tender, loving sex. Her orgasms were like honey through her veins; the feeling of Scott inside her made her want to cry. When they were done, they both lay back on the bed staring up to the ceiling. Scott reached for her hand and stroked her palm lovingly.

Maya snuggled into him. 'So where do we go from here?'

'How about nowhere and everywhere?'

They both laughed.

'That'll do just fine for now.'

Feeling an extreme peace wash over her, Maya kissed his chest and reached for her cigarettes.

FIFTY-SIX

Gracie felt like she was on the set of *Pretty Woman* as she entered the five-star central London hotel. The concierge took her up in the lift to the penthouse suite at the top of the building and let her in.

'Mr Grant will be with you in thirty minutes. He said to help yourself to anything you require while you're waiting for him.' He smiled as Gracie's jaw dropped at the room in front of her before heading back down the corridor.

Left alone, Gracie walked around the penthouse apartment. This really was how the other half lived. It was four times bigger than the flat she had shared with Lewis, full of sumptuous antiques and beautiful fresh flowers. The whole place oozed opulence. She went into the bathroom and gasped at the sunken marble bath. It was surrounded by speakers and two of the softest, whitest bath robes she had ever seen hung up to the side of the mirrored walls.

She checked herself out. She had thought plain was the best way forward, so she had chosen a black shift dress with a white collar and black, high strappy sandals. Her eyes were smoky and her lipstick bright red. Her St Lucia tan accentuated her green eyes and Noms had blow dried her hair so that it was sleek and straight to her shoulders.

She tried not to think about the text Lewis had just sent her, explaining that he hadn't seen or heard from Annalize since the night they'd had sex. Gracie was trying very hard to put the whole thing out of her mind. She hoped that seeing Leo would be a sufficient distraction – much better than waiting at home, worrying and seething until she could face talking to Lewis properly.

Looking at herself now, she realised that she wasn't even nervous. This wasn't 'a date'. She was by no means Leo Grant girlfriend material. Even the thought of having a casual sexual encounter – whether with a film star or anyone else – wasn't something she could cope with on top of everything else.

She hadn't given Ed much thought since the Cornish fiasco. She cared for him, but not enough to care that he hadn't followed her home. She wasn't angry; she hadn't even cried. She obviously didn't love him. She liked him, but it would be easy to say goodbye and she was sure that would be the outcome when they next met. A meeting yet to be arranged. And today, the shock of the Annalize 'babygate' situation had driven out most thoughts of anything else on the planet. Noms had been right, she needed to take her mind away from all that and throw herself into the fantasy world of a Hollywood actor.

She walked through to the bedroom and smiled at the size of the round bed in the centre. It was adorned in cream silk sheets and covered in sumptuous cushions to match the decor. There was a double bath at the end of the bed and French windows that opened to a magnificent view of the whole of the city.

Catapulting herself backwards on the bed she lifted her legs in the air and waggled them. Her laughter was matched by Leo's as he appeared in the doorway.

'Gee, my natural woman, that is quite a welcome.'

Gracie jumped up blushing. 'Shit! I'm sorry.'

Leo mimicked her English accent. 'Shit! I'm not.'

Gracie flattened down her dress. 'I thought you'd be longer.'

'Can I get you a glass of champagne?'

'That would be lovely, thank you.'

Gracie took in the actor's appearance. He was wearing dark denim designer jeans, hand-stitched dark brown shoes and a crisp white shirt. His hair was cut neatly and his skin looked like an ironed peach. He looked much younger than his forty years. He looked edible.

'As it's such a nice evening I thought we could sit out on the terrace, have a few canapés, have a chat and then Kingston can set the table for dinner. Sound like a plan to you?' Leo raised his eyebrows.

'That sounds like an amazing plan to me.' Gracie smiled, suddenly feeling shy.

'It's easier to eat in sometimes, what with the paps and everything.'

'And the fact you have a girlfriend,' Gracie added.

'You look great, Grace. A tan suits you. And as for the girl-friend, she's traded me in for two twenty-year-olds. But that's life, eh.'

Gracie's lips downturned. 'I'm sorry.'

'Are you really?' Leo smirked.

Gracie nodded. 'As mad as it may seem to a man of your calibre, I can assure you the last thing I want is another one to complicate my life.'

The sun shone as they downed their champagne. After two glasses Gracie felt quite heady.

She fanned her face with her hand. 'That's hit the spot.'

'Good.' He rang a bell and Kingston appeared with a delicious plate of canapés.

Gracie ate a couple, tipped her head back and shut her eyes. 'These are amazing!'

'So how are you, Grace? Not so good from your previous comment, I assume. But I have to say I've thought a lot about you since St Lucia.'

Gracie blushed. 'And me, you actually.'

'Really?' Leo smiled. Gracie bit her lip and nodded. 'And you were so kind to let me see Jack. I will never forget that. It made me realise that actions speak louder than words or money. I can be a shallow bastard sometimes.'

'I think we probably all can.' Gracie reached for a canapé.

'Being so privileged, it's bloody hard to keep your feet on the ground. But forget all the women, fame and this—' He panned his arm behind him. 'The most important thing to me now is meeting Jack and trying to be a good father to him, not just financially but emotionally. Do you think your sister will ever let me in?'

'I think she's just worried what it will mean for Jack if word gets out that you're his father. With the kids at school and all that sort of thing.'

Leo grinned. 'If I was a five-year-old kid I'd think it was really cool.'

'Maybe, but I understand Noms's way of thinking, too.'

'I see where she's coming from. But maybe she could introduce me as a friend and I could get to know him? I could call myself something else. I guess he hasn't seen any of my films?'

'No, but your face is all over the place at the moment, now that Working it Out has hit Netflix, so I'm sure he'd pick up on it.'

'Will you talk to her for me, Grace, please? My intentions are only good, you know that.'

He poured her another glass of champagne and pressed the bell again.

'You ready for dinner?'

She took a sip of champagne. 'Yes, I'd better soak this up with something substantial.'

'I took the liberty of choosing a tasting menu, so hopefully there's something on there you will like.'

'That's just perfect, I eat everything but aubergine and my words.'

'You're cute, Grace. Real cute.'

There was a different wine with each course and by the third one Gracie was feeling really quite drunk.

'I must drink more water.' She guzzled down a glass of sparkling in one go. 'And I should slow down. I'll be talking nonsense – well, less sense than usual anyway.'

'You should really stop doing that.' Leo was serious.

'What?' Gracie hiccupped.

'Putting yourself down.' Leo took her hand. 'I'd rather spend a whole evening with you than ten minutes with some of the shallow fame-hungry women who throw themselves at my feet. You're great, Grace. Never forget that.'

She could feel herself blushing. 'That's so sweet.'

'I mean it. And please don't think I wanted to see you just to chew your ear about seeing Jack. I wanted your company. Naomi said you'd had some more bad news. Do you want to talk about it?'

Gracie shook her head. 'I don't want to ruin the night.'

'There she blows again. I want you to talk to me. It's not all about champagne and roses, Grace. Real life quite often stinks. I'm a big boy; I can take it.'

Leo reached for this phone and Aretha Franklin's beautiful tones began piping out of the speakers as a complement to Gracie's tale of woe.

Gracie bit her lip. 'I'm going to say it quickly for fear of crying.'

'Cry me a river if you like, honey child.' Leo squeezed her hand and Gracie laughed.

'There you go again, Mr Original.' She sipped the dessert wine that Kingston the butler had just put in front of her. 'I told you about the twins and the hysterectomy. And my boyfriend Lewis cheating on me after saying that he didn't find me attractive anymore.'

Leo exhaled and nodded. 'Harsh, but yes.'

'This week, I thought maybe I would meet Lewis again, because part of me does miss him.'

Leo raised his eyebrows and turned his head to the side, not quite understanding why she would want to see her ex. He nodded again.

'While I was with him in a coffee shop the girl he had sex with that night walked in. And she was pregnant. About four months pregnant. Which would be perfect timing to make it Lewis's baby.'

'Whoa, that's big shit, man.'

'I know. Even if it's not Lewis's, I still feel bitter and twisted. What gives her the right to have children and not me? It's just not fair.'

'You can't be mad at everyone in the world who gets pregnant, Grace. You'd be mad forever.'

'I know that. I love it if people I care about are pregnant – it means more lovely babies to squeeze and smell. It's because it's *her*.'

'What does Lewis say?'

'We've only texted. I can't speak to him. I always run when I have to face confrontation. He assures me he hasn't seen or heard from her since. I'm going to meet him tomorrow.'

'Do you want to know if it is his or not?'

'I have to know or I would wonder forever.' Gracie sighed.

Leo looked thoughtful. 'Like Jack would about his dad.'

'Oh, Leo, when you put it like that... I will talk to Noms tomorrow, I promise.'

Aretha Franklin's beautiful voice sang out '(You Make Me Feel Like) A Natural Woman'. Leo guided Gracie out of her chair, held her close and began to dance with her, cheek to cheek.

'Sing it to me, Grace.'

Gracie, fuelled with champagne and wine, started to recite the lyrics, then pulled away, dancing animatedly from room to room.

Leo followed her to the bathroom where she missed a step, nearly falling headlong into the sunken bath. He caught her and swept her up in his arms. Her head rested on his shoulder.

'You, my little lady, are a little bit drunk.' He carried her through to the bedroom, laid her gently on the bed and within minutes she was asleep. He kissed her gently on the cheek, got Kingston to bring some extra bedding, put a pillow under her head and looked down at her tenderly.

'And you, my little lady, I could watch dance like nobody's watching, forever.'

FIFTY-SEVEN

Noms was giving Jack his breakfast when Gracie arrived home looking the worse for wear.

'Good night, was it?' Noms looked her exhausted-looking sister up and down.

'Nothing happened, if that's what you mean.' Gracie poured herself a glass of orange juice and downed it.

'Yeah, right,' Noms said with a wry smile.

Jack was engrossed in a cartoon on the TV.

'No, truthfully. We had an amazing dinner in his hotel room, I got drunk and woke up fully dressed on top of the bed. Bless him, he had slept in the other room. I woke to a breakfast tray and a note saying thanks for a lovely night. It's so embarrassing. I was dancing around like a madwoman.'

'Well, as long as you had fun, I'm happy.' Noms put her hand on her sister's arm.

'I felt like I was on a movie set. It's just a different world. One I don't fit into.'

'I honestly don't mind if you take it further, though, Grace. Our ship sailed long ago.'

'And what with you being on the path to pussy paradise, now and all that.'

Noms shushed her sister.

'Can I get down please, Mummy?' Jack pushed his cereal bowl across the table.

'Yes, go up and get dressed, darling. Your clothes are on the chair. We'll take Boris to the common when you're ready.'

'Are you coming, Auntie Grace?'

'Not today, sweet boy.'

'All right, then.' He stroked Boris, who was lying patiently in his bed, and scurried upstairs.

'Did he mention Jack?'

'Of course he did. He's adamant he wants to meet him.'

'I did have a long think about it last night.'

'And?'

'I still don't know what to do.' Noms looked pained.

'He suggested that he meet him without you telling him he was his dad. I guess at least then he can get to know him.'

'And then he'll be gone off again filming somewhere or other and he won't see him for months.'

'But if it's just a casual meeting, and you announce him as a friend, then Jack will be none the wiser.'

'Maybe. But I don't want anyone to see us and to end up in the bloody papers. We've kept it quiet this long and that suits me.'

'Well, it's your decision. I thought maybe he wanted to have dinner with me to get me on side about Jack but he told me categorically that it wasn't the reason. I think he likes me, Noms.'

'And why wouldn't he? You're good company and you're looking really beautiful. A tan suits you.'

'He could have any woman he wants.'

'And that, my dear sister, is why he likes you. You're down to earth and not throwing yourself at him.' Noms smiled knowingly.

'I probably won't see him again anyway. He's leaving in two nights for Vegas.' Gracie sighed.

'And how do you feel about that?'

'Fine, we haven't slept together, Noms. It's just like a lovely, romantic friendship. And if it were more, to be honest I couldn't deal with all the not knowing when I was going to see somebody and having to deal with all the tabloid scandal. I mean, I got jealous of a girl in a bar in Cornwall, for god's sake.'

Noms had to laugh. 'Well there is that.'

Gracie smiled. 'What happened between us was, well it was beautiful, and I have no regrets.'

'Aw, I'm so pleased.' Noms squeezed her sister's shoulder.

'Toast?' Noms shook her head as Gracie popped two slices of bread in the toaster. 'Lewis has already texted. He wants me to go to the flat for eleven. For just a few hours last night I amazingly forgot about the whole sorry situation.'

* * *

It felt weird to be knocking on the door of her old flat and not just letting herself in.

Lewis looked tired. He smiled weakly. 'Hey. How you doing?'

'I'm hungover.'

'Oh, right. Coffee?'

'A strong one please.'

Gracie sat awkwardly in the lounge as Lewis went to the kitchen. The flat seemed like an empty shell now that her things had been taken out. There was a lone empty beer can on the coffee table and the carpet looked like it hadn't been hoovered in weeks. She was desperate to see if he had cleared out the nursery but knowing the pain that would bring, didn't dare look. He had promised he would sort it out, sell the stuff and give her some money. She didn't care about the money.

Lewis put her steaming drink on the table and sat next to her on the sofa. He went to take her hand; she pulled it away.

'I haven't seen her since… since that night, you know. In fact, I haven't seen any other women.' Lewis blew out a huge breath.

'That isn't really the problem, though, is it?' Gracie took a sip of coffee.

'So what do you want me to do, Gracie?'

'Call her, say you saw her, and ask her outright if the baby is yours? As easy as that.'

'Is that what you really want, though?'

'I don't think I could go on not knowing one way or the other. And if you're honest with me, I bet you can't either.' Gracie felt slightly sick.

'She obviously doesn't want me to know if it is mine or she'd have been in touch long ago.'

'Maybe, but I can never be at peace if we don't find out. And I know you gave me all the "I'd happily adopt" spiel, but I'm not stupid, Lew, deep down I reckon you'd love it if you were the father.' Gracie felt tears stinging her eyes.

Lewis looked away. 'Don't be so ridiculous, Gracie.'

'I don't blame you. Who would want to be with a barren old bag like me? Men need to know they're virile.'

'Stop it, Gracie! You know I bloody love you…' He shot up and walked to the window and looked out. 'Sorry, sorry for shouting.'

'If you love me then be honest with me. Does part of you hope it's yours?'

Lewis shuffled awkwardly.

'I knew it.' She looked up to try and stop her tears.

'I'm so sorry, how can I make this better?' Lewis groaned.

'Ring her and find out.'

'I don't have her number.'

Gracie reached for her phone. 'Here!'

'This is so bloody awful. What am I supposed to say?' Lewis screwed up his face.

'Be a man, Lewis, for once. Go on. But don't ring her from my number; she'll never pick up.'

'I'm not going to ask her outright on the phone. I'll arrange to meet her.' The words flew out before Lewis had a chance to stop them.

Gracie put her hand to her forehead and sighed. 'Whatever, Lewis. Whatever.'

Lewis's hand shook as he dialled the number. He was praying inside that she wouldn't pick up. Gracie had asked him to put it on speaker so she could hear exactly what was said.

'Margaret Good speaking.'

'Oh, hello... I was after Annalize.'

'I'm her mother. Who's speaking, please?'

'It's Lewis Blair. I'm a...' He looked to an agitated Gracie. '... a friend of hers.'

'Lewis, you say? I've never heard her mention you.' A nosy mother wasn't what he needed right now.

'Yes, that's right.'

'What do you want?'

'Just a chat with Annalize.'

'Well, she's not here, I'm sorry.'

Lewis sighed with relief. 'When can I talk to her?'

'It's a really bad time actually, Lewis. She's not too well at the moment. I'll tell her you called.' And with that she hung up.

'She always was a bloody hypochondriac,' Gracie ranted. 'And as for getting her mother to answer her phone, what's that all about? Stupid bitch!'

'Well, we've tried. As soon as she calls back I'll arrange to meet her.'

Gracie drained her coffee. 'And so the nightmare continues.'

Lewis stood up to hug her but she pushed him away.

'Try not think about it too much, Gracie.'

Gracie huffed, 'And that comment shows why we are no longer together, Lewis.'

She walked through to the hallway and pushed open the door to the nursery. Just as they had left it: two empty little Moses baskets. The eerie silence of what could have been.

The grief monster surged its way through Gracie.

'And you can't even do the simple job of clearing this room, you lazy bastard. No babies are coming here, Lewis. Unless you and Annalize get it together. Then you'll have a ready-made bedroom!' Angry tears started running down her face.

'Gracie, stop it. You're only hurting yourself. I can't bear to see you like this.'

'And I can't bear to feel like this.' She wiped her face with the back of her hand. 'I can't see you again, Lewis. Every time I do I feel angry and sad and now this has happened, I just can't look at you.'

'But it was you who arranged to meet me the other day?' Lewis softened.

'Yes, in a moment of weakness. But going back is of no use to either of us. There's too much hurt, too much anger. Look, if you get hold of her, just text me. The way I'm feeling now, I don't know if I care if that baby is yours or not. You two shit heads are welcome to each other.'

Lewis's cry of 'I don't bloody want her' was completely ignored as Gracie grabbed her handbag and slammed the door behind her.

FIFTY-EIGHT

Ed smiled as Gracie walked into the pub and joined him at the bar. She felt unnerved by the faint flutter of butterflies in her tummy. He was a very handsome man.

'Hello, my stroppy little minx.' Ed smirked. 'What can I get you?'

'A large white wine, please.' Gracie felt suddenly awkward.

'Why don't you grab a seat outside, it's such a nice evening. I'll go to the bar.'

Soon after, Ed placed the drinks on the table and sat down opposite her.

'So, how are you, Ms Davies?'

'I'm all right, thanks,' she lied, really not wanting to discuss the Lewis situation.

Ed slurped the froth off his Guinness. 'You don't sound it. Look, I'm really sorry about what happened in Fowey.'

'It's cool. I overreacted.' Gracie took a large slug of her wine.

'No, I thought about it driving back. I get where you were coming from about me not telling you about my friends joining us. I just thought you'd be fine with it, that's all.'

'A woman's runaway mind and all that.' Gracie managed a smile.

'Alas, I feel I will never fathom the intricacies of the female psyche,' Ed laughed. 'I found it quite flattering that you got jealous about Skye.'

'I wasn't jealous.' Gracie's abruptness gave her away.

'Gracie Davies, your green eyes went even greener.'

She smiled. 'She's a pretty girl – that's what you said, anyway.'

'Come on, let's not go down that route. I was drunk and maybe I was flirting a bit, but give me some credit, Gracie. I was down there with you. I respect you. I have to say they did think it was a bit odd you clearing off.'

'I do feel embarrassed now.' Gracie took a sip of wine.

'Don't be. But you do understand why I didn't come back, don't you? I haven't had a holiday for bloody ages and it gave me time to forget about the court case.'

'Yes, I know. And it's not so far away now, is it?'

'First week of September. I'm shitting myself. I'm meeting my barrister later. She seems really positive about it all.'

'Well, you're not guilty, so justice will prevail.'

Ed took another swig from his pint. 'I hope so.'

Gracie's voice lilted. 'So did you enjoy the rest of your holiday? You're looking even browner than me so the weather must have been good.'

'It was amazing. I love waking up to the sound of seagulls. Being so near the sea really chilled me out. Glyn took a couple of extra days off, so we ended up going back to Newquay and surfing.'

'Nice.'

'And before you ask, I didn't see Skye after you left.'

'I wasn't thinking anything of it,' Gracie lied.

Ed groaned. 'Back to work tomorrow. How depressing.'

'Yep, I'm busy at the moment, got a birthday party at the hut and a Miscarriage Matters session tomorrow, myself.'

'I'm glad it's going well for you. Why can't we be on holiday all the time? This work lark really does get in the way of our social lives,' Ed laughed.

'Maybe I need to find myself a rich man.' Gracie laughed, suddenly thinking to Leo.

'Well, don't be looking at me with dollar signs in your eyes. All I can give you is a lot of fun and an extremely good seeing-to.' Ed raised his eyebrows.

Gracie felt a twinge in her nether regions. Despite everything that was going on, and her reasoning for never seeing him again, she did still fancy the pants off him. She smiled and shook her head.

'Another drink for the lady, at least?' Ed laughed.

'I'll get them.' Gracie wandered to the bar. Maybe he wasn't so bad. If she looked at their 'holiday' through his eyes, she could see that she had been oversensitive. Bloody Lewis, he had tainted her so much with his infidelity she was worried she may never trust another man again. Just as she was reaching for her purse she felt a text buzz through on her phone.

> Hey, my tipsy natural woman, fancy spending
> my last night in London together?

She smiled to herself. Just a text from a very famous Hollywood actor asking her out! But if she couldn't trust a normal bloke, how could she ever trust somebody as handsome and sought after as Leo Grant? He had never made her feel anything short of special. But he was the father of her nephew and was rarely in one place for long. Once he had lost sight of her, she was sure he wouldn't give her a second thought.

Noms was meeting him before he left to discuss some sort of compromise with Jack. She really hoped it would be a win-win situation for everyone. Leo might be famous and part of the jet set, but from what she knew of him, he seemed like good man and deserved to be happy, too.

Gracie walked back to the table. Ed was stroking a dog and speaking to a woman at the next table. She left as Gracie approached.

'Just another one of my bitches.' Ed smirked.

'The dog was quite sweet, too,' Gracie laughed.

'That's more like it. In Cornwall, I thought I'd lost you. I'd have been really sad if you hadn't wanted to see me again.'

'Really?'

'Yes, of course, really.'

Four drinks later, Gracie thought that she must have a word with herself about her drinking. She'd be putting all her weight on again, plus she wasn't good working with a hangover. The wine also made her extremely horny. And turned off her NO button.

'So, young Ed, what was it you were saying about being able to offer me a good seeing-to?'

'Gracie Davies, I thought you'd never ask. Let's go. I can't wait to kiss those white bits again.'

* * *

Gracie stumbled into Ed's flat and straight onto his bed. She felt reckless. *Fuck Lewis, fuck everything.*

Ed followed, jumped right on top of her and started kissing her hungrily. He pulled up her dress roughly, pushed her panties aside and stuck two fingers into her deeply. Gracie gasped.

'Careful.' Gracie put her hand on his.

'Sorry, sorry – did that hurt? I just want you so bad, Gracie.'

She felt his rock-hard cock through his boxers and got wetter in an instant.

'Let's just fuck.' Gracie loved feeling like this: enjoying pure animal passion with a man with a good body.

'I want you on your knees.'

Gracie quickly pulled off her dress and panties and did as she was told. Ed entered her from behind making her cry out in pleasure. But she squealed as he pulled back her hair sharply.

'You want it harder, you little minx?'

'Ow,' Gracie cried out as Ed pounded into her, the pleasure exceeding the pain. He eased up slightly.

'Go on, then, fuck me harder.' The dirty talk with Ed was arousing. He slapped her butt cheek and she cried out.

'I'm coming, I'm coming, keep going,' she said between pants.

She could hear from his deep breathing that he was about to come too.

She was shocked at how rude she had been. But it felt good. Really good.

'Blimey, where's Gracie gone?' Ed laughed, as he collapsed onto the bed. 'That was bloody amazing.'

'I don't know, but I'll tell you when she's back, shall I?'

'I quite like this new more promiscuous one, to be honest.' Ed grinned.

Gracie ran her tongue around her lips in faux-seduction style.

'Oi, you sexy little... I want to know something.'

'What?' Gracie reached for her discarded knickers with her foot.

'Are we still talking lovers?'

'It looks like it.' Gracie smiled. 'I do like you, Ed.'

'And I like you, too, but let's stop the jealous dramatics from now on, shall we? Let's tell each other when we are not happy. I won't cheat on you, Gracie. You deserve better than that.'

Gracie leant over to kiss him and then lay back looking at the ceiling.

She had been adamant that it was over between her and Ed, but she couldn't deny her feelings for him when she saw him. It frustrated her that her head couldn't be in charge of her relationship destiny. Fact: hearts have minds of their own.

Right now, her feelings were leading her a merry dance. Sex was an escape from the real world; Ed was an escape from the real world. And at this moment, she needed that.

FIFTY-NINE

Noms had thought that Windsor Great Park would be a good place to walk with Leo and Jack without being spotted. It was only a forty-minute drive out of Wimbledon and there wouldn't be a pap in sight. She remembered going there a few years ago with an ex. They had entered the park through a gate near a sleepy Berkshire village called Cheapside. Not many people knew about this entrance so she guessed there wouldn't be many people about.

That time, she'd ended up having naughty outdoor sex with the said ex. Today the outcome would be very different.

She had had a long chat with Leo on the phone that morning and after much deliberation decided that she owed it to him at least to let him meet his son. Jack would be none the wiser for the time being and, when she told him properly in a few years' time, she would hope that he understood. Leo would be Lee, a friend of his mum's.

Leo was wearing his obligatory cap and dark glasses when Noms spotted him waiting at the gate. She had seen his chauffeur drive off as she pulled up. He was carrying a kids' electric scooter. She sighed – he just couldn't help himself.

She kissed the handsome actor on the cheek. 'Jack, this is Lee.'

'Hi, cool scooter. Can I have a go?'

'Course you can, little man. Here. Let me show you how it works.'

Within minutes Jack was speeding ahead of them, yahooing as he went.

'Keep to the side of the road,' Noms hollered after him.

'He's fine, honey, don't worry. They bounce at that age anyway, don't they?'

'I hope so. You realise you won't get a word out of him now, don't you?'

'I've brought a picnic, too.' Noms had failed to spot the rucksack on Leo's back.

She laughed. 'I'm impressed.'

'Don't be. The hotel sorted everything.' He smiled. 'So how you doing, Noms? Coping?'

'I've managed OK for the past six years.' She realised how abrupt she sounded and tried to start again. 'Leo, I can't thank you enough for the money. It has made our lives so much easier.'

'I would never have not helped, you know that, one-night stand or not.'

'Well, it is appreciated.' Noms felt a sudden calmness.

'It was a bloody fun night we had. I still think about it sometimes.'

Noms thought back to the champagne and coke-fuelled night on the deserted beach in Croatia. 'I guess it was. My love life is so much more staid now.'

'We all have to grow up, even Peter Pan here.' Leo smirked.

'So, why the interest in seeing Jack now?'

'I'm not getting any younger. I haven't met "the one" yet and, to be honest, I'm not sure if I want to start a family now. I'm too frickin' selfish.' Leo looked ahead and smiled at his now-whooping son.

'Your honesty is refreshing, Leo.'

Jack was careering back towards them down the hill.

'Jack, slow down!' Noms shouted.

'Wheeeeeeeeee.' He met them at the bottom of the hill, gave Leo a high five then turned around and sped off again.

'It's weird, isn't it? People's interpretation of what a Hollywood superstar should be like.

I'm just a normal guy who happened to make it big. I eat, sleep, talk, walk. There ain't nothing special about me, sweetheart – it's everyone else who thinks there is.'

'The special thing is you are my boy's dad and that won't change.'

'Exactly. I'm rich in material wealth, Naomi, but blood and friendships are worth far more to me now. He's a great lad. It seems like you've brought him up really well.'

'Thanks. It's not always easy, but I try my best.'

'And I can hopefully help make it even better now, if you'll let me.'

'We can make it work, I'm sure.'

Leo's face lit up in a huge grin. 'You have a new man now, I take it?'

Naomi flushed slightly. 'Um. Not really.'

'Just an afternoon play date the other day, then?'

'Something like that. If you really want to know, I'm attracted to women these days.'

'Really? So you were in bed with a woman when I turned up. I wish you'd said, I've have jumped in too.'

Naomi replied in an American accent. 'Cock just doesn't do it for me anymore, honey.' She laughed out loud. 'Actually, that's probably a lie. It's all that goes with it that doesn't. I have had it with men.'

'Does Jack know?'

Naomi was sharp in her reply. 'Of course he doesn't and he won't. Unless something serious develops, of course.'

Leo smiled. 'This little fella's sure gonna have to grow up when it's time to reveal all, isn't he?'

'He'll be ready, it'll all be fine. I just want to protect him for now.'

'I hear you. It's cool. Even if I can maybe just pop and see you a few times a year, so I don't miss him growing up? I'd like that.'

'That's what I was going to suggest. I'll send you photos and email you updates too. And who knows, maybe the time will be right to tell him earlier than I envisaged.'

'Yeah. Maybe this dog will have had his day and no one will remember who I am.'

'I very much doubt that; I mean, look at George Clooney.'

'We'll see. It could be time I duck out anyway. I've made my millions, Naomi. I'll want for nothing for the rest of my life. It makes me laugh that all the kids nowadays want just the fame, for fame's sake. I tell ya, it gets to be a pain in the butt after a while.' He looked around them at the open fields and woodland areas. 'This is just exquisite out here, so peaceful and not a soul in sight.' As if on cue, a dark brown cow mooed her appreciation of the gorgeous weather.

They both laughed.

Leo started taking photos of the beautiful scenery on his phone.

Jack came belting back towards them and he took one of his son.

'Handsome just like his dad.' Leo flashed a film-star smile at Naomi.

Naomi tutted. 'Anyway, I'm hungry. What's in that bag of yours?'

Noms called to Jack to join them and settled him under a big oak tree as Leo laid out the five-star feast.

Jack scoffed mini open sandwiches and cream cakes.

'Isn't that scooter a bit little for you?' the lad asked Leo eventually with a burp.

'Jack, what do you say?'

'Pardon me. Well?' He looked to Leo.

'Jack, don't be so rude,' Noms scolded.

'He's fine. Actually, I was thinking maybe I had grown out of it. Seeing as you seem to be doing so well on it, would you like to keep it?'

'Yes, please!' Jack got up and started running around the oak tree, his arms out wide like he was flying. Despite Noms never being short of money, she had never spoilt him.

'You wait till I tell my mates, they'll be dead jealous. Thank you so much.'

Noms looked at Leo knowingly.

'Can I have another go, please?' Jack asked his mum.

'Go on, then, but make you sure keep to the side of the road. We'll sit here for a bit in the sun and wait for you.'

Leo poured Naomi a glass of champagne. She lay back against a big tree root. 'This is the life.'

Leo groaned in pleasure. 'Isn't it just? You can't beat the English countryside. Every time I come here I'm more drawn to it. I'm thinking of buying a house here, you know, either in the countryside or possibly near to the coast. I could do with advice on good areas – if you have the time, that is?'

'Sure.' Noms sipped on her drink slowly as she was driving later and wanted to relish the one glass.

'It would be somewhere else for you and Jack to holiday, too.' He paused. 'Or for me to holiday with Jack, if it suited.'

'You're so kind, Leo. I do appreciate everything you've done for us two, you know. You didn't have to believe me. You could have walked away.'

Leo kissed her on the cheek. 'But I didn't. You're a lovely woman, Noms, and even more awkwardly, I wanted to tell you how fond I am of your sister. She makes my heart happy. I feel so at ease with her.'

'Grace is amazing. She's been through so much. She needs some kindness, too. As for romance, I don't want her to get hurt again. She's been seeing this Ed guy, who's up on a rape charge.'

'What?'

'I know. I know. He seems nice enough, but I do worry.'

'Gee. And then there's Lewis and the new pregnancy saga with the woman he slept with. I'm surprised sometimes she doesn't just lock herself in her room and never come out.'

'Bless Grace. She doesn't deserve any of this.' Noms drained her plastic glass.

'I'm hoping she'll come and see me again. I really want to say goodbye before I go off to Vegas,' Leo added.

Jack came belting back on the scooter.

'Wait here a second,' Noms said. 'Let me put some sunscreen on your face.' Jack screwed up his eyes and wriggled as his mum applied the lotion. 'We need to go soon.'

'I don't want to go,' the lad whined.

'Go on, then, up the hill and back one more time.'

Noms started packing up the rubbish.

'It's been such a lovely afternoon, Leo. Thanks again.'

'It's a pleasure and thank *you* for letting me in. This is perfect, just getting to know him, without any big drama. I work on enough of those.'

* * *

Jack was knackered by the time he was back in the car.

'Mummy, is Lee your new boyfriend?'

'No, he's just a friend. Do you like him?'

'I think he's cool.'

'Good.'

'Can we see him again soon?'

'He works away a lot, but soonish I'm sure.'

Noms turned the radio up and smiled.

Sometimes the fear of things was a lot worse than the reality.

SIXTY

Gracie was amazingly upbeat as she opened up the hut for the children's birthday party. She was thankful it was such a beautiful day – perfect for excitable five-year-olds to run around outside and not make so much mess. She threw the doors open wide and began to put pink plastic cloths on the tables. It was great that most Wimbledon mums had enough money to pay for personal caterers; it meant she didn't have to worry about making sandwiches and cakes. The whole project had turned into a much bigger money-spinner than she had ever imagined. She liked the flexible hours, too. In that respect at least she felt she had got her life back.

She was just hooking up the last of the balloons when Ed appeared with a bunch of yellow roses. He handed them to her and kissed her lightly on the lips. 'For you, *ma chérie.*'

'Blimey, what have you done wrong?'

'The other night was amazing, Gracie. I tried to get daffodils but I thought these were a good compromise.'

Gracie was overcome at this thoughtfulness. 'They're beautiful, thanks so much.' She put them in the kitchen sink and ran in some water. 'How did it go with your barrister?'

'OK, I guess. I'm just worried about what the bouncer from the club might say.' Ed grimaced.

'He'll be on oath, Ed. He has to tell the truth.' Gracie remained upbeat.

'I guess so. What you doing for lunch? Have you got time to have a sandwich with me in the café?'

Gracie groaned. 'I'd love to, but I've got the mother of the birthday girl arriving soon, so I'd better not.'

'No worries. You around later?'

She had agreed to see Leo later. She felt that she owed it to him to say goodbye, after falling asleep on him the other night. 'I'm not, I'm sorry. I'm out.'

'Out? Is that it, just out? It sounds slightly cryptic.'

'Not at all.' Gracie reddened. 'I'm just meeting an old school friend for dinner.' Gracie wasn't very adept at lying.

'OK. I'll catch up with you tomorrow, then, I'm sure, sexy.'

'OK. And thanks so much for the flowers, Ed.'

Gracie rearranged the roses so that all of the stems were covered in water. Flowers for being good in bed, now that was a first. Maybe that's all it would be with Ed, a sexual fling. It was so difficult, as she didn't feel now like they were in a committed relationship, but if it was him saying he was going out and not telling her who with, she would no doubt be furious.

Before she had time to reflect on her double standards any further, Cecilia Beauchamp-Coil appeared carrying a Selfridges bag full of expensive gifts for little Amelia's party.

The next three hours passed in a whir of party games, sticky food, an appearance from Snow White and an ice-cream van, blaring 'Happy Birthday' from its speakers. Gracie was astonished at how much families spent on their kids' birthdays. She wondered if it was about how much they cared about their little ones' enjoyment, or really how far they could go to outdo the other yummy mummies.

She was just sorting out paying the caterers when Kate appeared.

'How did it go, Gracie?'

'I'm knackered, to be honest.' Gracie pushed her hands through her hair.

'Bless you. I'll make sure I sort some childcare for the next one and help you.'

Gracie took a sip from her water bottle. 'Don't worry. I can't expect you to be here all the time. I enjoy it.'

'I had to see you, anyway.' Kate sounded like an excited child herself. 'I've just done a pregnancy test and you'll never guess what!'

'Oh my God, Kate, that's just so amazing.' Gracie gave her a huge hug.

'I know. It must have been that one time we did it on holiday. Bingo! Mr Johnson's sperm must have got its skates on.'

'So when are you due?'

'March.' As much as Kate couldn't contain her grin, Gracie couldn't stop herself from bursting into tears.

'Oh, Gracie, what is it? I'm sorry. I had to tell you.'

'Of course you had to tell me. I'm just being silly. I'm truly happy for you, Kate. It's just still so hard, sometimes.'

'That's understandable. Let me get us some decent coffees from the café. You stay there, we haven't had a chat for ages.'

Kate was soon back.

'I've got about thirty minutes before I need to get ready for Miscarriage Matters. I need to get my head straight.' Gracie picked up her coffee. Kate had got her a flapjack, too.

'So come on. How are you?' Kate took her hand across the table.

'I'm fine, honestly. It's just...'

'Just what, Gracie?'

'I know it's the circle of life, women are going to get pregnant, babies are going to be born. It's just, well it's just... I will never be in that circle.'

'I can't even begin to imagine how you feel, Gracie, but you have to draw on all the positives. You have a great nephew and sister and a new friend in me, I hope. Ed seems like a good guy. The business is booming and you're looking really fantastic.'

'Yes, I know all those things – but Annalize is pregnant, too.'

'Annalize?'

Gracie took a tentative sip of her hot drink. 'The woman Lewis slept with. I saw her the other day. I thought I was going to be sick on the floor.'

'Oh, darling.'

Gracie broke her flapjack in half. 'I don't know if it's Lewis's – nor does he – but just seeing her made me so angry again and so bitter that she could become pregnant and I can't. I don't feel the same way about you being pregnant, it's joyous, but...'

Kate looked pained. 'What a nightmare. So does Lewis... do *you*... want to know if it's his?'

'I have to find out, I think. Because if it is Lewis's there is no way I could ever consider seeing him ever again. It would be too painful.'

'I didn't realise he was in the equation still?'

Gracie sighed. 'I'm so confused. I missed him the other day, when Ed annoyed me. I thought perhaps in time we could work it out. I shared so much with him, Kate.'

The common was heaving with mums and kids, cyclists and horse riders.

'Look around us, Gracie. So many people, so many men. I always think it's amazing we end up settling with one person when there is a whole world out there. Who says any of us end up with our soul mate? I love Kevin, but compromises are made all the time, especially now that we have Alice. It's not a perfect relationship by any means. You have the chance to find somebody, no compromises required. Maybe not going back to the safety of what you once knew was the right thing.'

Gracie took another sip of coffee. 'When you put it like that...'

'How's it going with Ed, anyway?'

'It is what it is. He brought me flowers today, but it felt like a reward for some amazing sex we had the other night. He's not the one, I know that.'

'Mr Right Now instead of Mr Right,' Kate laughed. 'Take the good sex and just enjoy yourself, I say.'

Gracie thought back to her night with Leo. He had been so kind, so caring. She felt more comfortable with him than any other man at the moment. But tomorrow he would be gone again, on to pastures new, and with another young model or actress on his arm, she suspected.

She looked at her watch. 'I'm not sure how many ladies will come today, the weather is so beautiful.'

Kate sounded concerned. 'Are you sure you're up to discussing loss today?'

'I'll be fine. It'll do me good not to wallow in my own misery.'

'Well, as long as you're sure. Sally, my author friend, is coming today; she can amuse everybody and I can do the refreshments.'

'We'll do them together. And thanks, Kate, for listening.'

'Always here, you know that.'

Gracie put her hand on top of her friend's and squeezed it. 'I cannot wait to meet that new bubba of yours.'

'Nor me. He or she has been a long time coming. And... I know this is premature, but if everything goes to plan, I'd love you to be the godmother, if you'd like to be, that is?'

Gracie felt tears welling again. 'It would be an honour,' she replied softly.

SIXTY-ONE

'You've caught the sun,' Gracie said to Noms as she and Jack walked through the front door. She was painting her nails a bright red.

'Look what Mum's friend Lee gave me the other day.' Jack proudly showed off his new scooter.

'Take it through into the garden, Jack, we'll sort out charging it once I've spoken to Auntie Grace.'

'But I want to ride it now.'

'Come on, be a good boy. Why don't you go and get changed out of those dirty clothes. You've had a lovely day.'

Jack harrumphed, abandoned the scooter against the fridge, and went up to his room.

Noms groaned. 'It beats me why schools you pay for have the longest holidays! I've got weeks more of amusing him. But at least I have the time to do it.'

'Lee, eh?' Gracie smiled.

'It's near enough.'

'Can't believe I haven't had the chance to talk to you about it. How did it go?'

'Better than I thought it would, actually. He is a decent

bloke, isn't he? Jack loves him, helped by the material bribe, obviously.'

Gracie laughed. 'I'm really pleased you agreed to let him meet him.'

'I've said that he can come and see him whenever he's around and then, I guess, we just see how things pan out.' Noms put the kettle on.

'Maybe he can take the school holiday pressure off, give you a break.'

'Hmm. He did say he was thinking of buying a place here, so maybe.' Noms was thoughtful for a second. 'He thinks the world of you, you know, Grace.'

'Really?'

'You know he does. His exact words were that you make his heart happy.'

'How sweet is that?'

'I know. He really is just a normal bloke under his famous face.'

Gracie laughed. 'A normal bloke, recognised by half the world, who's a multi-millionaire with women dropping at his feet and who is never in one country for more than ten minutes. Yeah, really normal.'

'He's got to settle down one day.'

Gracie frowned. 'Noms, you're the realist here. What's going on. Settle down? With plain old thirty-eight-year-old Gracie Davies, demonstrating a curvy figure and no womb? I don't think so.'

'Oh, Grace. Listen to you. You've got to stop this low-self-esteem rubbish. You are an amazing person. You are beautiful inside and out. Any man would be a fool not to see that. You make *my* heart happy, too, little sister. In fact, you make my world a better place to live in.'

'Stop it, you. Going all sentimental on me. Well, I'm seeing him tonight. You know how last minute he is. His driver is picking me up at seven thirty.'

Noms smiled. 'Hence the nail painting. I get it.'

'He's told me to pack an overnight bag but I'm not going to sleep with him. I can't put myself into that predicament. And it feels a bit weird because of you, too.'

'Don't be so silly. Enjoy the now, Grace, I told you I have no interest in him romantically anymore. In fact, I'm seeing Ali tomorrow night. I really like her. It's mad. I can't stop thinking about her.'

'Who's having Jack? Do you want me to?'

'No, he's having a sleepover at Mali's. He'll take his scooter, he'll be fine. And you might be too tired.' Noms winked and put two steaming mugs of tea in front of them. 'Have you heard from Lewis, by the way?'

'Thank you and erm... He texted earlier saying that he'd still had no word from her. Part of me feels like asking him to drop it. She obviously doesn't want him to know if he is the father. Maybe opening a new can of worms is not the way forward. What good will knowing do for either of us?'

Noms slipped off her trainers and joined Gracie at the kitchen counter. 'Maybe find you some peace. Can you honestly say that you don't care not knowing?'

Gracie shrugged. 'If Lewis is not going to be in my life anymore, then maybe.'

Noms tutted. 'I don't believe you.'

'I don't know. I'm so confused about everything and there's still Ed to think about. I do like seeing him and I can't deny the sex is amazing. What am I doing, Noms? I feel like I need to clear the cache of all men.'

Noms looked to her phone messages. 'Then do it. I've been saying that you need to take some time out. Leo, though, is good for you. You need a boost, you need somebody to show you a nice time and be kind to you. Have fun and you can worry about the others in the morning.'

'I don't want to sleep with Leo, though, I feel like it will taint things. And I don't want to let him get close enough to hurt me, either.'

Noms shook her head. 'If you don't let anyone in, how will you ever fall in love again?'

'Look at my big sis being all romantic. What's got into you?'

Noms smiled. 'The fact my heart is having a little dance of its own at the moment.'

Gracie laughed. 'I love you, Naomi Davies.'

'Right back at ya, sister. Now do you want me to blow dry your hair?'

SIXTY-TWO

Professor Princeton was about to walk into the betting shop when his daughter called. He could hear the panic in her voice.

'Daddy, it's me. You've got to come quick. Mummy's had an accident, she's fallen off her horse at Pearl's yard. I'm here with Josh. The ambulance is here. She's not speaking and you know how much she speaks.'

'Oh, God. OK. Calm down, darling. There's no point me coming to you there, it will take too long. Ask the paramedic which hospital he is taking her to, follow with Josh and I'll meet you all there as soon as I can.'

As he put the phone down, he saw Maya's name flash up on the screen. Dumping her call, he flagged a taxi.

SIXTY-THREE

Gracie felt like Carrie Bradshaw in *Sex and the City* when Leo's car arrived outside with its blacked-out windows. As it slowed, one back window wound down slowly.

'My very own Mr Big,' she laughed to Leo, as the chauffeur got out and put her overnight case in the boot.

Leo kissed her on the cheek. 'Are you ready for an adventure?'

'As I'll ever be.' Gracie laughed again. She could pretend she was rich and famous just for one night at least.

'You look gorgeous, Grace. Coral really suits you. It goes with your tan.'

'Thanks. I wasn't sure what to wear since I don't know where we are going.' She tried to sound casual, not daring to tell him that she had tried on at least seventeen outfits, settling for a coral sleeveless above-the-knee dress which accentuated all her curves in the right places – with

another five outfits crammed into her little case. Noms had also lovingly curled her hair into soft waves.

Leo handed her a glass of champagne as the Bentley zoomed to life down the M4.

'Not too much for me,' she laughed. 'You don't want me in a coma again, do you?'

'I don't know. You're really quite cute when you're sleeping.'

'Is that a compliment or not? I'm not sure.' She gently poked the handsome actor in the ribs. 'Where are we going, anyway?'

'All will be revealed, Grace, but not yet.'

Gracie sat back in the comfy seat and let out a massive sigh.

'Are you OK, baby?'

'More than OK, thanks. That was a sigh of relief. It's so good to be escaping.'

'Good. I want you to relax and enjoy the ride.'

After about an hour, they pulled into an airfield. Gracie looked at Leo quizzically.

'Not sure if I'm up for a flying lesson after two glasses of champagne.'

He laughed and pointed to a small jet. 'That's my plane over there.'

A private jet! Gracie was speechless.

'You and I, my lovely, are having an overnight stay with a difference.'

'We're staying on the plane?'

'Of course not.' Leo smiled at her innocence. 'Come on. Sam will bring your bag. He'll stick around to drive us at the other end, too.'

* * *

Gracie pinched herself. Before their trip to St. Lucia, she had only ever flown economy before. Here she could walk around or lie down, and eat and drink whatever she liked. It was simply amazing. The interior was so plush, the seats so comfortable. It was like being in a well-appointed hotel.

'We must be going somewhere in the UK, because I haven't got my passport.'

'That, doll, is where you are wrong. Check the front pocket of your handbag.'

Gracie couldn't believe it. 'How did you...?'

'I asked Noms to sneak it in there.'

'The sneaky...' Gracie couldn't believe that her sister had known about this all along. 'You're good, Leo Grant, very good.'

'Ain't I just, honey? I was going to come out with another cheesy line from a film then, but I thought you'd bust me so I held it in.'

'What the hell, say it anyway. But if one day you come out with something original I may faint.'

'I can't be responsible for your actions once I've said it, though.'

Gracie laughed. 'You're funny. Go on – what is it?'

Leo cleared his throat. 'No, I don't think I will kiss you, although you need kissing, badly. That's what's wrong with you. You should be kissed and often, and by someone who knows how.'

Gracie bit the inside of her lip. Her favourite scene from *Gone with the Wind*. She looked across the seat to Leo. The thought of being kissed by him made her toes curl. This was it, she would be brave; she would kiss him hard on the lips. She got up out of her seat only to be halted by the pilot telling them to fasten their seat belts: they were making their descent into Barcelona.

'Barcelona!' Gracie screeched. 'Oh my God! I've always wanted to come here. I've got a Miscarriage Matters meeting tomorrow at five, though.'

'Chill, baby girl, we'll be home by lunchtime.'

'I can't believe you,' Gracie laughed. 'And I'm so, so glad that I can't.'

SIXTY-FOUR

The beeps of the intensive care machine matched the rhythm of Scott Princeton's heartbeat. Scarily slow. He'd been sitting for six hours, holding and stroking Cynthia's hands, willing her to come round, to open her eyes and bark at him, like she usually did.

He'd been told that her riding hat hadn't been done up tightly enough, so that when the horse threw her at a jump, it had flown off. She had hit her head on a tree trunk. Surgeons had removed a blood clot from her brain. The twenty-four-hour wait until they could assess the success of the surgery seemed endless.

Emma and Josh had gone to get him a drink and a sandwich as he refused to leave his wife's side.

His red-eyed daughter put a packeted sandwich down gently next to him and stirred some sugar into his coffee. He took in her beautiful, young innocent face: the product of his relationship with the feisty, moral, driven, forthright woman who was lying here motionless, fighting for her life.

'Don't stay if you don't want to, sweetheart. I'm not going

anywhere, I promise. There is a room for me here, if I do need to sleep.'

'OK, Daddy. I'm so tired and I don't want to be asleep when Mummy wakes up. I'll go home now, have a few hours' sleep and come back early in the morning. You will call me if you need me, though, won't you. I won't turn my phone off.'

'Of course, sweetheart.' Feeling an intense surge of guilt, he stood up and held her to him – something he had not done for too many years. She felt frail, helpless – his baby girl.

'I'll look after Emma, Professor Princeton,' Josh added in grown-up fashion.

'Thanks, son.' He shook Josh's hand and pushed a wodge of cash into it. 'Take that for petrol and anything else you might need.'

When they'd gone, he paced slowly around his home for the night, stretching his arms high above his gangly body. He thought he heard the rhythm of his wife's breathing change and leant down so his face almost touched hers.

'Come on, old girl, you can do this. I know you're strong enough. Even if it's for Emma and not me.' His voice cracked.

A nurse came in and started doing the necessary regular checks.

He sat down and drank his coffee. He couldn't eat. He looked at Cynthia's bruised and swollen face with the tube down her throat helping her to breathe. She had always been so self-sufficient, never needy, and he felt an overwhelming rush of love for her.

What he and Maya had now paled into insignificance. Did he really love a twentysomething sex-worker? Somebody he would always have to look out for. Probably provide for. Or was it just the thrill of the sex, the naughtiness of the whole situation. Could he really see himself living with the girl, sharing wine, sharing memories? Did they really have anything in common? Did you need to have anything in common to be in love with someone? Actually, as you got older, he thought, yes, you did.

At whatever age a relationship starts, passion fades and then what are you left with? In twenty years' time, where would he and Maya be? He would be sixty-five, she would be just forty-two – not even the age he was now. She might have traded him in for a younger model by then. He wasn't ageing that well as it was.

Could he see himself sitting with her over breakfast? Opening *The Sunday Times*? Chatting about current affairs? About life in general?

Here, in front of him, was his future. An intelligent, still very attractive woman, the mother of his beautiful daughter. What had he become? A selfish middle-aged man, who had spent too much time thinking of nothing but his own sexual gratification. It was time he woke up to what he had and not what he thought he could or should be having.

It distressed him even more that it had taken something as dreadful as this to make him realise the truth.

He liked Maya. He had missed her when he hadn't seen her for a few weeks, and it really had been great to see her the other night. He couldn't deny how he felt when he was with her, but it must have been lust, not real love, and if he didn't face up to his responsibilities, he would end up a sad, lonely old man.

SIXTY-FIVE

To avoid any unnecessary rumpus at the hotel reception, Sam went ahead and sorted out the check-in. He spoke to the concierge in private and ushered both Gracie and Leo up a back staircase to their room.

'The Presidential Suite! Leo, this is just too amazing!' Gracie couldn't believe the decadence of the whole place. 'I have to jump on the bed.'

Leo laughed. 'Do exactly what you want. We are here for one night only, let's enjoy it. There are two bedrooms so you can choose which one you like best.' She loved the fact that he didn't expect anything from her.

The Gran Hotel La Florida was magnificent: set high on Tibidabo, twenty minutes above the city of Barcelona. It was the epitome of luxury. Gracie was in awe of the huge bedrooms and marble baths. But best of all was the vast terrace that overlooked the city and the Mediterranean, complete with hammocks and Jacuzzi. It was the sort of place she had only dreamt of staying at. And now not only was it her home for the night, but she was staying here with a beautiful and charming Hollywood actor. If somebody had told her six months ago that this would be happening to her, she would have thought they were mad.

'So, Grace, my proposal is that Sam gives us a whistlestop tour of the city. I've booked you a massage in the spa and then we'll have dinner up here overlooking the city. Is that OK?'

'That sounds just perfect. Thank you so much, Leo.'

'I hope you understand why I want to stay here and have dinner. I just love not being in the public eye when I don't have to be. It's not for one minute that I wouldn't be proud to have you on my arm.'

It had crossed Gracie's mind that the press might go crazy following a sighting of Leo with someone like her; she was certainly not the usual sort of girl he was seen with in the glossy magazines.

'This is the most beautiful hotel that I have ever set foot in. I'm more than happy to take in the amazing view... and not have to share you, to be honest.'

'Really? That's nice.'

Gracie couldn't believe he even questioned her. The more she got to know Leo Grant, the more she thought she'd be happy eating fish and chips with him in a one-bedroom flat in Cleethorpes.

By the time they had got back from their tour of the city and she'd had her massage it was nine o'clock. When she returned, glowing and relaxed, Leo was lying outside in a hammock leafing through a new script that had been couriered to the hotel. Darkness had fallen and a magnificent full moon filled the sky.

Leo looked up and beamed at her.

'That was so what I needed. The oils they use smell so good, too. I can't thank you enough.'

'Excellent. And nothing less than you deserve sweet cheeks.'

'I'd better get out of this robe.' Gracie went to walk back into the bedroom.

'Up to you, but if you're comfy stay like that, Grace. You don't need to impress me, you did that the moment I set eyes on you in St Lucia.'

'You say all the right things.' Gracie laughed as he handed her a glass of champagne and the melodic tones of Aretha Franklin filled the room. 'But OK, if you're sure.'

'Is tapas all right for dinner? I didn't think you'd want a big meal after a massage.'

His thoughtfulness was too much.

'Are you sure you're not gay, Leo Grant?'

'Ha ha. I've been called many things before but never that.'

They laughed and talked as they ate exquisite tapas while listening to the muted sounds of the city. The light of the moon, the soft music in the background, the warm evening and the twinkling lights of the city below made for a special ambience. Gracie felt heady with relaxation, rather than alcohol and for this she was pleased.

Leo pressed the button on the Jacuzzi.

'Totally up to you, of course, but I think it will be lovely to finish the night in here.'

'Yes, perfect.'

Gracie self-consciously slipped off her robe and quickly immersed her naked self under the moving foam. She couldn't ignore the actor's toned body as he stripped off and sat opposite her, entwining his feet with hers.

'You've got great skin, Grace. A real English rose. In fact, you have a gorgeous womanly body that you should be very proud of. Those curves of yours are so darn sexy.'

Her mind and senses rushed. He had just had to touch her feet and she felt like she was on fire. She thought of Ed, where physicality was what made up their relationship. Yes, good sex was important but to feel loved and appreciated was worth that tenfold. Whatever this was – wherever it went – she would never forget this moment with this man. She felt on top of the world.

'Leo.' She looked across the Jacuzzi at him intently.

'Yes, honey.'

'Thanks for helping to boost my self-confidence. I so appreciate the two wonderful nights you have given me.'

'What you've given me is so much more, Grace. You don't expect anything from me. You're always so sweet, gentle and appreciative. Your company is so easy, so honest. I love being with you.'

Gracie felt like she wanted everything to stand still. To stay safe and warm in this magnificent setting, never have to step outside and face the real world. A tear slipped down her cheek. She hoped he wouldn't notice, would think it was just steam from the Jacuzzi.

Leo moved forward in the bubbles so he was looking up at her and took hold of both of her arms.

'Let the tears go, Grace. Like I said before, let all those trapped words in your heart just flow out.'

Gracie began to sob. She sobbed for her lost babies, her lost relationship with Lewis, for the Annalize situation, even for her lost relationship with her mother. All the while Leo held her until she felt she had no more tears left to shed.

'I'm so sorry,' she blubbered. 'After all you've done for me tonight and look at me, what a mess.'

Leo reached for a towel and gently wiped her face. He cupped her sad face in his hands and kissed her, so passionately and lovingly that she thought if she died that minute she wouldn't care.

'I've been wanting to do that since the second I saw you at my villa.'

'Um. I think you did kiss me.'

'No, I mean really kiss you. That was my vain ego then, trying my luck.'

'And now?'

'It was my vain ego, trying my luck again.'

They both laughed.

'Come on, let's get out.' Leo took her hand and handed her a dry robe.

Leo snuggled Gracie into him in the hammock.

'I adore you, Grace. You're not like anyone I've ever met before.'

'I bet you say that to all the girls.'

He looked slightly hurt. 'I'm being serious.'

'Oh, Leo. I think you're a beautiful person, too, but me and you? It just wouldn't work.'

'Why not?'

'Look at you and look at me.'

'Just a boy looking at girl... just wanting her to love him... OK, I know that wasn't strictly original either but take the external out of the equation, Grace. There is nothing not to like about you. The whole you. Grace Davies, the complete package.'

Gracie sighed deeply. 'You'd soon want to take on a younger, prettier model.'

'I've been with most of them.'

'Oh, have you now.' Gracie laughed.

'You know what I mean, Grace. I know for sure that isn't what I want now. It's bad enough having one narcissist in a relationship.' He dramatically lifted his arm in the air.

Gracie managed a smile. 'I can't have children.'

'I have one. In fact, he shares your blood, which may sound a bit creepy, but it makes me all the happier.'

'Happier as you know you'll get to see him more?'

'No way! If that's what you think, you're wrong. I tell you, Grace, I like you for all the right reasons. Short of putting a ring on your finger, I'm not sure what to say to you.'

'What film is that from?'

'It was straight from the actor's mouth, completely un-romantic and un-scripted, for once.' Leo leant into her. 'Come to Vegas with me tomorrow, Grace. We can go to the Little White Chapel and Elvis can marry us.'

'Stop it now. We've only met each other three times.' Gracie shook her head.

'That's all it took.' He took her hand.

'I've got my Miscarriage Matters session.'

'Cancel it.' He picked up her hand and kissed it. 'Sorry, I know how important that is to you. 'I'm filming for two months, Grace. Come with me.'

Gracie shook her head. 'So you wouldn't have time to see me anyway.'

She reached up to his lips to kiss him. Their lips fitted together perfectly. She always felt that if your kissing was compatible, then it was a sign of whether a relationship would work or not.

'I want to make love to you. I've never wanted to make love to anyone more than you in my life.' Leo kissed her forehead.

She smiled up at him. 'This is so romantic, so amazing, that it feels too good to be true. I can't accept that it is real. Go to Vegas. I will carry on with my normal life. When you come and see Jack again, let's see each other again and see how we feel. I want you to be absolutely sure that you mean what you say. The thought of making love to you takes my breath away but, for once, I'm thinking ahead. I still have healing to do and I want to make sure that I'm not being swept away by the moment. Do you understand?'

'Reluctantly, I do.' Leo nodded. 'But I'm coming to see you the moment I finish filming, you hear me.'

'I hear you, Mr Film Star. Come on, let's go to bed.'

'Together?'

'If you like. You can cuddle me all night if you can manage that.'

'It will be too hard.'

'What the cuddling, you mean?'

'You saucy gal, now get here now.'

Leo pulled her towards him and hugged her tightly.

'I mean it, Grace, I won't ever let you down.'

SIXTY-SIX

What do you mean Cynthia Princeton can't represent me anymore?'

Ed held his hand to his head as the posh voice at the end of his phone continued.

'Exactly that, Mr Duke. Due to unforeseen circumstances, we are having to put your case in the hands of Mister Dominic Westley.'

'But he knows nothing about me. Or about the case. This is not good at all.'

'Mister Westley is a very experienced member of our team here. Please don't be concerned. Now, when can you come and meet with him?'

Ed put his phone back in his pocket and threw himself down on his sofa.

'Fuck, fuck, fuck,' he said aloud.

He needed de-stressing; maybe he could catch Gracie between events and persuade her to come back to his. He tried her mobile but it went straight through to answerphone. Strange, he noticed she'd been offline for hours as well. His instinct had already told him that she was not really with a friend last night. Not picking up his phone would be exactly what he would do if he was up to no good, too.

What was she playing at? Surely she hadn't gone back to Lewis? It was bad enough losing his trusted barrister, let alone the woman who he was beginning to have real feelings for.

SIXTY-SEVEN

A tired but happy Gracie smiled as a couple of ladies appeared for the Miscarriage Matters session. One was a familiar face who had repeatedly miscarried at six weeks and another was new: a well-dressed woman around her own age.

She had arranged a talk today on health and nutrition from somebody Ali had suggested, who worked at the same hospital as she did. Gracie was happy with the attendance of eight today and busied herself making teas and coffees as the talk commenced.

A few of the group stayed on for general chat after the talk but just one – the new lady she had seen earlier – came and sat with Gracie. She had a doll-like face with almost perfectly round red circles on her cheeks, steel-blue, almond-shaped eyes and wore her hair in a neat plait. Her buxomness suited her. Gracie, although not short herself in the chest department, felt a little in awe of the woman's peachy looking breasts poking over her green T-shirt.

'Gracie Davies? That's you, isn't it?' She was softly spoken.

'Hello, yes. The one and only.' Gracie grinned.

'I'm Renee. I've heard such good things about this group, I had to come along. I think you should be really proud of what you've achieved. In fact, I think groups like this should be set up around the country. Women need to talk about fertility issues, about loss. It's a big part of a lot of our lives.'

'Well, thank you, Renee, that's really sweet of you to say and I think you're right. No more sweeping miscarriage aside as if it means nothing. It's everything if it happens to you.'

Renee stood up.

'Thanks for coming, Renee.' Gracie could tell the lady had more to say. This happened quite often, people wanting to talk to her but not being able to release the words that had been trapped for so long. Usually the thanks-for-coming line jolted them back into telling her what they had really come here for in the first place.

'I don't want this to be painful for you, Gracie, and I hope you don't mind me coming to you about this, but I'm going through IVF and one of the other ladies told me you'd been through it, too.'

'Yes, been there, done that.' Gracie smiled. 'How are you feeling?'

'Scared,' Renee replied, bluntly.

Gracie nodded. 'Now, that's a feeling I do understand. Are you at the injecting stage?' The whole painful process flooded back to Gracie and actually made her feel slightly glad that she didn't ever have to do it again.

'Yes, well, I'm four weeks away from egg collection. Hopefully they will get enough this time to make it work.'

'It's your second time?'

The attractive woman took a deep breath. 'No, my fifth.'

'Wow, I commend you, it's so much to put your mind and body through.' Gracie looked slightly downcast.

'I know. But we – that's me and my husband, Andy – we

won't give up until we get a child. It's what we have always wanted.'

Gracie thought back to the pressure of wanting to conceive so much it had taken over *her* life and Lewis's.

She thought for a second before she delivered with a shaky voice, 'And what if that doesn't happen, Renee?'

'That thought doesn't enter my head. I'm keeping everything positive around me. The thought of never being able to have children of my own just devastates me.'

'I apologise for the negativity, it's just I know exactly how that feels, I'm afraid. The longing, I mean.' Her voice faded. 'The desperation.'

'Oh, Gracie, I'm so sorry. I didn't know that was the case with you. I heard about the loss of your twins – for which I am so sorry – so tragic.'

'Yes, they were IVF. Sadly, a hysterectomy followed, too. After I... we, lost them.' Suddenly a vision of Lewis's shocked, white face when he realised what had happened rushed through her mind.

'Oh, Gracie.' Renee looked pained.

'I'm coming to terms with it now.' Her voice lilted. 'And today is not about me.' She sighed deeply. 'So why are you here today, Renee?'

'The nutrition talk, I think it will be of use to me. And I guess it's also good to talk to other women who've been in the "IVF club".'

'The club of joy and sorrow.' Gracie stated dramatically. 'And I'm not a very good advert for it, really.' Gracie felt tears spring to her eyes. 'Actually, what am I saying? I conceived the twins through it without too much effort. It was hanging on to the little darlings that I struggled with.'

'Oh Gracie, I'm so sorry for what you've been through.'

Gracie cleared her throat. 'What doesn't kill you makes you stronger and all that.'

Renee squeezed Gracie's arm. 'It's amazing what you are doing here. Thank you.'

'No, thank you for coming and I wish you all the luck in the world with it.' Gracie paused for a second to order her words correctly. 'Renee. I will say, though, that trying over and over again can be a little damaging not just for your body, but your soul too. All that heartache... you need to let it out, even though you are taking positive steps to try again. Make sure you do, won't you? I'm here if ever you need a chat.' Gracie put a comforting arm on the woman's shoulder.

'Thank you, Gracie. It's lovely to talk to someone who understands.'

'One other thing which might help or not, because this is your journey and not mine, but after recovering from the hysterectomy physically, I felt a sense of relief that the decision about having children of my own had been taken out of my hands. Relief that I would never again have to be tied to my ovulation dates. And most of all, relief that I would never have to feel the atrocity of losing another baby again.'

Gracie felt good to have said that out loud. Then she cringed. 'I'm sorry, maybe that wasn't the right thing to say to you, now.'

Renee welled up. 'It's OK. I understand every single thing you just said. And I can't believe I'm saying this, either, but if the decision were to be made for me it would be the best thing. I'm thirty-seven. I could go on trying to conceive for another five, maybe even ten, years. Ten years in which I could be looking to adopt or foster or just be at peace with myself.'

Gracie handed her a tissue.

'Let's will those eggs to be all plump and juicy when they come to be collected and that you and your husband make a beautiful bouncing baby.'

Renee sniffed. 'Yes. Positive thinking breeds positive happenings.'

Gracie smiled warmly. 'Indeed. Let me know how you get on, won't you?'

'Yes, of course, and thank you, Gracie, thank you for... for being so candid. It's good to say it how it is. In fact, if this round of IVF isn't successful, then I have a lot of thinking to do.'

SIXTY-EIGHT

Maya walked back from her shift at the café, her legs almost as heavy as her heart. She couldn't believe that since the last magical time with the professor, he had not once spoken to her. He had even dumped one of her calls. He never dumped her calls. Men! Why, when they suddenly got close, did they have to pull away again?

If the professor was going to be like this, she might as well carry on seeing her clients – at least she was then earning decent money enough to save.

She was putting her key in the door when she heard her phone ringing in her bag. On seeing who it was, she felt a rush of relief flood through her.

'Little bird, it's me. Sorry I've not been in touch. We need to talk. Are you around later?'

Maya's relief turned to alarm. Needing to talk? That sounded serious. Hopefully serious in a good way. Maybe he was going to discuss moving in with her or how best they could carry on while he was still married? She wasn't stupid, although the other night had been just so lovely, the reality was that he still lived with his wife and daughter, so she didn't expect things to move forward that fast.

Truthfully, part of her was a little scared about being in a full-time relationship with just one person. But the thought of being financially stable was all that she had ever wanted and the chance to have this with somebody she did actually love was like a dream coming true.

'What time? At my place?' Maya replied casually.

Say seven? I'll come to you and we can walk somewhere from yours.'

Maya kept her voice as upbeat as she could. 'Sure. See you then.'

Walk and talk? Maya thought. *How things had changed.*

SIXTY-NINE

Annalize was sat in one of the two booths right at the back of Marcy's Café when Gracie arrived. The perfect one stood up to greet her and, at the sight of the very flat stomach of the woman who had helped to break her heart, Gracie let out an audible gasp.

It had taken a huge inner strength to agree to meet her and now that she was confronted with this surprise non-pregnant version, she wasn't quite sure how to react.

She had been amazed, after Lewis's many failed attempts at contact, that the perfect one had suggested meeting her, but after a short, sharp text exchange, here they were, sitting in Marcy's just like in the old Lemon Aid days. Maya brought a menu over and discreetly squeezed her friend's hand.

Without a word Annalize sat down, then burst into tears and began to blurt between snotty sobs.

'I lost a baby. I've been really sick. I lost so much blood that they thought I might die. Gracie, I'm so sorry for what I did. I just didn't understand... until now that is... what you must have been through.'

Suddenly, Gracie was confronted with not the hard-faced

person she had been hating for so long, but another woman who had suffered the insurmountable loss of a child.

Gracie hoped the massive deep breath she had just taken would allow her to impart the compassion that she normally felt in this situation.

'How pregnant were you?'

'Sixteen weeks,' Annalize blubbered.

'Oh, Annalize, I know what it's like when you see that the little soul dancing around on the scan and it is taken from you.'

Annalize noisily blew her nose. 'I don't think I'll ever get over it.'

'You will, I promise. You'll never forget the horror of the physical event, I don't think, but time is a healer in all cases of grief and anguish, even something as devastating as this,' Gracie replied matter-of-factly. She then paused for thought. It was time to ask the million-dollar question.

Her voice wobbled. 'Was it Lewis's?'

It was Annalize's turn to bring the little compassion she had within her to the fore. Her final deceit towards the woman in front of her could now be taken to the grave with the soul of her unborn baby. What use would it be for anyone to know that she had chosen Lewis as the father of her baby, thinking that his dark, good looks would make a beautiful child? And also that she would amazingly get pregnant at her first attempt at it.

'God, no! I mean, what use would Lewis have been to me? I knew how much he loved you, Gracie. He would never have left you. Lewis was a drunken mistake and I will be forever sorry for what I've put you through.'

Not having realised the extent of relief she would feel on finding out it hadn't been Lewis's baby, Gracie felt strangely euphoric. 'Do you want a coffee?'

Annalize sniffed. 'Do they sell anything stronger?'

* * *

They sat drinking white wine.

Annalize checked her blotchy face in her hand mirror. 'Thank you for giving me this time, Gracie. I really don't deserve it.'

'How are you and Lewis doing, anyway?'

'As if I would have stayed with him after him being unfaithful. Come on, Annalize, give me some credit.'

'That is so sad to hear. He loves you, Gracie, and you him. I can't believe you've wasted everything good that you could have together. That whole night, it was me, not him. I was drunk. I came on to him. If I'm honest, I guess I was jealous of what you had with him. Something I've never had. See, I'm wicked. I deserved to have lost that baby of mine.'

Gracie shook her head. 'Nobody deserves that, Annalize, not even you.'

Annalize drained her glass. 'Do you hate me, Gracie?'

'Hate is a very strong word.' Maya swept by to pick up the empty glasses and gave Gracie a supportive smile. 'I *am* very sorry for your loss, Annalize. I can't say you will ever be my friend again, but I now run a club called Miscarriage Matters.' Gracie took a flyer out of her bag. 'The door is always open there, Annalize.'

Annalize replied quietly, 'Thank you.' She got up. 'There is nothing more I can say, but I'm truly sorry. Goodbye, Gracie.'

'Goodbye, Annalize.'

SEVENTY

Maya put on shorts and a little flowery top. She applied her make-up carefully and put gel through her blonde spiky hair. As usual, the professor was on time.

He seemed preoccupied when he arrived, edgier than usual. His smile was weak.

'Shall we?' He beckoned her to follow him down the front steps.

Maya felt uneasy. She sensed something was wrong. Even the warm summer's evening couldn't melt the cold atmosphere that she felt between them. They reached the park close to her house and found a quiet place to sit on the grass.

Scott couldn't even look at Maya; he took her hand and gently rubbed her palm with his fingers.

'My wife had an accident.' Maya said nothing. 'She has been in a coma. The prognosis is good, but she is going to need a lot of care and rehabilitation.'

'Now I understand your silence.' Maya felt herself welling up.

'Yes.' He let go of her hand and starting picking randomly at blades of grass. 'I do love you, Maya.' Maya felt like every breath was being sucked out of her body. She gulped. 'But...' A lone tear ran down the young woman's cheek. 'Just say it and get it over with, I'm not a little girl, Professor.'

Scott put his hand to his heart. 'I know you're not. You're a clever, quick-witted, desirable woman who deserves more than anything I can offer you. But when I saw Cynthia lying there, it was a wake-up call. I'm the one who needs to grow up and stop playing with people's emotions. I can't leave her, Maya. I'm so sorry.'

'Then why say what you said? Fill me with hope when you know that I love you?' Maya spat.

Scott blew out a big breath. 'I was blown away by you, flattered by the fact you do love me and, well, maybe if the accident hadn't happened then... Oh, I don't know, Maya but what I do know is the last thing I wanted to do was hurt you.'

'What we felt together that night was not an illusion. I can tell you love me, too.'

Scott ruffled his hair with his hands. 'I do love you, but there are many aspects of love and I have to listen to my head for once and not just my loins.'

'I think you might be making a big mistake,' Maya blasted.

Scott's voice remained level. 'Maybe I am, but I owe it to my family to try and do the best by them.'

Maya couldn't stop her tears. 'I can't not see you again. I simply couldn't bear it.'

'It has to be this way, Maya, it's not fair on anyone otherwise. You will get over me. I can't see what you see in an obnoxious old fool like me, anyway. Look at you. You are beautiful, you will find somebody else much worthier of your love straight away.'

Maya sobbed. 'But I want you. I love you, Professor.'

'And in twenty years' time, would you? Would you really? When I'm in my sixties and you are still a vibrant fortysomething. Come on, we need to be realistic.'

'My heart chose you, not my bloody birth certificate. Age is just a number. I know what I feel.'

'Oh, Maya. I don't want more children either. I'm certain about that.'

Maya's tears subsided. 'When did I ever mention children? And if it can't be forever, why can't we just enjoy the now? Carry on as we were.'

'Because my "now" has to be with my wife and my daughter.'

Maya sniffed, then leaning in to Scott, hung on as if she would never let him go. Scott discreetly checked that nobody could see them. The last thing he needed was a nosey student spotting them.

'Maybe when your wife is better?' Maya pleaded.

'No, Maya. I've made a decision for once that I must stick to. I've been playing a young man's game for too long. It's time I grew up.'

Maya pulled herself away from him and covered her face with both hands as if not looking at him would make this whole dreadful situation disappear.

'I have to go now. I need to go back to the hospital. I'm truly sorry that I have hurt you.'

'Can't we go back and go to bed just one more time?' Maya urged.

Scott was short in his delivery. 'As much as I want to, it would do neither of us any good. This has to be the end.'

Scott coughed to remove the huge lump that had formed in his throat. Saying goodbye to his little bird was possibly one of the hardest things he had ever had to do. But he was clear in his mind what he was doing was the right thing for him, for his family and ultimately for Maya, too.

He got up and helped Maya up off the grass. No fuss, no bother, he just had to go and go now. He knew if he got within a metre of her front door, he would not be able to resist her and all the temptations she had offered him for so long.

As he walked away Scott didn't dare look back for he knew if he saw Maya's sad, beautiful face he might well be tempted to change his mind. His psychology studies had said that it *was* possible to love two people at once; he could now teach this with conviction.

* * *

Maya pushed open her bedroom door and threw herself face down onto her bed.

Even if he had wanted to be with her, he had just said he was certain he didn't want more children. And what use was that to either her or the little bundle of cells that was now growing inside her.

SEVENTY-ONE

Lewis flicked through the TV channels. Not even a weeknight football match could keep his mind focused on anything but Gracie and the Annalize situation. He got himself a can of beer from the fridge, took a sip and put it to one side. Drinking wasn't the answer, either. He felt like he was going mad. As much as he tried, he couldn't *make* Gracie love him.

He took his toolbox from under the sink and made his way to the nursery. Slowly and painstakingly, and with tears running down his cheeks, he took the two little Moses baskets apart and placed the frames and mattresses neatly against the wall. He boxed up the soft toys and ceiling mobile and gently pulled off the teddy-bear border. All that was left was a white-walled empty shell. The promised warm, happy family of four that could have laughed and grown together in this space was reduced to one sad, lonely man with huge regrets.

He put away his tools and sat back down in front of the TV. At least Gracie would be pleased he'd sorted the spare room. Maybe it was better to see if one of the mums she knew could make use of everything, rather than sell it to a complete stranger on eBay. A good excuse to ring her. He was just about to dial her number when a text flashed up.

> Saw Annalize. She lost the baby. It wasn't yours. G

Lewis phoned her immediately.

'Wow, OK. Thanks for letting me know.'

'Kind of a relief for you, I guess?' Gracie was curt.

'Gracie, don't be like this.'

'Like what?'

'You know what I mean. At least we can move on now, can't we? I want to see you, Gracie, I miss you so much.'

'I texted, not called, because I'm on my way out.'

'With lover boy, I take it?'

Gracie chose to ignore his comment. Yes, she had arranged to see Ed, but just for a drink and a catch-up. She was confused about how she felt about him, too, especially after her night with Leo. In fact, she felt like her heart and head had been put in a blender and they were whizzing around at one hundred miles an hour. If only the end result could be a love potion that led her to happiness with the right person.

'I sorted the nursery tonight. Everything is taken down, even the border. I wondered if any of your ladies might have use for it?'

The finality of it all caused Gracie's heart to break a little bit more. 'Well, at least that's something. I'll ask Kate if she wants anything.' She croaked.

'See.' Lewis spoke softly. 'I can do some things right.'

Gracie flipped to curt. 'It's only taken you a year.'

Lewis sighed. 'I just can't win with you at the moment, can I?'

'No, Lewis, I'm afraid you can't. Anyway, I'd better get on.'

'So, when *can* I see you?' His voice was soft and low.

'See me for what, Lewis? All we do is argue.'

She could feel his pain at the other end of the phone and softened slightly. 'Look, why don't I come round Saturday morning and I'll put some of the stuff in my car. At least it's out of your way then.'

'OK. Before twelve would be good as I'm going to the cricket in the afternoon.'

'Yep, fine, must get your priorities straight, eh, Lewis?'

Lewis said goodbye, hung up and sighed deeply.

However she behaved, it was as if Gracie was tied to him by an invisible thread and he couldn't bear to cut her free.

At least there wasn't the added stress of Annalize's baby being his. What a bloody relief! That would for certain have been the end of anything he might still be able to salvage with Gracie. He wondered, too, how he would have coped if he had found out he had lost yet another baby.

Despite everything, he hoped that Annalize was feeling OK. For fear of getting his head bitten off, he hadn't dared ask Gracie where she had seen her to be told the news.

He stretched out on the sofa. He felt tired of everything. He would see Gracie on Saturday, make his last attempt to win her back and then, maybe, he would do his best to move on. She was seeing somebody else after all.

In fact, he thought, maybe he should follow the age-old adage of setting her free. If she came back to him, then it *was* meant to be? Perhaps he should start dating other people, too. Maybe he was just hanging on to the good memories in their relationship. He took a slug of his now warm beer and flicked on the TV.

An advert came up for an online dating site.

Who was he bloody kidding? He hadn't actually even thought about sex since the split, which was very unlike him. There was only one Gracie Davies in this world and he was going to do everything in his power to get her back.

SEVENTY-TWO

Ed was already halfway through a pint of Guinness when Gracie arrived at the pub. He stood up when he saw her and kissed her on the cheek.

'Hey, sexy. Sit down. White wine?'

'Yes, perfect; make it a large one.'

'Bad day?'

'You could say that.'

'Aw, that's no good. Take a seat, I'll get you a drink.'

Ed put a glass of chilled wine down on the table. 'Wanna talk about it? Your bad day, I mean.'

'No, I don't. I want to relax now I'm here.' She didn't want to go into the sorry details about Annalize and her conversation with Lewis.

'Fair enough. You look great, by the way.' Ed smiled warmly.

'Thanks. But more importantly, how are you?'

'Not so good either, to be honest. Cynthia Princeton can't represent me anymore.'

Gracie frowned. Princeton? Now why did that ring a bell? Of course, it was the professor's surname.

'She's your barrister, right?'

'Yeah.'

'I was seeing a therapist – to go through the baby stuff – his surname was Princeton.'

'Yeah, that's right. She said her old man did that shit.'

Gracie thought back to how Scott had been quite sharp when she mentioned Ed and the rape case... it made more sense now. And, of course, because of the ethics of it all, he couldn't discuss it, she guessed.

'So why can't she represent you?'

'All I've been told is that there are unforeseen circumstances. It's pissed me off, to be honest. She seems a bloody good barrister and I'm worried now.'

'You're innocent and that is what a jury is for. Try not to worry.'

'Yes, but Cynthia – well, she just seemed to have every avenue covered.'

Gracie finished her drink.

Ed lifted his half-drunk pint. 'That was quick. Do you want another or do you want to come back to mine and really de-stress?'

Gracie knew she had to be straight with him. 'Look, Ed. As much as that thought is tempting, I really don't think this is going anywhere.'

'Does it have to? I mean we have a good time together, right? The other night, you blew my mind. Come on, let's just go and get naked. You know it makes sense.'

He winked at her.

'I haven't been totally honest with you.' Gracie felt a bit sick.

'Oh?'

'I... err... I went on a date with someone else.'

Ed's face fell. 'The night your phone was switched off? I

bloody knew it. Thanks, Gracie, thanks a lot. I thought you could at least be honest with me.'

'I'm sorry, Ed. I'm just so mixed up about everything at the moment.'

'Lover boy Lewis, I suppose? You just couldn't help yourself, could you?'

'A date doesn't have to mean sex, you know?'

'No wonder you were so hot the other night. Got a taste for it, have you?'

'Ed, you don't have to be quite so vile.'

'Good, was he?'

'Stop it now. I was having my reservations about us after Cornwall, to be honest. I don't want to be worrying about trusting you, especially after Lewis.'

'You trusting me!' Ed's voice raised an octave.

'You're the one who's just run back to the man who shagged someone else, nice.'

His voice was getting louder.

'Ssh, not so loud.'

'Don't shush me, Gracie.'

'It wasn't Lewis anyway.'

'So, you've got three of us on the go now, then? Great!'

'That's it, I'm trying to be honest with you here but I've had enough. It was fun, Ed, and you have helped me through a really bad time and for that I'm really grateful.'

Gracie got up and rushed towards the door, Ed followed swiftly.

On reaching her car, Ed beckoned for her to wind down the window. She did so hesitantly.

Ed looked less angry now, more forlorn. 'Look, Gracie, I'm sorry for shouting. I kind of hoped we might make a proper go of it, that's all.'

Gracie let out a slow breath. 'I know,' she said softly. 'I wanted that, too. For a while.'

'OK,' he murmured.

'I never wanted to upset you, Ed.'

'You haven't.' He shrugged. 'See you around, Gracie Davies. Be happy, heh?'

With a sad smile, Gracie wound up the window and, without looking back, drove off.

SEVENTY-THREE

Maya smiled warmly as Gracie pulled up outside her flat. Boris was wagging his tail furiously in the back seat.

'It's so good to see you.' Maya gave her a big kiss on the cheek. 'It's been too long.'

Gracie beamed. 'Yes, it has. I've got so much to tell you.'

'Are you sure you're all right going to the common? I mean, it's your workplace now.'

'I need a long walk and Boris needs to let off steam, so it's perfect.'

'It's such a beautiful day, too,' Maya added.

Gracie pulled into the car park and was relieved that Ed's van wasn't there. She hadn't heard a word from him since the episode the other night, and was really glad that she hadn't. She'd just have to avoid the main car park from now on and hope she didn't bump into him too often.

'Coffee first?' Gracie suggested.

'Yes, why not?'

Boris barked. 'We won't be long, Muttley, I promise.'

Gracie headed into the familiar Windmill Café while Maya

waited outside on a bench with the dog. She had asked for a smoothie instead of her usual black coffee.

'We can sit up at the end so nobody sees you smoking, if you like?' Gracie offered as she put their drinks down on the table.

'No, here is fine, we are in the sun.'

'So... tell me what's happening with you. Still working hard at the café?'

'I'm pregnant, Gracie.' Maya was never anything short of direct.

'Shit. And by the look on that face you really don't want to be? Whose is it?'

'He's a married man.'

'Oh, Maya.'

'I know. Tell me about it. I'm on the pill but had had a bit of a stomach upset that week. It must have affected it – how's my luck?'

'Have you told him?'

'No bloody way. He had already said that he didn't want children. This would tip him over the edge.'

Gracie looked pained.'Oh, god. I'm sorry you are going through this.'

Maya started to rush with her words. 'I know you must think of me badly as he's married... especially after what you've been through, but the really sad thing is I love him, Gracie. Like properly love him. I feel like my body and mind is taken over when he makes love to me. And I really don't know what to do.' The usually tough-as-nails Maya started to cry.

'Oh, baby girl. Don't cry.'

'And... this is so cruel for you, too, someone who would die to be in my position, right now.'

'Don't even think about that. These things happen and it wasn't like you trapped him or anything.'

'I really didn't. And as much as I love him, he came and told me that he was making a go of it with his wife just the other day.

I am nobody's second best, Gracie. In fact, I always used to say I'm far too big to be a bit on the side – and then I fucked him. I've been fucking him for months.'

'Sadly we don't always choose who we fall in love with, Maya. Have you thought about what you want to do?'

'I've got so many plans for the future. I'm twenty-two, Gracie. I would have to go back home if I had a baby. I would never be able to afford to stay here and I'm too proud to take benefits.'

'So are you thinking of an abortion, then?'

'I can't do that either. My mother would kill me. She is so religious.'

'She wouldn't have to know.'

'OK, my mother is an excuse... I can't do that. I would never forgive myself.'

'So you have to tell the father and he must support you.'

'No. I can't be beholden to him. I want him to want me for me and – as much as I could still have him in my life if I told him this, he made it clear that he doesn't want to see me again.' Maya took a deep breath. 'It would just be too painful.'

Gracie sighed. 'There has to be a solution. Have you thought about adoption?'

'I did consider it but I don't know where to start.'

'OK. Things got so bad with Lewis that it was never discussed further than that it could be an option, but I'll happily get some details for you. I'll help you as much as I can, Maya, I promise you.'

'Gracie, you are such a lovely person. I'm glad you are in my life.' Maya sniffed loudly.

Gracie took a sip of her coffee. The past few months had certainly pushed her to her limits. Lana wanting a miscarriage; Renee's struggle with her IVF journey; Annalize losing the baby that she'd thought was Lewis's; and now Maya not having any choice in her mind other than to give up a child for adoption. So many women, so many difficult issues to face in their lives, and she had helped them or was helping them all.

She had learnt and listened and been able to convey the pain she had felt and put it to good use. It made her feel happy in a way, happy that her babies hadn't died in vain.

'You are a beautiful person too, Maya Bakova. You gave me the kick up the arse I needed to move on from Lewis. Ed hasn't worked out, but he was good for me initially. He did show me the affection I was craving at the right time.'

'Is it over with him, then?'

'Yes, I finished it the other night, he wasn't happy.'

'I'm sorry, Gracie.'

'I'm not. It was the right decision, for both of us, and he will see that eventually.'

'And... Lewis?'

'I think about him every day. Mainly what could have been. We'd have our little family now. How different life would be. A few times when Ed was mean, I did think about what Lewis and I had. I felt a pure love for him, safe. It is just so sad that I can't forget what he did.'

'Sex is so different for men, Gracie. We get so much more involved, I reckon. They can just stick their cocks in and out of whoever they please, and then walk off with no emotion.'

Gracie smiled. 'You so have a way with words, Maya.'

'Think of it as a function men have to perform. Like drinking or going to the toilet. It has nothing to do with their hearts or feelings, just their dicks. Think of it like that with Lewis. He wanted the sex, not the person. A throw-away shag.'

'But the deceit will never go away.'

'Were you having sex at the time?'

'That's not the point.'

'It is. Just think that instead of him having sex, he went out for a drink. Quenched his sexual thirst and came back again.'

'That makes it sound so simple.'

'It is that simple. Men are animals; they are physical. Lewis didn't stop loving you for one moment, I'm sure of that. His heart and his head weren't connected that night. He was drunk.'

'And how would I know he'd never do it again?'

'How do we know anything, Gracie? I don't even think we should be monogamous, to be honest – it's a strange concept in my view.'

'I would never be unfaithful.' As she said it, Gracie thought back to her night with Leo, that not a single soul, apart from Noms, knew about. She had done the same to Ed, really. Gone behind his back.

'Anyway, it's you we need to be talking about. How you are feeling and how far gone are you?' Gracie looked to Maya's tiny tummy.

'I've literally just missed my period so just feel a bit sick, but that's all.'

'OK. Let me make some enquiries. I will just find out the process for you, won't give any details. Are you one hundred per cent sure this is what you want?'

'No, none of the scenarios are right. But at least with adoption, the child will have a chance. If I abort, I give up their chance of life. If I tell the father, I give up my chance of life as I know it.'

'Well, I'm here for you all the way. If you need to talk, call me whatever time it is.'

'Gracie, you are a special lady – don't ever let anyone say any different.'

Just then, Boris barked from under the table.

'Sorry, Boris, we forgot about you, you've been so patient. Come on, boy.'

'Oh, before I forget, Gracie. I got this for you.' Maya handed her a small black jewellery box.

Looking confused, Gracie opened it slowly, then let out a

cry of surprise and gave Maya a hug. For there inside, on a little red piece of velvet, was tiny faux-diamond nose stud.

'I know you've always wanted one. Go on, be brave. I think it will suit you.'

Gracie laughed. 'Oh shit, I have no excuse now. Thanks, Maya, that's so thoughtful of you. But don't you think I'm a bit old for a nose piercing?'

'Gracie, age is just a number. Besides, you're never too old to do something that makes you feel bold and beautiful.'

Gracie felt a warmth run through her. 'And just look at our friendship. Age hasn't even come into that.'

'Exactly!' Maya smiled.

Boris was now whining very loudly.

'Come on, mister. Let's walk you, before you internally combust.'

SEVENTY-FOUR

Two months seemed to pass in a blur for Gracie. She'd been so busy that she'd not sat down with Noms properly for a catch-up for what seemed like an age. It was easier to find quiet time together now Jack was back at school, so they had arranged a relaxing lunch at the local Italian.

Gracie sat back in the restaurant seat with a dramatic sigh.

'This is just what I needed. I'm bloody knackered.'

Noms smiled. 'Yes, agree. It's so good to do this. Jack can be a handful during the holidays.'

'Bless him.' Gracie laughed. 'I do love that kid and always ask me to do more, if I can, I will.'

'You've been crazy busy, it's fine.'

A waiter appeared to take their food and drinks order.

'Yes, the business couldn't have gone any better. It makes me so happy to have a focus, that I can call my own,' Gracie enthused. 'Kate's both delightful and delighted, too. We're making far more money out of it than we ever imagined and, now word is spreading, I can only see it getting busier.'

'I'm so proud of you, too. Of how far you've come, you know.' Noms put her hand across to her sister's.

'Thank you. Time has definitely been a healer. I don't wake up every day and think about the twins like I used to. More like, how on earth am I going to fit everything into the day? Anyway, more importantly, how's it going with Ali?' Gracie raised her eyebrows.

Noms smirked. 'Great, actually. It's so weird that I am officially in a relationship with a woman. She just does it for me, though. I get on so well with her, it is like having an amazing girlfriend with benefits, who just seems to get me.'

'I'm so pleased for you, Noms. You deserve every happiness. I don't suppose you've heard from Mr Film Star, have you?' Gracie asked tentatively.

Noms screwed up her nose. 'He emailed last week just to check up on Jack but that was it.'

'No mention of me, then?'

'Said to say hi to you, but no more than that. Sorry, I forgot to tell you. Have you thought much about him and what happened in Barcelona?'

'Yes, of course, but the more I think of it the more I have to be realistic. Did you see him in *Hola* magazine last week with that young brunette on his arm? She's the daughter of someone in a heavy metal band, apparently.' Gracie waved her hand dismissively.

'No, I didn't see it. It's funny, when I first had Jack, I used to stalk him online, but I don't care what he gets up to now. Although, if it involved him hurting you, of course I would.'

'The *Hola* article was on the gossip-column page so who knows the context, but I don't think I could live with that every day. I was jealous for a second and then had a word with myself. I'm so glad I didn't sleep with him before he left. He was adamant that he wouldn't let me down and would contact me when he got back from Vegas, but I won't hold my breath.'

Noms took a sip of her fizzy water. 'I'm impressed you're being so measured about it all, Grace.'

'I think I have to be with him. He did seem to be so into me. He even slipped in that he'd take me to a chapel in Vegas and we'd get married, but I know what it is – it's the fact that I didn't put it on a plate for him. Don't get me wrong, Leo boosted me no end. He gave me two amazing nights, but...'

'But what?'

'He hasn't contacted me once: no text, no mail, no nothing. If he had cared just a little bit, then he could have made some sort of effort.'

'He's like that though, Grace. On set, it's full on. And if you had chosen to be with him, it would always have been like that.'

Gracie shrugged. 'Out of sight, out of mind, more like. If he really liked me, he would still be keeping me interested.'

'Hmm.' Noms cocked her head. 'He isn't a bad person, just a busy person.'

'Yes, but it takes two seconds to send a message, so I'm more peeved than hurt. My gut told me it would never be right, and hurrah, I listened to it, for once.'

'Bless you.' Noms took another drink.

'And I don't think he could give up that lifestyle,' Gracie added, 'much as he professes he wants a quiet life.'

'I agree, it's in his DNA.' Noms sighed. 'I'm waiting to see if it's nature or nurture for Jack. He could be the next Leo Woodall, who knows.'

Gracie fanned herself with the menu. 'Now he is *another* film star called Leo, I would entertain.'

Noms laughed. 'What are you like!'

Two big plates of spaghetti bolognese arrived at the table.

'Wow, that looks amazing.' Gracie picked up her napkin and put it on her lap.

'Good to see you tucking in to something decent, Grace. I was worried you might be getting too skinny.'

Gracie laughed. 'As if. I've just cut out all the crap and although I've ditched the running club, walking Boris on the common allows me to have my wine and the odd flapjack at the weekend.'

'Well, you look great for it. In fact, this is the best I've seen you looking in a long while. No men and hard work must be the answer. Talking of no men, any word from Lewis?'

'Not for over a month... it's weird. He was so full-on and now nothing. Last time I saw him, he was bringing the twins' stuff to the hut so that other ladies might make use of it.' Gracie's voice wobbled.

Noms put her hand on top of her sister's. 'Oh, Grace.'

Gracie pulled away. 'I'm fine, it had to be done and it allowed us to leave each other on amicable terms.' Gracie spun a big swirl of spaghetti around her fork. 'But if I'm honest, I don't like not having him at the end of a phone. I hate to say it out loud, but I am missing him. Even when we were rowing, I knew he still loved me. The fact that he's got over me, thinking that he might be moving ahead with someone else, well... it kills me, actually. The worst thing will be if I find out he is having a baby. I don't think I would ever want to know. It would destroy me.'

'Contact him, Grace,' Noms said boldly.

'Oh, I don't know.'

'If he truly loves you, whatever situation he is in, he will come back to you.'

'Do you think so?'

'I know so. From my past experiences, men are like bloody rubber bands. They always ping back and sting you when you least expect it.'

'He hasn't replied to two of my texts and that's so unlike him. He must be seeing someone.'

'Well, you won't know if you don't ask, is all I can say.' Noms scraped her plate of the last morsel of her lunch.

Gracie did the same. 'I told you that seeing Annalize helped me to move on from everything, didn't I? He never would have ended up with her, I know that. She even told me just how much he loved me!'

'This life lark is a funny old game, Grace. Those cards keep getting dealt, whether it be an ace or a joker, everything usually does work out for the best in time. Pudding?'

'God, no, I'm stuffed. I am happy, though, Noms, so don't worry about me. And I promise to get out from under your feet soon, now I've got some decent money coming in.'

'You could live with me forever, sister, if you wanted, you know that? Right, I'd best get down the school and pick the little terror up.'

Outside, Noms looked at Gracie and screwed her face up.

'Gracie Davies, is that a nose stud!?'

In that minute the diamond had caught the light.

'Yes. Isn't it cute?'

'So when is the tattoo coming?'

It was Gracie's turn to laugh. 'I'm not having a midlife crisis, don't worry. I've always wanted a nose stud and just never had the balls to do it. This is the new me. Taking control of my life.'

'Well, I like the new you, but make sure the old one still pops up sometimes, because I liked her too.' Noms hugged her sister in the street. 'I love you, Grace.'

'Back at ya, sister. Right, gotta run, I've got some balloons being delivered at four.'

SEVENTY-FIVE

Professor Princeton gently fluffed up the pillows behind his wife's head and kissed her on the forehead. She had been home for a month now and was beginning to show distinct signs of recovery.

'There you go, old girl.' He put a fresh glass of water by her side.

She smiled at him. 'Did you go down for a lobotomy while I was in surgery?'

'No, but I needed to. Now, anything else I can get you, before I put the racing on?'

'No. I'm fine, thanks, darling.' Cynthia reached for her water. 'Actually, it's that lad's rape case today, remind me to ring the office later, I'd like to hope Westley can get him off.'

'Will do.'

Scott went downstairs and opened up his *Racing Post*. He smiled as he scoured the runners and riders and saw a horse called Maya's Magic. It was a rank outsider but he'd still have to have a little each-way punt on it.

Giving up gambling would have been easier than giving up the beautiful Czech girl and he often wondered what she was up to. He had no doubts that she would forge a successful life for herself and also knew that she was too proud to ever come knocking at his door again.

For once he felt he had made the right decision. For once he felt almost content.

SEVENTY-SIX

Edward Duke was sweating profusely as the jury took their seats in the courtroom. The loud, deep voice of the judge boomed across the court.

'Do you find the defendant guilty or not guilty of rape?'

Trudi Simpson glared at him from the viewing area.

'Not guilty.'

'He bloody did it!' Trudi shouted as her friend took her arm and ushered her outside.

The case had fallen apart without the bouncer's evidence, just as Cynthia had predicted it would.

Ed tipped his head back, shut his eyes, then punched the air.

SEVENTY-SEVEN

Gracie was blow drying her hair when she heard Boris barking madly downstairs. She turned off the dryer and went downstairs to see what all the fuss was about.

'What is it, boy?' Boris was scrabbling at the front door. 'You need a wee?' On opening the door, she nearly jumped out of her skin – for there looking up at her from a white dog crate, wearing a pink bow around its neck, was the most beautiful little Yorkshire terrier puppy she had ever seen. On the top of the crate was an envelope with the words, *To my Natural Woman.*

There was water and food in the crate and a supersoft cream cashmere dog blanket with a bone pattern embossed in it. She lifted the crate gently, put it on the kitchen table and reached for the tiny animal.

'Hello, little one.' The doggy snuggled into her. Boris sniffed around in the front garden with no care for his newfound housemate.

An intrigued Gracie sat down and opened the envelope.

Dear Grace, I ended up only being in town for a couple of days as had to get an early flight to Geneva. I so wanted to catch up with Jack, yourself and Noms but my schedule changed and I didn't think you'd appreciate me waking you up at 5 a.m. on a Sunday morning. So... meet Hetti... your new baby. I hope you love her.

I loved our time together in London and, of course, Barcelona. In fact, that beautiful night will remain etched on my mind forever. But I guess you were right not to give yourself to me. I was praying you didn't see the tabloids and think badly of me. I do adore you, Grace. You are a beautiful person inside and out. You taught me that you don't have to have sex to have a good night. You also taught me that I have to stop being so shallow when it comes to women. I need to look within.

I expect you're thinking: then why was he out with Peony Fox the other night? I guess despite all I've just said the playboy in me will always be there. You deserve better than me, Grace. I don't want to give up the films yet, and to have a committed relationship with somebody when I am forever travelling and filming would not be easy.

Maybe I'm also trying to say that I got swept away with the moment with you. I hope you don't hate me for leading you on, but I think you are clever enough and also maybe slightly relieved to understand exactly what I'm saying.

What I do know for sure is that you will find somebody who will love you for the true beauty that you are. And when you find that person I want you to be the happiest girl in the world.

The minute I set my eyes on Hetti, I immediately thought of you. You may not be able to have children of your own, but she can be your 'baby' for now – until you adopt a house full of chil-

dren who will be more than blessed to have a mom in you, that is.

Gracie sniffed back a tear.

I feel honoured to know you, Grace. I also feel safe in the fact my beautiful son has such an amazing auntie and mom.

I also hope that Hetti brings you pleasure. She's small enough for you to take to work, so I hope you're not cursing me for such a random gift that holds so much responsibility. My assistant got her jabbed and chipped to this address, so you don't have that worry.

I will see you again, but I just wanted to get down all of this on paper as you know how bad I am at coming out with original lines on the spot. :)

'On that note, you really do make me want to be a better man, Grace. And for that I will always truly be grateful.'

I hope you find your peace and happiness. You truly deserve to.

Lots of love to you, you beautiful, natural woman.
Leo X

Gracie sat in silence for a second. She could feel the tiny heartbeat of the little puppy pumping fast against her chest and found it strangely comforting.

Deep down she always knew that Leo Grant would never love her like she wanted to be loved. But she hadn't regretted a single moment of her time with him. He had made her feel like a million dollars.

She had always believed that people came into your life for

a reason, a season or a lifetime. And the reason for meeting Leo was to boost her self-confidence. He had done that in spades and for that *she* would be eternally grateful.

'Hello, little lady… I'm your new mummy.' With tears in her eyes, Gracie gently held Hetti in her right hand. 'We'd best get you settled in, hadn't we?'

SEVENTY-EIGHT

Gracie was just finishing up putting chairs into a circle in the event hut when Kate turned up. She was glowing and now had a visible baby bump.

'This looks very organised.' Kate went to the kitchen and put the kettle on.

'Yes, I'm doing an open forum today. Thought I'd let people tell their individual stories. Hopefully women will learn from sharing each other's experiences. If they don't want to talk, they can just listen.'

'That's a great idea, Gracie.'

'How are you feeling now? You were a bit ropey last time I saw you.'

'Fantastic now I've stopped throwing up. The twenty-week scan was all fine. I'm having a boy.'

'How lovely, one of each.' Gracie said, and meant it.

Kate did a little dance on the spot. 'Yes, I'm getting excited now.'

The first of the Miscarriage Matters ladies started filing in and Gracie chatted to her to see if she was happy with the day's planned activity.

Within half an hour all the seats bar one were full and Gracie cleared her throat to introduce the session.

'It has been a pleasure to meet you all this year and I love to see new faces coming through the door every week. It has also been my privilege to impart my little bit of knowledge after what I have been through personally. I now have a true insight, not only into the strength of sisterhood, but it has also made me realise exactly what motherhood really means. Motherhood is not just a title; it is a force, a calling, a bond that goes beyond biology and beyond boundaries. So tonight, we celebrate every woman who has ever mothered, whether by blood, by adoption, by circumstance, or simply by the power of their presence.'

A ripple of applause went around the room. Gracie flushed.

* * *

Renee was the first to speak. 'Hi, I'm Renee. I've just been through my final unsuccessful bout of IVF.' There was a sad murmur from the group. 'Final – because after numerous attempts, I've made the decision that I can't put myself through any more heartache. And I wanted to say that thanks to having a very candid chat with this wonderful woman' – she nodded and smiled towards Gracie – 'the decision was made much easier for me. I am now looking to go through the process of adoption.'

Gracie stood up. 'Renee, what a brave lady you are and thank you for sharing. I'm so glad you have come to a decision. It takes a while to make one, but when you've done it – you must feel so much better.' Renee nodded as Gracie continued.

'So, it's Briony, isn't it? How about you?'

The pretty twentysomething blonde nodded, then spoke quietly. 'I feel almost guilty being here as I want to share the news that after five miscarriages, I am now three months pregnant.'

Everybody clapped, allowing a tall figure quietly to enter the hut and sit at the back of the room unnoticed.

Briony went on. 'I wanted to come today, not to tell everyone that I'm pregnant but to share that without the support of everyone here, I couldn't have got through the dark times. Gracie, you're an inspiration. For someone to have suffered so much loss yourself and be able to impart the care and compassion that you do, well... well... I think you're amazing.'

Renee shouted out, 'Hear, hear!'

Gracie bit her lip. 'Just to know I've helped you means so much to me. It also helps me, that by understanding your pain first hand, I did not lose my baby angels in vain.' There was barely a dry eye in the hut.

The tall figure then walked forward and took a place in the circle. Gracie's heart jumped into her mouth. She was fearful of opening it in case it jumped right out again and did a dance of joy.

'Excuse me for being late. I guess it's OK for a man to join in?'

Guessing who it was from the look on Gracie's face, Kate took control. 'Of course. Have you got something you want to share with the group?'

The handsome man nodded, stood up and stared right at Gracie.

'Hi.'

The group acknowledged him with a united, 'Hi.'

'I just wanted to say that I can only imagine how hard it is for all of you here and I commend you for sharing your stories. I also wanted to say that although men play a lesser part in this whole baby business, we feel loss, too. Me and my partner lost twins, you see.'

Kate went to Gracie's side and held her hand as Lewis continued.

'We lost them at five months in. It was almost the worst day of my whole life, so far. I loved my partner with all my heart, but when it happened, she withdrew from the world.' His voice went quiet. 'But mainly she withdrew from me. We didn't really talk – we didn't even make love anymore. We effectively fell apart.' Everyone was listening intently. 'And then I did something unthinkable. I slept with someone else.' The group gasped. 'Not just someone else, actually, someone who worked with my partner. It was an unthinkable act of deceit which I have regretted ever since. I say that losing the twins was *almost* the worst day of my life. Almost, because actually the worst day of my life was when my partner walked out of my life.' Gracie shut her eyes and ran her hands through her hair. 'I love her, you see. I love her so much that still, months later, every day without her feels like an eternity. Some days I still feel like my heart is literally breaking in two.' The man's voice cracked.

'Can't you try and make it up with her?' Briony put in from the circle.

'Oh, I have tried. I've even proposed, but she just won't forgive me.'

Gracie could not stay quiet any longer.

'Maybe if he tried again – maybe after a few months apart and not having any contact with him – she might be thinking differently, might realise that she is still so in love with him that she can't ignore it either.'

'Really?' Lewis looked at Gracie. She could see tears in her eyes.

Gracie whispered. 'Yes. Really.'

'Even though his behaviour was despicable?'

Gracie nodded. 'I believe that grief is a monster that makes us react and do things that are completely out of character.'

Lewis smiled. 'Love can be a little bit like that, too.'

He stood up and walked towards her, took her hand and led

her to the middle of the circle. Everyone wondered what on earth was going on. He got down on one knee.

'*How do I love thee,* Gracie Davies? *Let me count the ways. I love thee to the depth and breadth and height / My soul can reach, when feeling out of sight...* My true love, my soul mate, the intended magnificent mother of a huge adopted family, please will you marry me? Because I'm not going to bloody ask you again.'

Gracie felt a complete loss of emotional control.

'Yes, yes, of course I will.'

He leapt up and pulled her to him.

Everybody clapped and cheered, while Hetti ran around in circles barking.

* * *

Kate took the helm as Gracie walked outside with Lewis. Although by now, everyone was so emotional about the whole situation that there seemed no point in carrying on with the group.

'I think for those who can partake, champagne is due, everyone.' Another group 'hurrah' ensued. 'There's still some left from our open day. And plenty of softies for those of us lucky enough to be with child.'

Gracie overheard Kate and smiled. What a year it had been! Full of loss, new starts, new loves, new dogs and even a Hollywood actor to boot.

As soon as they were out of sight of everyone, Lewis hugged Gracie tightly. He thought she had never looked more beautiful.

'Oh, Gracie, I'm so happy. I promise I will never let you down again. I never realised what it was to be heartbroken until now. I cannot believe that you said yes.'

'I missed you, Lewis. When I realised you weren't at the end of the phone, it suddenly hit me. It hit me that I couldn't bear never to see you again, I couldn't imagine growing old with anyone else.'

'It's all going to be all right, you know, Gracie.' He kissed her on the forehead.

At that moment Hetti came running out of the event hut barking wildly.

Lewis laughed. 'Yours, I take it?'

She lifted Hetti to Lewis's face.

'Meet your new daddy, Hetti. He's all right, as men go.' The Yorkshire terrier jumped out of her arms and proceeded to have a poo.

Lewis laughed. 'Uncontrollable, just like his mother! But you'd better get used to it as I guess there's going to be a lot more of that to clean up when we start adopting babies.'

'Let's get ourselves back on track, eh, Lewis? I mean, we have a wedding to arrange first. And a honeymoon.'

'Where do you fancy going?'

Gracie grinned. 'I know a fabulous villa we can rent in St Lucia. We'll have staff and everything...'

EPILOGUE

The toddler squealed in delight as Jack pushed him on the swing.

'Not too hard,' Lewis shouted over. 'Or Little Scott'll fall out.'

Gracie and Maya chatted animatedly over their Prosecco-and-pie picnic, leaving Lewis with one eye on the boys and the other on his newspaper. Noms and Ali were playing with Boris and Hetti over on the other side of the common.

The adoption process had been a lot easier than Gracie had ever imagined.

Maya was happy that her baby boy was now in the safest of hands and the fact she could see him whenever she wanted had made the decision a whole lot easier. She had even helped choose his name.

Lewis moved towards Gracie and gave her a kiss. 'Are you happy, Mrs Blair?'

'Never happier, Mr Blair.'

Maya refilled their glasses. 'On that note, time for a toast. Here's to mothers, in every beautiful form they take. Cheers!'

The three of them chinked glasses.
'To mothers... in every beautiful form.'

A LETTER FROM THE AUTHOR

Don't miss out on all my news!

A huge thank you for taking the time to read *How to Fix a Broken Heart* and I hope you enjoyed Gracie's journey.

If you want to join other readers in hearing all about my new releases, you can sign up for my newsletter:

www.stormpublishing.co/nicola-may

And if you want to keep up to date with all my other publications and other writerly goings on, you can sign up to my mailing list:

www.nicolamay.com

Your review is like gold dust!

If you could also spare a few moments to leave a review that would be hugely appreciated. Even a brief review can make all the difference in encouraging a reader to discover my books for the first time. Thank you so much!

Why I wrote this story

How to Fix a Broken Heart was born from the heartache of losing twins myself and having to undergo a hysterectomy. Just because we never get to hold our little ones doesn't lessen the pain of their absence; in fact, the 'could have beens' can be even harder to bear.

I poured my heart and soul into this book, hoping it will resonate with others who have faced similar grief or are navigating the challenges of fertility treatment. I owe a deep debt of gratitude to my beloved family and friends – who know who they are – for their unwavering support, encouragement, and love that guided me back into the light and inspired me to write this story.

Thanks again for being part of this amazing journey with me and I hope you'll stay in touch – I have so many more stories and ideas to entertain you with!

Nicola May

www.nicolamay.com

 facebook.com/NicolaMayAuthor
 x.com/nicolamay
 instagram.com/author_nicola

Printed in Great Britain
by Amazon

61106242R00190